PEARL OF

WISDOM

Rob Wassell

Pearl of Wisdom

First published in 2016 by RAW Publications
www.rawpublications.co.uk

Copyright © 2015 Rob Wassell
www.robwassell.com

Pearl of Wisdom
www.pearlofwisdombook.com

International Standard Book Number

978-0-9569912-2-5

978-0-9569912-3-2 (eBook)

RAW
Publications

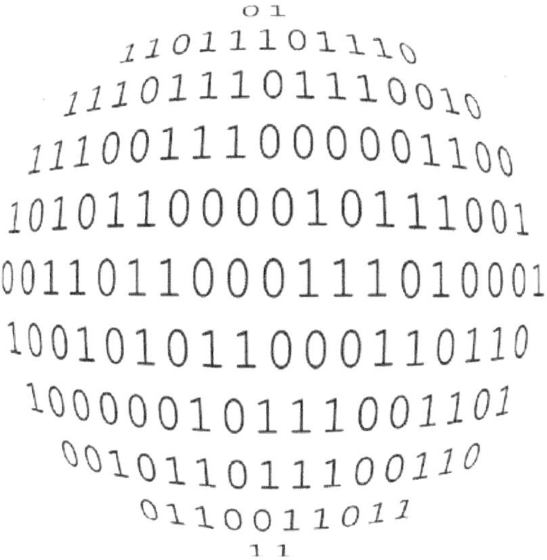

Chapter 1

The Debate

"Twenty seconds ..."

Trevor could hear the voice of the producer in his ear.

He stared into the blackness of the camera lens. It was a big show today, with big guests, and the producer had big expectations.

"Ten seconds ..."

Trevor flattened the hair on the side of his head with a nervous palm and clasped his hands tightly around the clipboard. He listened to the countdown.

"Five, four, three, two, and – we're live!"

"Hello and welcome to *The Political Debate*. I am Trevor Whiting and this evening my guests are the Prime Minister, George Clarke, and the Deputy Prime Minister, Greg Willis. The topic of discussion isssSSSS ..." Trevor said with rising intonation, "...Europe!"

Applause erupted from the audience behind the cameras.

The producer barked orders to the production crew as an intro reel began to play. The theme music started and animated graphics filled the screens in front of them. He ordered the cameras to get ready for one of the most divisive programmes the BBC had ever aired.

The clapping stopped. Trevor looked up from his notes.

"The Conservative party is enjoying a successful high at the moment and the Government seems to be the most consistent and cohesive that it has been for years, but there is a rift developing and that rift is over whether to pull Britain out of the EU."

The presenter looked at camera two when prompted in his earpiece.

"Prime Minister, perhaps you could explain a little more."

"Thank you, Trevor. Well, you are certainly correct and it is fair to say that in previous years and in successive governments the team hasn't always seen eye to eye or agreed on every policy. Yet, today, the party is the most joined up in its thinking that it has been for a long time."

"Apart from Europe," the Deputy Prime Minister interrupted.

"Camera three!" the producer barked. "This is brilliant – he's already starting to lose it. I know he can be hot-headed but I really hope he goes for it this evening."

"Yes, thank you, Deputy Prime Minister, apart from Europe. But, before we talk about Europe, I would just like to say ..."

"No, no, it doesn't matter what else you want to say, we're here to talk about Europe. It's an important issue – that is why we're having this debate," the Deputy Prime Minister said, looking at the camera. He looked behind the camera to the audience.

The audience started to clap. The Deputy Prime Minister raised his hands to rally their support. Shouts of 'hear hear' erupted and the applause persisted with fierce intensity.

"My ... My ..." The Prime Minister struggled to be heard over the roaring crowd. As the cheering died down, he carried on, "My concern is that, with so many countries failing in the EU, Britain will be brought down with them. Plus we pay so much money into the EU each year to get very little back from it except restrictions and laws that sometimes defy sensible logic."

"No, no. We pay money in to be part of a team, a team that has benefits, and those benefits affect everyone in every EU nation."

"But you're missing the point," the Prime Minister said. "I am not against Europe, I am for Europe, but I want a Europe that will work for Britain not against it."

The dialogue continued – rhetorical tennis as they both had their say, each deriding the other as eloquently as they could.

As the presenter watched the exchange carefully he could hear the producer's voice in his ear.

"This is good. This is very good. We've got four and a half minutes left. I want you to really stir it up."

The presenter interrupted, "I think we have an understanding on the main points of your argument, but, Prime Minister, if I may ask you first, where do you see Britain in five years' time?"

"My concern is for Britain. Sure I want it to be part of Europe, just as we are a part of Europe, but I would like to see our debt reduced. I would like to see our economy boom and welcome in an era of prosperity for Britain that sees the people with more jobs, more money in their pockets, and a

Britain that is helping to lead the world with its technological and scientific advances – just as it has in years past."

"Three minutes, keep it going." The excited producer's voice echoed in the presenter's ear.

"And the same question to you, Deputy Prime Minister."

"Don't get me wrong, I want the same. I want Britain to be successful, to have more people in jobs, for them to have more money and for Britain to be on the map with advancements in technology and science, but Britain can't do it on its own. Like it or not, Britain is part of Europe and needs to remain part of the EU. We need to be involved and have a say; we need to be part of it and to help shape the Europe of tomorrow. How can we have a say if we're not involved - not involved in policies that will affect Europe, one of our largest trading partners? To leave is suicide!"

"To leave is not suicide, don't be dramatic. To leave is to ensure our survival."

"One minute – this is going to be good!"

"It's not survival, it will be cutting our ties with our closest allies," the Deputy Prime Minister pleaded.

"You *are* being dramatic. The restrictions and rules imposed on our country cause us real problems and it is important the British people understand what's going on."

"Then why don't you ask them to decide?" the Deputy Prime Minister said, leaning forward in his seat, his hands clutching his knees.

"The public vote for us to make their decisions for them. This does not need a public referendum."

"I disagree. It's one of the biggest decisions to face Britain since the Second World War, of course they should have a say." The Deputy Prime Minister's fingers tightened, his knuckles turned white.

"Thirty seconds!"

"Britain is my top priority. Its future and success will be better served by leaving the EU."

"No, no," the Deputy Prime Minister said, banging one hand into the palm of the other. "This is crucial." His face was red with fury. "When I am Prime Minister – there will be a referendum!"

"Wind it up!" the producer barked.

"And on that note," the presenter cut in, "we really must say thank you to the Prime Minister, George Clarke, and the Deputy Prime Minister, Greg Willis, for a very interesting debate on Europe."

The Prime Minister sat back in his chair, mystified at his colleague's closing comment. He looked at his Deputy who was smiling for the camera and waving. He seemed confident, pompous, determined.

"Next week we'll be joined by the leaders of the two main opposition parties when we will be talking about the popular topic of education. See you then."

"Roll credits," the producer ordered.

He tossed his pen onto the control desk and sat back in his chair. "When I am Prime Minister – interesting ..."

***

"That went well, sir," Veronica said.

"Hmm, we'll see," the Prime Minister replied.

"Don't forget you've got that eight-thirty meeting in the morning."

"Oh yes, remind me again – what is it?"

"The French Minister for Business arranged it, some kind of envoy for Commerce."

"Okay, probably timed to coincide with all these discussions about Europe," the Prime Minister said. "See you in the morning."

Chapter 2

Pursuit

Aden Fitch pushed his way through the busy commuters crossing London Bridge towards the station. It was a cool March morning – the air was crisp and the sun was low in the sky.

He pulled the collar of his jacket up around his neck. His River Island brogues hit the pavement firmly as he walked.

He looked at his watch. Seven-thirty. He was so pleased he didn't have to do this every day. He looked around. There were people everywhere, marching forward, solemnly, quickly – all trying to get to work.

The discreet radio crackled in Aden's ear followed by a familiar female voice: "Target should be up ahead. White male, dark suit, pink shirt, red tie and brown shoes ... nice ensemble," the voice quipped.

"That could be any one of the men in front of me," Aden replied.

"Someone has given you a helping hand," said the voice in his ear.

Aden unzipped his jacket, reached into an inside pocket and put on a special-issue pair of sunglasses. He looked through the crowds and there about ten metres in front of him was a man with a fluorescent handprint on his right shoulder.

"Nice one," Aden said.

"One of our cabbies brought him down from Heathrow and managed to leave his mark before he left the car."

"Strange he didn't get the cabbie to take him directly to the station."

"Maybe he's suspicious of being followed," the voice replied.

"I wonder what would give him that idea. Okay, Blue One, I've got him from here."

"Roger, Blue One, you have control. We'll be listening."

Aden kept his eye firmly on the target.

"Blue Two?"

"Roger, Blue One," Mike replied.

"Where are you?" Aden asked.

"Right behind you."

"Quicken your pace, overtake me. Stay off his shoulder, to the right. Keep your distance."

"Roger."

After a few seconds Aden saw Mike come into view from his right, inching closer to the target.

Mike had only graduated from Hendon three months ago. He had been assigned to the Special Intelligence Agency due to his outstanding performance and family connections. He had been so keen to get involved in an operation and Aden considered tailing a target to be the least dangerous thing he could do. He had passed his firearms training and Aden had insisted that he was armed, just in case.

"Blue Three – location?"

"South side of the bridge, holding hands with Blue Four," Tim replied.

"Blue Three and Four, canoodle near the end rail of the bridge. When the target passes you'll realise you're about to miss your train and walk along behind him."

"Roger."

"Blue Five – report?"

"South side of bridge, on the stall," Steph said.

"Roger, get your special bar prepared, we should be on you in ninety seconds."

Aden caught glimpses of the target through the masses. Blue Two had moved well forward and was just behind his right shoulder. The workers continued to surge over the bridge, all heading for the station.

"Sixty seconds. Blue Five, get ready."

Aden smiled. He felt exhilarated. He inhaled. The cool air filled his lungs. He loved the thrill of the chase. He felt alive.

He didn't know much about this target. He had received a call at 5am to report that a known assassin named Mykola Liski had disembarked a flight at Heathrow earlier that night. He was ordered to assemble a team and tail him to find out what he was up to. The chocolate bar was an emergency measure. The wrapper contained a low power tracking device. As long as they were within 500m they would know exactly where he was.

The man moved swiftly. There was something about the way he walked – he was confident and assertive, definitely ex-military. The fact he'd got out of the taxi a few blocks from the station troubled Aden. Was he suspicious of being followed?

Aden suddenly noticed Mike's position. "Blue Two, you're getting too close. Back off a bit."

"I want to make sure we don't lose him," Mike replied.

Aden was about to reply when he noticed the familiar branding of the Mars pop-up stall.

"Blue Five – get ready."

"Roger, target in sight," Steph replied.

"Get ready."

Steph was all smiles as she handed the Mars chocolate bars to the commuters who streamed by. Some passed with open hand, accepting the bar as if it were routine, and others just slid by, none of them making eye contact.

Steph reached down behind the box and selected the special bar.

"Here you go, sir, a nice start to the day."

As Steph thrust the Mars bar towards the man, he ignored her completely. His pace remained unchanged, his gaze fixed ahead.

"Blue Five – mission failed."

"No problem, Blue Five, we'll follow on foot. Pack up. See you back at base."

"Roger. Blue Five, out."

Aden watched as he got closer to Blue Three and Four. They were sitting on the railing of the bridge. He could see Blue Two was still too close.

"Blue Three, Four – get ready. Blue Two, slow down, back off, you're too close."

"It's okay. I don't want to lose him," Mike replied.

The target was almost alongside the couple canoodling on the side of the bridge.

"Shit, we're gonna miss our train, come on, babe," Tim said, grabbing Gabby's hand. The target walked briskly past them, peering out of the corner of his eye as they jumped off the railing.

"Standby, Blue Team. Target could break left and go down the steps along the river or he might go straight on. Get ready."

Aden's heartbeat began to quicken.

"Get ready ..."

Aden struggled to see the target with the handprint on his back. *Come on, report*, he thought to himself.

"Target going straight on, down Borough High Street," Mike whispered.

"Roger, got that, Blue Two. For God's sake back off, you're only feet behind him."

Aden was worried he'd made a mistake bringing Mike on this job. His mind had said yes, it would be good for him, great experience, no way to screw up – an easy job. But his heart had said no.

"We'll take the target at the station. The crowd will make it easier for us to grab him and slip away. Repeat – take him at the station."

"Blue Two – Roger."

"Blue Three – Roger."

"Blue Four – Roger."

"Steady, he could take the walkway or the road," Aden said.

He realised Mike was even closer.

"Blue Two! For Christ's sake slow down, you're too close, if he ..." Aden cut off.

Then something completely unexpected happened: the very thing Aden feared.

The target came to a dead halt. Mike ploughed straight into the back of him. The man turned and grabbed Mike, preventing him from falling to the floor.

He read Mike's panicked expression. He felt Mike's gun in the shoulder holster under his jacket. The man reached inside, snatched the gun, spun Mike round and pushed it into his back.

With his other arm around Mike's chest, the man held him tightly. He watched, peering over Mike's shoulder. His eyes scanned the bridge, reading the faces and expressions of everyone in front of him.

"Blue Two – stay calm, don't do anything hasty," Aden said, lowering the sunglasses from his face.

"He's made us. We need to do something," Tim said.

"Negative, Blue Three, you and Blue Four stand by. Let him make the first move."

The target stood perfectly still and shifted his gaze between the three of them.

"Don't move," Aden ordered.

The target looked Aden firmly in the eye.

Aden shook his head from side to side.

The target pushed the gun firmly into Mike's back, smiled and fired.

There was a loud, muffled crack. Aden saw Mike's head tilt upward, his mouth wide open, his eyes filled with horror. His body slumped to the ground.

The target raised the gun and fired into the air.

Everything was happening in slow motion. It was as though all the commuters had suddenly been woken up, their half-sleep march brought to an abrupt end. There were screams and shouts from every direction: "He's been shot!", "Oh my God!", another scream, another shout – pandemonium.

"What's going on? What's going on?" Aden heard a voice in his ear.

He struggled to see. There were too many people in the way, running in all directions.

"Report. Report!" repeated the voice.

"Wait," he snapped.

His eye caught something move. The target – he was running, still heading towards the station.

Aden was almost knocked off his feet as panicking people surged against him.

"Mike! Blue Four, check on Mike. Blue Three, with me!" Aden said, raising his arms in front of him and pushing his way through. Side-stepping he leapt over a woman lying on the floor and it was then that he saw Mike. He wasn't moving.

"Control, Blue Two down. Chaos on bridge. In pursuit towards London Bridge station."

"Roger, sending back-up," the female voice said.

The target was quick. Aden put the sunglasses back on. He had difficulty keeping his eye on him as he shoved his way through the people.

"Blue Three, we can't afford to lose him."

"Roger," Blue Three said, fighting to catch his breath.

The target bolted along the road, veering around traffic, onto the pavement and back into the road.

With his gun still holstered, Aden was close behind. He followed in the target's wake.

Cars and buses sounded their horns and people jolted to the left and right as he thrust his way past.

"Let me through – police!" Aden shouted.

Out of the corner of his eye he saw Blue Three collide with a bicycle.

"Blue Three down, collision with bike. On my own."

"Control – Roger."

"Target just entered station, going in."

The station was packed. Like one huge organic mass, the crowd oozed through the turnstiles to get to their platforms.

The calm flow was disrupted by the target forcing his way through any gap he could find.

"Target heading for the Northern Line."

"Control – Roger. Back-up just pulling in outside station."

The man leapt the turnstile and reached the top of the escalator. There were too many people and there was only one way down. He jumped up onto the central panel between the escalators, took a step forward and began to slide downwards.

"Police, police!" Aden shouted, vaulting the turnstile. "Shit, I can't believe I'm going to do this!" he said as he, too, jumped up onto the central panel, took a step forward and began to slide down behind the target.

While commuters turned their heads in surprise, the man ahead was waving his arms around to maintain balance. Aden found it surprisingly easy, thanks to many years of skateboarding in his youth.

He skilfully slid past the little notices and emergency stop buttons.

As the target reached the bottom, he slipped and top-pled. He glanced behind, hurried to his feet and kept run-ning towards the platform.

"Bottom of the escalator. Not sure if he's going North or South at this point."

"Roger. Back-up in station, with you in twenty seconds."

The bottom of the escalator approached with speed. Aden took a deep breath and jumped. He landed on his feet, slipped but managed to steady himself and raced ahead after the target.

"North, North."

Aden followed his trail onto the Northbound platform.

The air was hot and thick with the breath of a thousand commuters – densely packed, huddled up against one another, bodies touching.

Aden could see the target. He had worked his way through to the edge of the platform. Aden had to get closer. He pushed through. Passengers turned their heads in disgust. *They were there first, how dare he.*

In the distance the distinctive sound of railway carriages echoed through the tunnel.

"Police, let me through. Let me through."

The target looked round. He could see Aden approaching.

"Let me through!" Aden said, struggling through the resistant crowd. The gap behind him healed up with opportunistic passengers, bettering their chances to get on the train first.

The target was now on the edge of the platform.

Aden was four rows back. "Excuse me – police!" He

stopped. "I've got him," he said over his radio.

The target looked straight at him, smiled and grabbed one of the passengers.

"What are you doing? Let me go," the woman said.

Aden gave him a pleading look and shook his head.

The man's smile was evil . He held the woman just as he had held Mike in the street above. Aden didn't want anyone else to get killed today. The woman struggled to get away but the target held her tightly.

"Oy, what are you doing? She asked you to let her go," a man shouted from beside her.

There was a sudden whoosh of air as the train approached. With a clattering of carriages it emerged from the tunnel.

Aden watched as the man raised his gun and pointed it at the Good Samaritan.

"He's got a gun!" someone screamed. People started to push and shove. The Good Samaritan reached for the woman's hand with his own. She clutched it. The assassin was pushed backwards to the edge of the platform, he struggled with his footing and toppled.

There was a sudden screech of brakes as the train roared along the platform. A blinding spark from the rails and a dozen faces gasped at the same time. He was gone.

"NO!" Aden shouted.

Screaming erupted from all directions. Commuters surged forward, desperate to get out of the way. A woman bent double and was sick on the legs of those around her. The next thing Aden knew she was on the floor, toppled by the sheer force of the crowd. He stepped forward, took her arm and lifted her to her feet.

"Target down, repeat target down. He fell in front of the train."

"Roger. Back-up with you now, will evacuate the station."

Within a few seconds there was an announcement.

"Due to unforeseen events on the Northern Line Northbound Platform, will all passengers please evacuate via the nearest exit. Due to unforeseen events on the Northern Line Northbound Platform, will all passengers please evacuate via the nearest exit."

Aden stood – elbowed, shouldered and manhandled as panicked commuters rushed to exit the platform. The train had stopped short of the end of the tunnel and passengers bled from it as quickly as they could.

Amongst the commotion Aden could hear a voice from his left. "But I need to get to work, can't you just get the train moving again?"

Aden turned. A man was talking to a conductor. "Sorry, sir, there's been an accident and the platform needs to be evacuated."

"But I need to get to a meeting." The man flung his arms in the air. "Bloody madness, bloody madness."

More voices, from all around, the crowd speculating.

"Was someone pushed?"

"Someone jumped, that's all I know. A woman, I think."

"I heard it was a suicide attempt."

Aden let the voices echo through his head. His thoughts were transferred to Mike, lying above on the pavement, most likely dead.

Chapter 3

The Dream

In a far off land, a beautiful woman lay in bed.

Her peaceful, almost angelic face revealed nothing of the dream she was having.

She felt hot powdery sand under her feet. She was on a beach. Palm trees lined the edge. The sound of the surf lapping onto the beach filled her aural senses. She could feel something in her left hand – it was the reigns of a horse.

She could feel something in her right hand but, before she could look, she heard a distant sound. She heard it again. She looked up. It was her father, calling her name and waving to her. "It's your mother!"

The woman's head jolted on the pillow. Her peaceful expression changed, her brow became furrowed and her eyes twitched.

Up ahead, her mother broke through the tree line. She was in her nightdress, but there was something wrong. She stumbled. Her father was panicking and her mother was struggling. The nightdress was blood-stained, as though she had bled from her groin.

"Mother!?"

She could still feel something in her right hand. She looked down. It was a knife.

There was blood on the blade which had run down onto her hand.

In her dream she screamed and the scream echoed through into real life.

She awoke.

Chapter 4

Debrief

Aden sat down outside the office of his superior, Inspector Caren Taylor.

He watched through the window as Chief Inspector William Headley paced backwards and forwards in front of Caren's desk.

The Chief Inspector was waving his fist and speaking in a loud voice. Aden couldn't hear exactly what was being said but he obviously wasn't happy.

It was about Mike, Aden knew it. He blamed himself for Mike's death. Mike hadn't been ready, but Aden had no way of knowing he would get himself killed.

Aden wondered if the Chief Inspector's reaction wasn't so much about an officer dying in service, but more the threat of a potential backlash due to Mike's family's connections.

The door swung open and the Chief Inspector appeared. Aden looked up to meet his gaze. It was as though he was about to say something, but instead he let out a disappointed sigh and walked off.

Aden stood up, stepped into the office and closed the door.

"Looks like that went well," Aden said, sitting down wearily.

"No shit, Sherlock!" Caren said, sitting forward and resting her arms on the desk. "How are you?"

"I keep blaming myself for Mike's death."

"Well, don't, it wasn't your fault. You did everything by the book. He made a mistake – he got too close."

"Yes, but if I hadn't have taken him along he'd still be alive."

"Don't beat yourself up. No one likes to lose an officer, but to be honest – most of the problem is due to his well-connected family."

"Thought so – and we didn't get the target either! Double disappointment."

"Tell me about it. This is going to reflect badly on my appraisal next week."

Aden rolled his eyes up to the ceiling and shook his head.

"I know you don't agree with appraisals but they are a reality in our modern world. We're all graded on our performance."

"I understand performance. Protecting our country and its people is what it's about. Sitting in an office and telling someone what your goals are while they criticise you and tell you what you could have done better is – well – a complete waste of time."

"I am not going to go through that again – it's just the way things are."

"It doesn't mean I have to like it though, does it?"

"Well, it will be your appraisal soon too."

"Can we get back to some real work now, please?"

Caren adjusted herself in her chair and smiled. "Yes, Cuddlebug."

Aden blushed and looked round to make sure the office door was closed. "I thought you weren't going to call me that anymore."

Caren winked and began to organise some paperwork in front of her.

It had been nearly a year since they'd separated. They had been involved with each other beforehand but senior ranks suggested two officers 'seeing each other' was unprofessional unless they were married. The pressures of working and living together in Caren's apartment took their toll and the marriage only lasted six months.

"Go on then, fill me in, Mrs Fitch," Aden teased. She'd hated having his surname. She said it sounded like some kind of skin condition.

Caren looked up. "Touché."

She pulled out a printout and held it in front of her.

"As you know, the guy you chased into the subway was called Mykola Liski – a known assassin. In fact, he was due to have a meeting with the Prime Minister this morning."

"Really? Were we aware of a threat on his life?"

"We had no prior warning – and, believe it or not, the meeting had been arranged by the Minister of the Economy, Finance and Industry in Paris. A certain François Begnaud no less, with whom you're already acquainted."

"Ah, François, yes, on that job last year. He was meant to be working with us, but we suspected he was passing us misinformation – couldn't make it stick though."

"Well, now he's missing."

"Oh, that's interesting."

"He made a few calls after his meetings – they're still

trying to trace those – then went out and hasn't been seen since. He didn't turn up for work this morning and they can't track his mobile either."

"Hmm, anything more on this Liski character?" Aden sat back with his arms folded.

Caren checked the printout. "He is believed to have been involved in seven killings. He's been off the radar for a couple of years. Ex-Ukranian Special Forces apparently."

"He looked the type. Short cropped military haircut, the way he walked, the air of confidence, superiority." Aden unfolded his arms and sat forward. "So, have we got anything to go on?"

"Shortly after the minister met with Liski, he met with a woman called Pearl." She turned the page over and back again.

"Who's Pearl and what's she got to do with it?"

"Well, she's is a bit of a mystery really. The French have no record of her visit that day but we managed to get this CCTV grab of her," Caren said, handing him the picture. "Tech ran this through the computer and only got one hit – a blog for the Church of Wisdom. It appears to be some kind of group formed to campaign and promote free speech and the freedom of information."

Caren handed Aden a piece of paper.

Aden studied it. It was obviously a printout from a web page full of sensationalist topics such as 'You're not safe on the internet', 'Big Brother is spying on you' and 'Search for truth'. At the top he noticed the line art logo was of a building on top of a mountain.

Caren picked up a glass from her desk and took a sip of

water. "And that's not all," she said, taking up another piece of paper. "Tech continued to run searches through the internet archive and found this."

Aden took it from her. "What is it?"

"Apparently it's some ancient blog post written years ago. I have a transcript here if you want to read it. She was obviously going through a sensitive time due to the death of her parents. She deleted it soon afterwards. She probably had a change of heart after her emotional outburst judging by the content. But, when we have access to the great internet archive in the sky, everything ever published is at our fingertips."

"And the picture?"

"An old family photo by the looks of it. Tech managed to match scenery and background objects from photos and satellite imagery – it's an island called Tikehau. North-east of Tahiti."

"Wow, that's clever."

"So that's where you're off to. French Polynesia."

"That's an awful long way to go – is it really worth it?"

"We have nothing else to go on. If the assassin met with this French minister, came over here – presumably to kill someone – and failed, where does Pearl fit in? She's obviously a driven woman, a campaigner who lost her parents and, from what she's written, full of anger and resentment. She suddenly pops up the same time as this Liski chap – who's to say she's not an assassin too? And did she have something to do with the disappearance of the French minister – she was the last person to meet with him so maybe to cover her tracks? Perhaps if you could find some evidence from her past it might help you to find her."

"Worth a try," Aden nodded.

Caren picked up an envelope from her desk. "You'll be travelling under the name of Miles Jenkins, independent marine biologist on a small break. It's always been your intention to visit the island but you just never had the chance – until now, as you've taken a sabbatical from Plymouth University."

Aden smiled, "I love my job with all my heart."

Caren feigned a sad face. "Well, I hope there's still a little bit of room for me."

"Of course, my dear, somewhere. Down around there." Aden pointed towards the bottom of his heart, smiled and winked.

"Take care," Caren said.

"Yep. See you in a few days."

Chapter 5

Change of Plan

Greg Willis sat in his office. He stared at the itinerary in front of him and turned his mobile phone over and over on the desk whilst muttering something under his breath.

He went through the text messages, searching for one in particular.

He dialled a number from the message.

"Yes?" said a man with a French accent.

"Oh hello, this is Greg Willis, Deputy Prime Minister. You were arranging a consultant for a very important joint EU project we are working on and I just wanted to let you know that, unfortunately, the consultant is no longer able to carry out his duties."

After a moment the man said, "Okay, we will make other arrangements," then hung up.

Greg deleted the message and sighed.

He pressed the intercom on his desk.

"Yes, Deputy Prime Minister?"

"Jenny, I'm going out for a bit. Hold my calls."

"Yes, sir."

Chapter 6

Departure Lounge

Aden sat in the departure lounge at Heathrow Airport awaiting the call for his flight to Papeete, French Polynesia.

He sat with his arms folded and smiled. He had been so rushed off his feet for what seemed like ages, he rarely had the time to just sit and think. He watched the information board update, taking in all the interesting names of the various flight destinations.

He loved his job. He had worked for SIA for just over three years, originally transferred from the Metropolitan Police at the request of Caren after they had worked together on a job in London. They hit it off straight away, not just professionally, but also spiritually and emotionally. They became firm friends and then lovers, stealing every opportunity they could to spend time together – that was until their superiors found out. They had got married, because they thought it would be the right thing to do. But it just wasn't the same; perhaps it was the secrecy and excitement that had made it so appealing. Living and working together and being in the SIA just didn't work. Aden did still have a special place in his heart for her though and he knew she felt the same way. They were best mates.

Aden had been involved in some of the most exciting

cases without the public being any the wiser. They had no idea what went on behind the scenes to keep the country, and the rest of the world for that matter, safe and secure. MI6, Special Branch, they were high profile, all spy gloss and glamour, but SIA was where the real action was.

Aden looked around at all the other passengers waiting for their flights. He had been in the job long enough to recognise most people's professions. The guy sitting in front of him with the stylish glasses and the polo neck sweater was obviously a designer of some sort, probably an architect. The other guy to his left was a surfer or lifeguard. His hair had been bleached blonde by the sun and his skin was tanned; his clothing said the rest.

The woman to his right was more of a mystery. She was either a high-class prostitute or high-level management, and of a certain age where she felt the need to try to hang on to her youth by wearing clothing more appropriate for a younger woman. He watched her for a moment – definitely high-level management. She lacked confidence and covered up for it with a firm hand and a firm tongue. She was probably bullied at school.

Aden noticed the display board refresh. No change to the status of his flight.

At home, prior to leaving, he had gone through the details of the file and something didn't add up. His senses told him they could be on to something big here.

He pictured the assassin in his mind, the way he walked and moved. His expression before he shot Mike. This was a trained killer, a professional. What would he be doing meeting a French government official? And then there was Pearl.

She could have been meeting the minister to discuss internet policy or freedom of information, but now she was connected with the investigation by association.

She'd lost her parents when she was younger, just like he had. Perhaps the loss of his parents had influenced him in becoming a policeman. Maybe it had had a similar influence on Pearl, moving her to campaign for freedom of information and her work on the future of the internet. Surely it didn't make her an assassin or a kidnapper.

He looked at the display board again. Still no change.

He enjoyed travelling; it was often the cherry on the cake in what was an amazing job in the first place. But he liked the fact you travelled from A to B and you were there, so he wasn't looking forward to this trip. In the photos he had seen the sand, the sea and the palm trees. What he hadn't seen was the monster of a journey to get to his destination. This was more like travelling from A to F with every other stop in between.

He unfolded his ticket and re-checked the route. Heathrow to Chicago, then Los Angeles and then finally to Papeete, French Polynesia – a total of twenty-four hours and five minutes' flying time, not counting the waiting at the airports and the boat to get to the island of Tikehau. He really hoped this wasn't a wild goose chase.

Beep. Beep. Beep. He had a text message.

Another hit – Pearl is CEO of Pearl Technologies. Very successful, key player in internet networking stuff. We'll keep looking. Take care C X

Interesting, Aden thought to himself.

"Would passengers for the American Airlines flight to

Chicago please make their way to the departure gate."

Aden looked up at the display board.

Finally, he thought. At least he would soon be in the air.

As he grabbed his bag his phone began to ring. He was receiving a call from a number he didn't recognise. He looked around the airport departure lounge. People hurried to the gate whilst others sat reading or playing with their phones. He looked at the number again. He definitely didn't recognise it. But who would be calling this number?

"Hello?" Aden said hesitantly.

"Is that Aden Fitch?"

Chapter 7

Tikehau

The little transfer boat slowly approached the jetty.

Aden rubbed his face with his hands. He was tired. It felt as though he had been travelling for a week.

He chuckled to himself as he thought of the phone call he'd received in the departure lounge. He had been so suspicious of the caller, only to find out it was simply the phone operator calling to confirm his roaming package upgrade had been activated.

The boat thumped into place alongside the jetty. The only other people on the transfer boat were the captain and a young couple – obviously newlyweds on their honeymoon as they just couldn't get enough of each other. They had hardly stopped touching on the whole journey. *It won't last*, Aden thought to himself.

"Okay. Depart," said the captain, fastening the last rope to the jetty.

Aden let the couple go first and moved forward to step off the boat.

"Merci, monsieur," he said, fumbling in his pocket for some spare change. The light was starting to fade and he hadn't really got any idea how much was in his hand but he gave it to the boatman anyway.

"Monsieur, monsieur, c'est trop! Je vous remercie. Je vais vous attendre ici," the boatman said as he raised his hands, smiled and did a little jig.

Aden suspected he had given too much.

He walked up to the end of the jetty and stood for a moment to take in his surroundings. The sky was a lovely mix of hues: dark reds, purples and blues. It was magical. He lost himself in his thoughts for a while and then turned to find his hotel.

Aden was headed to the Hotu Guesthouse. He was booked in for two nights with the possibility of extending if necessary. He fully expected to be wound up in a day. Nice as the idea was to have a break on this idyllic island, he loved to keep busy and there was a case to solve.

The island was amazing. Aden had never been anywhere like this before. There was a huge lagoon in the centre and the land was oval shaped. There were palm trees, white surf, sand, little buildings made out of driftwood: the quintessential tropical island.

As he walked between the palm trees, he could see a sign for the Hotu Guesthouse.

"Bonsoir, monsieur," the cheerful lady on reception said, as she saw Aden walk through the doorway. "I hope you had a pleasant journey. Welcome to Hotu Guesthouse," she added in her best English.

"Yes, thanks. You have a room for me – my name is Miles Jenkins."

The receptionist didn't even have to check the guestbook. "Yes, yes, we have been awaiting your arrival. Please complete this registration card and leave your passport with us."

Aden reached into his pocket and gave the lady his passport. He filled out the form, signed it and pushed it back across the reception desk towards her.

"Merci. Auguste will take you to your room. Here is the key."

A young lad appeared from a doorway to his right and offered to take the bag. "It's okay, I'll carry it," Aden said.

"Yes, sir." The young boy nodded, gave his best smile and took the key from the receptionist. He beckoned Aden to follow.

The boy waited expectantly in the room. Aden understood, reached into his pocket and took out a few more coins. He gave them to the boy. The boy's expression was as if Christmas had arrived early. "Merci, monsieur, bonne soirée, bonne soirée."

"I'm just a generous guy."

The boy smiled and left in a flash.

Aden put the bag down on the bed and inspected the room. The term they'd use in England would be 'rustic' but it was comfortable enough. There was somewhere to hang his clothes, go to sleep, go to the toilet, wash – everything he needed.

He walked over to the window. It was almost dark. The palm trees moved gently back and forth in the breeze, illuminated from below by the lights of the hotel.

He sat down on the bed and bounced a couple of times. He hadn't slept properly for days. He could never sleep on flights. He was looking forward to bed.

He reached for his bag, opened it and sorted through his clothes. Spare pair of trousers, three shirts, jumper and fleece. He'd had no time to research the climate prior to leaving and he'd been to other places where the temperature dropped after sunset so he figured he'd play safe. In fact, he couldn't have been more wrong. The beads of sweat clung to his tired skin in the warm, humid air. He hung his clothes in the wardrobe and removed his wash bag.

The bathroom was also rustic with shower, toilet and sink. He turned on the hot tap and tested the water – it was hot. No waiting. Very impressive considering where he was.

He washed his face, savouring the feeling of cleanliness he got with every splash. He wiped his face and brushed his teeth.

He started to undress as he walked out of the bathroom, then noticed something had been pushed under his door. Instinctively he looked around the room – no sign of anyone. The bag was still on the bed; nothing had changed. He moved towards the door and looked closely at the delivery. It was an envelope. He bent down and picked it up.

He turned it over. There was no writing on it. He didn't understand. It wasn't a cloak and dagger trip by any means, but there was a lot of mystery surrounding this case. It was standard procedure to go undercover until they knew what they were dealing with. No one knew his real name or why he was here. Aden swallowed hard and opened the envelope. He peered inside and pulled out a piece of paper.

Interesting ...

Chapter 8

The Next Day

Aden woke up in the morning feeling completely refreshed. He put his hands behind his head, lay back and stretched. This was the life. No alarms or sirens, no urgent call from the office requesting him to come in. He could get used to this.

Or maybe not. A good night's sleep is one thing, but the lack of action would kill him.

He looked to the bedside table. There, standing against a bottle of water, was the complimentary 'Discover Tikehau' boat trip ticket that had been pushed under his door last night. He really must stop being so suspicious he thought to himself, but it came with the job – being suspicious had kept him alive.

He picked up his phone and checked the time. 8.30. The hotel stopped serving breakfast at 10.00 so he had plenty of time. He yawned, stretched and lay for a while longer. He thought of Caren.

***

The dining room was very picturesque. The kind of picture you'd see on a postcard.

There were six tables arranged near a balcony overlooking the sea. They were all laid out ready. An older man sat in the corner. Aden couldn't quite place where he was from. European certainly, perhaps French.

Aden approached one of the middle tables. The man looked up.

"Good morning," Aden said and nodded.

"Good morning," the man replied with a smile.

From out of nowhere a young girl appeared. "Morning, sir, would you like tea or coffee?"

The first thing Aden noticed about the girl was her accent; it took him by surprise. It sounded English but with a twist of the Black Country – not at all what he expected on a small island in French Polynesia.

Aden had obviously conveyed something with his expression.

"You're impressed with my English," she said proudly. "I went to school in England. My parents own the hotel. It will be my hotel one day."

"Yes, I am impressed. When did you come back?"

"Last year. I did a diploma in travel and tourism at University College Birmingham. My family are very proud."

The penny dropped. "And so they should be. Well done."

"Thank you. What can I get you?" the girl said as she raised her notepad to begin writing.

Aden picked up the menu in front of him. There was a lot of fish. He couldn't quite get his head around having fish for breakfast. "I'll have a pot of tea, please. And ..." He studied the menu further. "I think just some toast, please."

"Okay, sir, a pot of tea and some toast," the girl smiled.

"Coming right up."

Aden returned her smile and watched the girl disappear out the back. He dropped the menu back on the table and looked out at the sea.

"First time in Tikehau?" the man in the corner asked. Aden was right, he was French.

"Yes, it is. You?"

"No. I come every year. Have done since the seventies."

"It is a lovely place. Idyllic."

"Yes, it is."

The man sipped his coffee. "What do you do? If you don't mind my asking?"

"I am a marine biologist."

"Interesting. Lovely reefs round here."

"Yes, indeed. It's a fleeting visit but somewhere I have wanted to come for a long time. And you? Why Tikehau?" Aden asked.

The man took another sip of his coffee and placed the cup down onto the table. It was as though he was preparing his response in his mind before speaking.

"I used to be in the navy. I was stationed around here in the seventies. Fell in love with the place, hence I come back every year."

Aden looked out of the window and back towards the man. "Some kind of naval outpost was it?"

"Something like that," the man replied.

Aden was surprised at the sudden end to the conversation; it seemed there was something the man didn't want to talk about.

The girl reappeared with his pot of tea. "Here you are,

sir. Your toast will be with you in a moment. Would you like me to pour?"

"No, that's fine. Let it brew. I like it strong."

"Yes, sir, back in a moment."

Aden sat up in his chair. He felt his back crack. It was doing that more and more these days. It reminded him he wasn't so young anymore. He moved the teapot and cup nearer.

"Sorry for being so vague."

Aden looked up as the man spoke again.

"It's just that there was some controversy about us being stationed here. The locals had a lot of resentment, especially with the damage to the reef and all. You're probably aware of that, being a marine biologist."

Aden nodded.

"It was a period of discovery – just a few years after the moon landings. Scientists with their fantastic ideas. The Government was looking for the next big thing." The man suddenly stopped. "Most of it's classified of course and I am still bound by secrecy laws, even now."

Aden wondered what the hell had happened here. He continued to nod.

"Sorry, I can't say any more. You understand."

"Yes, I understand. No problem."

Aden poured his tea and looked back out of the window.

The girl appeared with his toast and the rest of breakfast was spent in silence looking over the balcony out to sea.

Aden stood up to leave.

"Are you going on the boat trip around the island?" the man asked.

"I hadn't decided. Have you done it?"

"Yes, I've done it a few times. It's worth going if you can make it."

"Okay, I'll keep it mind. Thanks."

"Have a nice day."

"You too."

***

As Aden walked up the dusty street between the palm trees, a child ran up to him. He had a cheeky smile, a determined face and a handful of handmade jewellery.

"Necklaces, bracelets – great prices – you want to buy?"

Aden smiled. The boy had developed a mixture of accents. Part American and part Australian by the sound of it.

"Okay. I'll buy a bracelet if you can tell me who is the oldest person in the village?"

"Sure, that is Monsieur Aguillard. You find him at Chateau Aguillard – North." The boy pointed and showed off his selection of necklaces and bracelets.

Aden picked through the bracelets. He had a specific person in mind.

"I'll have this one."

"Two hundred francs, please," the boy said, with open hand.

Aden pulled out his wallet, and gave the boy a 500 franc note.

The boy's eyes opened wide. "For me?"

Aden nodded.

"Thank you, monsieur, thank you!" He grabbed the note and ran off.

Aden walked in the direction the boy had pointed. He felt a million miles away from London.

After about ten minutes he could see some houses. He read the roughly engraved signs and could easily make out Chateau Aguillard.

Aden smiled. He had expected something grand. It was hardly a chateau.

He opened the gate and walked up the short path. A modest home, bamboo framed with shutters for doors and windows, nestled in amongst the palm trees that covered the small island.

He knocked.

He knocked again and could make out a voice in the background call out, "Entrez."

Aden opened the door and walked in.

The house was effectively one big room with a couple of palm partitions to help divide the building. In the corner to his right sat a frail old man in a rocking chair.

"Bonjour, monsieur." Aden continued in his best French, "Puis-je parler avec vous?"

The man smiled. The wrinkles on his face showed his years. "You are English. I speak English." He beckoned to the chair in front of him. "Yes, you may speak with me. Sit down, please."

"Thank you, Monsieur Aguillard. My name is Miles Jenkins. I am a marine biologist and I just wanted to ask you a few questions," Aden said as he sat in the chair.

"Could you pour me a glass of water, please?" the man said, looking towards a jug and glass beside him.

"Yes, of course." Aden reached across and poured the

man a glass of water.

"Thank you. Remind me, why are you here?"

"I am here to ask you some questions."

"And what is your name?"

Aden looked a little confused, but put the questions down to the elderly man's memory or hearing, or both.

"Miles Jenkins. I am a marine biologist."

"And where are you from?"

"London, England."

The old man looked at him with a knowing expression. "I don't believe you. You are from London but that is not your name and not what you do."

Aden looked at him but didn't say anything.

"It is information you seek but you do something else. I think you are a policeman."

Aden smiled.

"You see, I am right. Am I not?"

Aden's smile turned into a grin and he nodded. "Yes, I am a policeman. My name is Aden, but please don't tell anyone; I am here in secret."

"I understand, but what information could you possibly want from me?"

"I am trying to find out what happened to someone who lived here. Her name is Pearl. She used to live here with her parents." As Aden spoke, he watched the man's expression change as he shifted uncomfortably in his chair.

"I know of what you speak. This was many years ago."

"Yes, it was."

The man looked down, as though deep and painful memories had been stirred up from within.

"Atoni Kalua had farmed for pearls on this island for many years and his father before him, many years. A marine biologist, Elizabeth ..." He paused and brought his finger to his temple in thought. "... Er, Wilson, she came to examine reefs. Beautiful reefs we have here. They fell in love, had a child – Pearl – and were very happy. Much love we had for them."

The old man paused to catch his breath and shuffled in his chair. "The French navy came and began to conduct tests, secret tests. Strange things started happening. The harvest getting smaller, this his livelihood, very difficult times."

The man's voice became hoarse. He cleared his throat. Aden listened intently. "Of the rest I am not sure. Elizabeth believed reef problems were caused by the navy. Atoni found her drowned near his pearl farm. He was sure it was not an accident. She had got too close to finding out what was going on. Atoni managed to get Pearl off the island in a small boat before Atoni also disappeared. Bad times. Lot of secrecy. We know not what happened to Pearl."

Aden sat forward in his chair.

"Monsieur, thank you very much. That is very helpful. But don't worry, Pearl is fine."

The man smiled. "Pearl is okay?"

"Yes, yes. She is okay." Aden remembered what Caren had said in the text message: *CEO, successful, key player, internet.* "She has become a very successful woman, very respected, a pioneer in many ways. She has done much good for the world." It might be true.

The old man clasped his hands together, almost in prayer, and brought his fingers to his lips. A tear formed in the corner of his eye.

"Dieu merci," he sighed and sat up in his chair.

Aden smiled, reached forward and placed a supportive hand on his.

"Thank you again." Aden stood to leave.

"Wait, monsieur. Would you do something for me in return?"

The old man attempted to get out of the chair. It seemed such a struggle that Aden stepped to his side and helped him.

"Here." He pointed to a beautiful writing desk against the wall. It was the most exquisite piece of furniture in the whole house.

The man pulled open a drawer and fumbled inside. He reached towards the back.

"Voici," he said. "I want you to give this to Pearl," and he thrust a box into Aden's hand. He opened it. Inside was a beautiful pearl necklace.

"This belonged to Elizabeth. It was made by Atoni himself," he explained in a faltering voice. He prodded the necklace in its box. "Natural pearl, very rare, not farmed. Very precious." He cleared his throat. "After the disappearance we could smell fire. We rushed out. Atoni's house was burning. I went in to make sure no one inside. There was no one. I noticed the necklace. Atoni had taken it from the body of his wife. It could not be destroyed, too precious. It is in memory of Elizabeth."

"Oh monsieur, I couldn't, really."

The man held Aden's hand and looked into his eyes. "It is Pearl's by right. It was her mother's. It is precious."

"You don't understand ..."

The man cut him off and squeezed his hand. "There is goodness in your heart. It is wonderful to know Pearl is alive. These belong with her, from mother to daughter. It is providence."

Aden was touched by the moment. He had no idea what he would do with the necklace or whether he could honour the man's request but he felt he couldn't say no. He put the box in his pocket and decided to worry about it later.

"Okay, of course. I will give it to Pearl."

"Monsieur, thank you, thank you."

Aden helped the man back into his chair.

"Sorry, monsieur, I have one more question while I think of it. Do you know where Pearl went when she left the island?"

"The currents would have taken her." The man pointed. "They flow towards Asia."

Aden nodded, "Merci. Au revoir, monsieur."

Chapter 9

Return Journey

Aden sat in the departure lounge at Papeete airport.

Only another 24 hours to go, he sighed.

He reached into his pocket, pulled out his phone, tapped a message and pressed send. He wondered how long it would be until Caren received the text. He imagined the little packets of data flying halfway around the world.

He looked around – a huge difference compared to Heathrow, but so many things were the same. It was just the scale that differed.

His phone vibrated. *Damn, that was quick*, he thought. He read Caren's reply: `Cool, see you tomorrow. Come round to my place, got more information and a surprise!`

Go round to her place; she's got a surprise?

Aden read the message again. In a previous life that would have meant something quite specific, but that hadn't happened since they'd separated. He convinced himself it wasn't that. It would just make things complicated.

He looked up. A rather beautiful woman sat in the row of chairs opposite.

She beamed a wide smile to him. She had long, black, curly hair and her dark brown eyes seemed to draw him towards her.

Aden smiled and nodded. Their eye contact lingered for a moment. He was no stranger to a woman's attention, at least not since reaching the other side of puberty – after the acne had cleared up. He had been a dorky looking child and at school his nickname was 'Boil'. He smiled as he thought back to the petty taunts that used to cause him so many sleepless nights. He was bigger and wiser now. They had covered the Black Death in history, and when the teacher mentioned how itchy the boils were, the kids in the class had their inspiration – Fitch was that itch and Aden became Boil.

The lady's gaze returned and another smile was beamed in his direction.

Aden was about to lean forward to say something when a man appeared and put his bag on the chair beside her. He looked at his wife then looked at Aden.

Aden smiled, nodded to the man and looked back down at his phone.

The next time he looked up, the couple had gone.

Aden toyed with his phone for a while, going through the menu. He skipped past one application and then another. He remembered the e-book reader.

There was only a small selection of books he had added, with the intention of reading one day. He scrolled down to Chris Ryan's *The One That Got Away* and opened it. He had read it in paperback form when he had gone on holiday with Caren. It was the only real time he had to read books. He used to hate just lying around – better to be doing something, seeing sights or walking. But on that occasion he had really got into relaxing and reading.

He remembered what a good read it was. A tale of survival, being stuck behind enemy lines, split from the rest of the group in a desperate attempt to reach the Syrian border on foot – remarkable. He felt quite excited at the opportunity to read it again. He began to immerse himself and shut out the world around him.

Chapter 10

Caren's Apartment

Aden walked up the steps.

He hadn't been to Caren's place in ages. He noticed the outside had been painted; he could smell it. The building looked bright and fresh, even in the orange glow of the street lamps. It was good to know the maintenance money she paid to the managing agent was being put to good use.

As he walked up to the front door he looked at the keypad beside it. He remembered there was something strangely familiar about the names against the flat numbers.

Flat 1 – Connery

Flat 2 – Lazenby

Flat 3 – Moore

Flat 4 – Taylor

He jabbed number four and waited.

He heard footsteps run towards the door and it swung open.

"Wow, you look knackered. Still can't sleep on flights?" Caren stepped forward and gave him a peck on the cheek.

"You guessed," Aden said, walking into the hallway.

"Well, it's good to see you, thanks for coming. Did it go well?" Caren closed the door and led him upstairs.

"Yes, very well in fact. I thought I was on a bit of a wild

goose chase at first but, yes, it was interesting."

"Interesting?"

"Well …"

Caren cut him off. "Actually, before you continue, I've made us some dinner. I figure you haven't eaten yet?"

"No, I haven't. I'm starving actually."

As Caren opened the door to her apartment he could smell something nice.

"It's chilli. It's simmering at the moment. Let me just give it a stir and then you can fill me in."

Caren disappeared into the kitchen. Aden walked down the hallway and casually glanced around.

It was a very well-appointed, good-sized, two bedroomed flat. He looked up; he was sure the ceilings got higher every time he visited. He walked into the living room. It had a fireplace with a sofa and two chairs, and a divide at the front of the building which formed an office area on one side and a library on the other.

Then he realised. There were no candles and no incense. His intuition was right. It wasn't a romantic get-together like the old days – it was business. He felt quite relieved.

Caren's voice announced from behind, "Here you go, I poured you some wine – white, cold, just how you like it."

"Ahhh, brilliant." Aden took the glass; it was chilled, straight from the fridge. "Thank you. Cheers."

Caren raised her glass of red wine. "Cheers. Welcome back."

She sat down on the sofa in front of the fireplace and placed her glass on the coffee table.

"Go on then, you were saying. You think it went well?"

"Yes." Aden sat in the chair opposite her and took a sip of wine. "Well, I've had plenty of time to mull this over and there is definitely something strange going on. I'm not sure how this fits in our investigation as a whole but basically ..." and Aden sat forward, "Pearl's father, Atoni was a pearl farmer, as was his father before him. Elizabeth arrives as a marine biologist, meets Atoni, they get together, get married and have a child. Years later the French Navy arrive and they start to do some kind of super-secret experiments which end up destroying the reef and the pearl farm. Elizabeth starts to investigate and winds up drowned – suspicious I think you'll agree. Atoni suspects she was killed and manages to get his daughter off the island before he disappears without a trace."

Aden sat back in his chair and, as he did, he felt the box with the pearl necklace in his pocket.

"Oh, and ..." He was about to say something but decided not to. He still had no idea what to do with the necklace or whether he would ever be able to get it back to its rightful owner.

"Oh?" Caren prompted.

"Oh, and her surname is Kalua."

"Hmm," Caren reflected. "So, top secret French naval experiments, destroying the coral reef and silencing people by having them killed when they suspect something is wrong. And when was this?"

"Seventies," Aden replied, remembering what the man in the hotel had told him.

Caren took a sip of wine.

"Can you elaborate on your text about Pearl being a successful CEO?"

"Oh yes. She didn't have a photo on her website which is why we couldn't get a hit but Tech continued to run the name Pearl, plus searches based on word usage and sentence construction, and got a match to a company called Pearl Technologies. The company is a world leader in the development and supply of computer networking equipment, and Pearl has been instrumental in the IPv6 strategy to move over to the new internet numbering standard."

"She's obviously done well for herself."

"Only, in more recent years she has stepped back from her day-to-day work and has been concentrating on the Church of Wisdom."

"So what do you think?" Aden asked.

He could see the thoughts going through her mind. He knew what she was going to say. They were still very much on the same wavelength.

"Fascinating as this is and curious she met with the same French minister as the assassin did, I'm not sure this has anything to do with us." Caren looked up, waiting for his agreement.

Aden nodded.

"She hasn't popped up on our radar for anything before. She's obviously vocal about free speech and all that stuff but it doesn't make her a person of interest, does it?"

"No, that's right," Aden concurred.

Caren took another sip and contemplated the situation. "I'll update the Chief Inspector in the morning. We'll decide whether to hand this information to the French or not."

Aden sat back in his chair and raised his glass. He smiled. Caren smiled and raised hers.

In many ways it reminded him of old times; sitting here, in her apartment, just the two of them, drinking wine.

"What is it?" Caren asked as she noticed Aden's glance flick towards the window.

"I thought I saw something."

"What?"

"I don't know. It looked like someone's head moved by the window."

"But we're on the second floor," Caren said. "The window cleaner doesn't come this late at night," she quipped.

Caren watched Aden's expression change. It frightened her. She swallowed hard. She could feel her heart sink to the pit of her stomach. Aden leapt from his chair towards her.

A deafening boom echoed through the room. Her ears rang and she could feel a massive pressure wave envelop her. Aden's hands grabbed her. She felt herself dragged forwards, a huge force pushing downwards, the edge of the coffee table, a sharp pain in her forehead, squashed, winded. Then it went black.

Aden strained to see through the smoke-filled room as he crouched behind the upturned sofa which was lying on top of Caren.

He heard a loud crack and something whizzed past the side of his head. Then another and another.

He could see the muzzle flashes through the smoke. The gunfire was coming from in front of the window, behind Caren's desk on the office side of the partition.

He looked to his left. The fireplace was purely ornamental but up inside, behind the surround, was a small shelf where Caren used to hide her gun. It was as though it was intended for a moment just like this. He only hoped it was still there.

The smoke was thick enough to afford him some protection but time was running out.

He ducked. Another bullet whizzed overhead. Bullet after bullet struck the solid wooden frame of the sofa.

He hoped Caren would be okay.

He had to act quickly.

He looked at the fireplace. It was six feet to his left. He noticed the solid metal coal scuttle to the side of the fire.

He dived forward, reached for the coal scuttle with his right hand, crouched and held it to his side. With his left hand he reached up underneath the fire surround and fumbled behind. A ricochet nearly deafened him as a bullet bounced off the scuttle, and another.

His hand made contact with Caren's Glock 17.

Another ricochet and, as Aden turned, a bullet passed straight through his makeshift shield. He dropped the scuttle in the fireplace and sprang back behind the sofa.

As the smoke cleared, he could make out two shapes behind Caren's desk.

He pulled the top slide back on the gun, saw a round enter the chamber, raised the gun and fired. The shapes dropped themselves behind the desk and this was Aden's opportunity.

He fired again, again and again and kept on firing as he rushed across the room. He fired one more shot and dropped to the floor on the other side of the partition.

For a moment there was silence.

As Aden crouched behind the old leather chair, he looked

up towards the partition separating him from the armed intruders. Caren proudly referred to this area of her apartment as the library.

Although ornate and in keeping with the original styling of the building, with its coving and wallpaper, he knew the wall separating them was not original. It was a simple stud wall and he hoped that this would work to his advantage.

In his mind he pictured the office area on the other side. He kept low. He moved quietly, raised his gun and pointed it towards the wall just above a line of books.

He pressed the trigger five times in quick succession, punching holes through the plaster.

He heard a shout from the other side, a groan and a body thumping to the floor.

A split second later a burst of gunfire erupted and bullets sprayed through the partition.

Shattered books flew off the shelves and fell to the floor around him.

Whoever it was, he or she was firing high, well above his head. He knew he had to act. Keeping low, he crawled along the floor to the corner of the partition. He knew there was one other person in the room and that person was obviously still alive.

He knew precisely what he would do. He would reach around the wall, fire a few more shots, rush round and grab whoever was there.

As he prepared himself he looked down at the gun. The slide was locked open. He was out of bullets. *Shit*. And he knew exactly where Caren kept her spare clip: locked in a drawer in her desk – in the office directly in front of the remaining gunman in her flat.

The shooting stopped.

Aden very quietly stood up. His breathing was slow and measured. He waited. His ears were ringing but he listened for the slightest sound.

Almost in disbelief he saw an inch of gun barrel come into view from around the side of the partition. As the man lunged forward, so did Aden, grabbing the muzzle. It was as though the weapon came alive. He wrestled with it, pushing the gun upwards towards the ceiling as it rattled bullets all around him. The man rushed towards him; the weight unsettled him and they toppled over the leather chair.

The gun went silent as they fell.

Aden was finally face to face with the intruder. He was surprised by what he saw: a well-equipped soldier, complete with gas mask, MP5 machine gun and dressed completely in black. It was a surreal moment as he stared through the visor of the mask at the pair of steel-cold eyes staring back at him.

The intruder pushed. Aden pushed back.

Aden blocked a punch with his free arm – and another. He brought his knee up towards the man's stomach, but the man curled to protect himself.

The man freed his other arm and pushed himself back. He shuffled backwards on the floor raised the gun and fired – click. He was out of bullets too.

Aden struggled to his feet and tried to run to the office on the other side of the partition. The intruder kicked at his feet. Aden tripped and fell to his knees.

The attacker leapt up and reached for his sidearm. Aden

saw the move, stood, turned and grabbed his wrist as the pistol came free of its holster. The man fired – Aden pushed the gun upwards. He fired again. Plaster landed on their heads as the bullets hit the ceiling. Aden looked down at the intruder's well-equipped belt: a combat knife.

He lunged forward using all of his bodyweight and turned slightly to the side, unbalancing the intruder. As they both fell, Aden reached down for the knife. The intruder struggled to stop him but not before Aden had been able to pull it from its sheath. With a heavy thump he landed on top of him.

Aden gathered his breath. The assailant didn't move. Aden prodded him – no reaction. As he slowly raised himself to his feet, he looked down. The weight of the fall had pushed the blade of the knife deep up under the intruder's body armour. Aden turned the knife in the wound – he was definitely dead.

Kneeling next to the lifeless body on the floor, Aden struggled to get his mind around what had just happened.

"Caren!"

He rushed over to the sofa.

It was riddled with bullet holes; tatters of material hung off the sturdy wooden frame. She had spent an awful lot of money on it after they had split up, but it was probably too much to hope it was bulletproof.

Aden grasped the sofa and paused for a moment, terrified of what he might see. His throat was dry. He swallowed hard and lifted it up.

Caren was lying perfectly still, curled up, embryonic. He looked her over. From her feet up, her calves, thighs, waist, back, her stomach – all fine. Wait – her head. Her head was bleeding. On the floor in front of her a small pool of blood had collected on the rug.

"Oh no, Caren!" He feared the worst. He reached down. With two fingers outstretched he checked for a pulse on her neck.

"What the hell happened?" Caren groaned. She raised her hand to her head. "Why does my head hurt so much?"

"Careful, it looks like you've banged it."

"What happened?"

"We were attacked."

Caren tried to sit up. Aden helped her.

"By who?"

"I don't know, but whoever they were, they were well-equipped. I don't know if they came for you, me or both of us." Aden examined her head. "Are you sure you're okay?"

"I just hit my head that's all." Caren touched her forehead. "Thanks."

"What, for making you hit your head?"

"No, for saving my life, you arse."

Aden smiled, leant forward and hugged her.

Caren held him tightly.

"We'd better go. We'll call a clean-up team on the way." With his arm around her, Aden helped her to her feet.

As they stood, Caren could suddenly see the scale of what had happened.

"Oh my God."

The window was gone. Woodwork was shattered. Everything seemed to be covered in broken plaster.

She saw them. A dark shape slumped next to the desk

and another in front of the library. Dressed in black with gas masks, utility belts and God knows what else, Aden was right, they were well equipped.

"You did this?" she said.

"It's all thanks to the training," Aden smiled back.

"My hero." Caren kissed him on the cheek as something caught her eye in the direction of the desk. "That's strange."

"What?"

"Oh it's probably nothing." Caren rubbed her head. "I thought I saw the one by the desk move but that's impossible. He's dead, isn't he?"

"Oh shit, I didn't check the other one."

Aden turned his head and saw the dark shape rise to its feet behind the desk. From the way the man moved he was obviously wounded, but that didn't make him any less dangerous.

Aden remembered the other intruder had a sidearm. Without another thought, he let go of Caren and dived towards the weapon in the man's hand. The dark shape in front of the window raised his submachine gun and pressed the trigger, click; he pressed it again, click. He raised the weapon and ejected the magazine.

Aden landed hard on the ground, found the other gun and picked it up.

The man fumbled to find another magazine. As Aden brought the gun to bear the intruder made his decision.

Before Aden had a chance to pull the trigger, he dived out of the window.

"What the ...?" Aden stared in disbelief and looked round.

Caren was staring wide-eyed. "But we're two floors up!"

Aden rushed over to the window, expecting to see a lifeless corpse on the pavement. Instead he saw a high-powered BMW with its lights off racing down the road.

"Is he dead?" Caren asked as she staggered over, trying to avoid the lumps of plaster and rubble on the floor.

"He," Aden emphasised, "is not there. Someone was waiting for them in a car below. BMW, 520 series, probably dark blue or black, didn't make the number."

"But ... how did he survive?"

"I have absolutely no idea. Come on, let's go," Aden said, putting a supportive arm around her.

***

Aden was driving. He listened to Caren on the phone.

"Yes, sir. Two intruders, well-armed and equipped with assault gear. One got away in a waiting car. BMW 520 series, dark blue or black. The other one is still in the flat. We left everything as it was. Aden took him down with my Glock ... I think it's still in the flat?" she said looking over at Aden.

Aden nodded.

"Yes, still in the flat. We locked the door, you'll have to break it. We're on our way to Aden's place ... We did think about that – yes, we'll be careful. Yes, sir ... Yes, sir. Okay, we'll see you at 8am sharp."

"Chilli!" Aden said loudly.

Caren looked round bemused.

"The chilli is still on the hob."

"Oh I forgot. Sorry, sir, we left in a hurry and there's a

pan of chilli simmering on the hob – if someone could turn it off, please …Great, thank you … Yes, thank you, sir, see you in the morning." She hung up.

Caren placed the phone in her lap.

"Two minutes," Aden said.

"Do you think they'll be waiting?"

"Dunno. They might have checked out my place first and gone on to yours, or there could be two teams, of course."

She nodded. Aden glanced as she sat slumped in the seat with her arms folded tight around herself.

"I've been in the job years but never had anything like that happen to me."

Aden navigated the busy evening traffic and looked over again. Car headlights were flashing across Caren's face and he could see the tears in her eyes.

"They came to my home," she sniffled. "I've been shot at before, but it's always been where the action was, on the street, in warehouses, even on the river during that drugs bust last year," she said wiping a tear from her cheek. "But that was different. Out of the blue – they came to my home!"

Aden touched her thigh and squeezed. "You're fine, I'll look after you. We made it. We'll be fine. Nearly there," Aden said as he turned into the top of his road.

"Can you even park?"

"Dunno yet. Trouble is, by this time of night most of the spaces are taken."

They drove down the road tentatively. "There." He saw a space on the left, pulled in and turned off the lights.

Caren reached for the door handle.

"No. Wait," he said, with an outstretched hand to stop

her. "Other side of the road, further up."

Caren looked over, unsure what Aden was looking at.

"White Transit van."

"So?"

"Do you know anyone in this street that would have a white Transit van?"

"Ahh, I see. Detective Fitch is on the ball."

"During the day, yes, but this time of night is residents' parking – how many people living in this street would drive a white Transit? Also, look at the windows – steamed up. There's someone in there."

With the engine still running, he revved gently and pulled out of the space. He turned the lights back on.

"One way road. I can't turn round, I'll just drive by. Hopefully they don't know what car I'm driving so they won't follow."

Aden looked at Caren. She had a determined and angry expression on her face.

"I know what you're thinking."

"Bastards."

"I know."

"I want to know what this is all about."

"Me too. Me too."

They approached the white van.

Aden could feel the nerves in the pit of his stomach. He glanced at the speedometer: twenty-five mph. Was it too slow, should he speed up? Would it attract attention if he went too slowly? Would it attract more attention if he went faster? He made a decision. Aden pushed on the accelerator. By the time they were level with the van, he was doing thirty-five mph.

"Right, fingers crossed, act natural, look straight ahead."

As they passed the van. Aden glanced across. There were definitely people inside but he couldn't see how many. He stared into the rear-view mirror, desperately hoping he wouldn't see it pull out and come after them.

"I think we're okay."

They kept going. Still no sign of movement. "Yep, I think we're okay."

"Look out!" Caren screamed as she braced herself in her seat.

Aden almost jumped out of his skin. He looked ahead and slammed on the brakes.

"Oh shit!" he said as he held the wheel tightly and stared in disbelief.

Blinding them with its headlights, a car was heading towards them.

"But ..." Caren stated, "... this is a one way street."

"Yep, I think we've had it."

"What can we do?"

Aden looked ahead. He looked behind. He looked at Caren.

"The road's clear behind. I could try slamming into reverse and going for it but if they pull out it's game over."

The car in front had slowed down and stopped. The driver's side door opened and someone got out.

"Can you see who it is? Are they armed?"

"I can't see. The lights are dazzling me."

Just as Aden decided to put the car into reverse gear, his worst fears came true. In the rear-view mirror he saw the Transit van's lights come on.

"It's too late. The Transit's pulling out."

Caren reached across and clutched Aden's hand. "We could run."

"They'd cut us down."

Aden looked ahead. A man approached.

She squeezed his hand. "You know ..." Caren looked into his eyes. "I still ..."

Aden squeezed back. "I know, I still ... too."

Aden glanced in the rear-view mirror.

"What is it?"

"The space is too tight."

"What?"

"The space is obviously too tight, they're having to keep moving forwards and backwards to get out."

Suddenly there seemed to be a light at the end of the tunnel. Aden was about to slam the car into reverse when a man's face appeared at his window.

The man tapped on it.

Aden and Caren exchanged a glance. "You know," Caren murmured, "he doesn't look like a killer."

Slowly, Aden opened the window part way.

"You go wrong way. You in my way," the man said.

Aden suddenly felt the knot in his stomach loosen. "No, *you* go wrong way, this is a one way street." He pointed forwards with his hand.

"I go wrong way?"

"Yes, you go wrong way."

It was as if the penny had dropped. "Very sorry. First time driving here. First visit. Me from Beijing."

Aden was briefly distracted as he looked behind. The van

was halfway out of the parking space and still edging backwards and forwards.

"That's quite okay. Return to your car and reverse."

"Weverse?"

"Go backwards. Get in your car and go backwards."

"Ahh yes, yes, I go backwards."

The man walked back to his car, giving a little wave as he did so.

Caren watched Aden look in the mirror.

"Status?"

"They're almost out of the space, definitely no way back. Let's hope Charlie here is a good driver."

Aden eased the car into first gear and moved slowly forwards.

The man had got back into his vehicle.

"Come on. Come on," Aden said quietly, watching.

The Transit was clear of the space and advancing towards them.

"Come on. Come on."

All of a sudden the car in front jerked backwards and stopped, jerked again and stopped. Aden felt his stomach tighten and again the car jerked. Steadily it started to roll backwards towards the top of the road.

Aden looked behind as the Transit approached. "This could take some time."

The Transit van's headlights were illuminating the cabin as it sat behind them idling.

"They obviously don't know it's us or it would be over by now." Aden stared in the rear-view mirror. He inched forward.

Instinctively Caren made a move to look around.

"Don't. Just keep looking forward. We don't want them to see us."

Caren sat deadly still, watching the car in front move slowly and painstakingly backwards.

"Can you see the driver?"

"No, they're too close," Aden sighed. "Come on, Charlie," he urged as he continued to edge forward in convoy with the reversing car in front.

"Oh no. What's he doing?"

Aden shook his head. "I have no idea."

They watched in disbelief as the car started to turn in towards the cars parked on the side of the road and then stopped.

"What the hell is he doing?" Aden said.

He drummed his fingers on the steering wheel. He looked at the Transit. He looked in front. The car didn't move.

"Come on. Come on."

They both heard the sound of a door opening. Aden checked the mirror. It was the passenger door of the Transit.

"Oh no, just what we don't need."

"What?" Caren desperately wanted to turn but kept herself firmly facing forwards by gripping the edge of the seat.

"They're getting out."

"There's nothing we can do, we're trapped. If they see us ..."

"I know, I know. Just hold still."

The car in front jerked forward, stopped, jolted once more and straightened up. Once clear of the parked cars, it started to crawl clumsily backwards.

Aden stared in the rear-view mirror. The Transit door slammed itself shut.

"Thank God for that." Aden slipped the car back into first gear and moved forward.

Slowly they approached the top of the road.

"Nearly there. Come on, Charlie. Come on." Aden reached across and patted Caren's thigh. Caren held his hand tightly.

"We've made it. Well done, Charlie."

The man from Beijing turned the car backwards into the main street and waved. Aden and Caren both raised their hands and waved back. At last he was gone.

Aden looked behind. The Transit's right-hand indicator started to flash.

"In that case, we're going left."

Aden flicked the indicator left, turned the wheel and blended in with the traffic.

"That was tense," Caren said, feeling her body begin to relax a little.

"Yep," Aden replied. The knot in his stomach faded.

"Where to?" Caren asked.

"I know this rather nice hotel a couple of miles away," Aden smiled and glanced across.

"I think I know just the one you mean," Caren replied.

He pushed his foot firmly on the accelerator and sped away.

Chapter 11

What's Going On?

"That's better. I actually feel awake," Aden said, placing his empty cup on the table as they sat in the interview room. He looked up at the clock: 07:55.

"Thank heavens for strong coffee," Caren said, sipping hers gratefully.

Aden sat upright in the chair. He stretched and yawned. "What a night. I don't think I got off to sleep until about two."

"Yeah, I was the same," Caren said, "Oh, by the way ..."

Aden turned to look at her.

"Sorry about last night."

"What? About the attack?"

"No, in the hotel room."

"Oh don't worry," Aden said, shrugging it off.

"I was just ..."

"All forgotten. Never happened," Aden smiled.

Caren nodded and smiled back. She took another sip of coffee.

The door to the interview room swung wide open and the Chief Inspector appeared with a drink in one hand and a file in the other.

Caren and Aden waited for him to settle. He was a formidable fellow but he did have a heart.

He pulled up a chair and sat down. He placed his palms with fingers outstretched on the table and looked up.

"Good morning. How are you both?"

"Okay, thanks, sir," Caren replied.

"Fine, thanks, sir," answered Aden.

"From top to bottom I want to know what happened. Aden, you start."

***

Aden stared at the file in front of the Chief Inspector. Caren was nearly up to date with her account of what had happened and he wondered if they would soon find out what was in it.

He glanced up at the clock. It was 08:55. He shifted in his seat. His body felt as if it had been sitting there far too long, especially on the intentionally uncomfortable interview chairs.

The Chief Inspector, still sitting bolt upright in his chair, looked directly at Aden.

"We don't need to go through it all again, but I just want to double-check on that van outside your flat. Are you sure they were waiting for you?"

"Yes, sir, pretty sure. It was too much of a coincidence. It looked completely out of place and we could see there were people inside. They must have been staking out both our flats, got the call that we'd escaped and waited to see if we'd turn up at mine. When we didn't, they drove off."

"And you didn't see the registration plate?"

"No, sir, couldn't see when it was parked and it was too close when behind."

"Okay, we've already spoken to Traffic and they're going to send through what footage they can from any cameras in the area. So, Caren, what are your thoughts on this and how does it fit into the case?"

"Well, sir, at first we thought it didn't. A seventies' French government cover-up of naval experiments gone bad, a known assassin coming to London – we couldn't see a connection. But that attack on us last night obviously shows that someone wants us off the track and is willing to go to great lengths to do it."

The Chief Inspector slammed his hand down on the file in front of him. "Great lengths indeed."

Aden looked at the file. Finally, they were going to find out what was inside.

The Chief Inspector turned to Caren. "Recommendation?"

"That we dig deeper. But we can't do this on our own."

"Exactly what I was thinking. Caren, your office now."

Caren, startled, stood up and left the room with the Chief Inspector.

Aden, alone, sat staring at the clock. He yawned. "I think it's time for another coffee."

He stood up, opened the door and walked into the corridor. Dozens of fellow officers milled around – the admin staff just turning up for work.

He felt someone touch his arm.

"Aden. I heard about last night – are you okay?"

"Yeah, yeah, fine thanks."

"I heard you took out two of them. Well armed too."

"Yes, I did. Well, one of them escaped, but we're both fine."

"Well, I'm glad to hear you're okay," Tim said.

"Thanks."

"Oh, good luck by the way."

Aden was bemused. "Good luck with what?"

"With your new partner, of course," Tim said matter-of-factly.

"But, I don't have a new partner."

Tim raised his hand to his mouth. "Oops. See ya!" he said as he turned and disappeared in amongst the milling officers.

Aden turned to go up the stairs to his office. *What the hell was going on?*

Chapter 12

The New Partner

"How do you pronounce that? Padraig? Pad-raig? Raig? Is that really his name?" Aden asked as he read a page from the file.

"It's Irish for Patrick. I think he just calls himself Pat. It's easier." Caren looked up from the paperwork in front of her. "I can see why."

"He's got a mad looking face and wild hair."

Caren thumbed through the file. It's probably just a bad photo.

"So, do you know anything about this guy?"

"Not a lot. I've only just been given his file. Looks good though, very experienced."

"So, tell me about him," Aden said, handing the page back to Caren.

"He can tell you himself; he's here."

Caren beckoned to the man who had just arrived outside her office. They stood up. The door swung open.

"All right, mate, how ya doin'?" Padraig swooped in, grabbed Aden's hand and shook it enthusiastically.

Aden was startled. *He really is just like his photo.*

"How ya doing, darlin'?" He stepped forward and reached for Caren's hand.

"Less of the darling, thank you. Sit down." Caren beckoned.

"Aye, right you are, ma'am, sorry." He sat down.

"Aden Fitch meet Padraig Brogan."

"Call me Pat." Pat looked at Aden and winked.

Aden nodded.

"Pat is from Northern Ireland. He was with the RUC for many years before moving over to London to work in our anti-terrorism branch. He's very experienced and more importantly he's here because one of the men you shot last night was ex-IRA."

Pat chipped in, "To be fair, ma'am, it's a breakaway group called the Continuity IRA. They still receive support from overseas but in return they'll be guns for hire, especially for any jobs against the establishment."

"Thank you." Caren raised her hand in a 'there you go' kind of way.

"Mmm, the plot thickens. Polynesian, French, Irish," Aden said.

"Aye, I've been briefed already. It's an international tangled web of mystery, so it is indeed."

Aden looked bemused. Caren smiled.

"Right, well I don't have all day. You two get to know each other and I'll see you both in the briefing room in thirty minutes."

Pat shot out of his chair and opened the door for Aden. Aden nodded with a hint of suspicion and walked out. He turned to Caren, gave her a wink and closed the door.

Pat walked off down the hall.

"The briefing room is this way," Aden said.

Pat turned. "Aye, I know. I just need to visit the little boys' room. I'll see you there."

Chapter 13

Briefing

Aden sat in one of the chairs at the front of the briefing room, with folded arms. He yawned. Clearly the coffee hadn't worked its magic yet.

Tim, Gabby and Steph sat in separate rows behind. Tim sat toying with his phone. Gabby and Steph were whispering to one another.

The board had already been laid out with photos, labels and pictures. Aden stared and pondered.

Top centre was a picture of the French government advisor. To the bottom left a picture of Pearl, beneath that, lines drawn to her father and her mother. To the right there was a picture of the assassin. Aden saw both his face and Caren's on the board, together with a line to another label which had the name 'Dougie Malone' written on it.

Aden tried to keep his mind on the 'tangled web' on the board in front of him, but his thoughts kept returning to his new and rather annoying Irish partner. He was dreading working with Pat. With his bombastic cheery attitude, wild hair and mad face, Aden just didn't know how he'd cope. Pat was the quintessential Irishman stereotype.

As if perfectly choreographed, the door opened and Pat appeared.

"So, there's me new partner," Pat said, rushing forward and placing his hands firmly on Aden's shoulders.

Aden squirmed. It was a bit much. Aden had encountered his type before, ex-services, usually army, very touchy-feely.

Still holding tightly on to Aden, Pat looked up at the board. "So, what have we here then?" He walked up to the board and rubbed his chin. "Interesting ... I'll tell you what, I wouldn't trust this fella."

Tim, Gabby and Steph looked on in surprise. Pat pointed a finger at Aden's picture on the board.

They looked at each other in disbelief and watched the new lunatic member of their team. Aden sank further into his chair.

Pat spoke in a hybrid Irish-American accent. "Listen up, officers, we're on the lookout for this deviant miscreant. We're going to put an APB on this cat's ass for committing a three-one-one and being a five-oh -seven."

As Aden sat speechless, the rest of the team cracked up laughing. It was all the encouragement Pat needed as he reviewed an invisible file in front of him.

"Tut, tut. It makes for a sad reading, so it does. He's got a sheet as long as your arm." Pat thumbed through the invisible file, then looked up at Aden. He could tell his new partner was not amused.

"But that's enough of that," he said, closing the invisible file and tossing it over his shoulder. "Now, let's get back to the case at hand," he added, pointing at the board. "French government man ... Pretty girl ... Pretty girl's mummy and daddy ... Nasty man who killed people for money ... Man who doesn't smile much." Pat looked round at Aden.

Aden frowned.

"Boss lady."

As Tim, Gabby and Steph sat spellbound, Aden wanted the men in white coats to come and take the man with the mad face away.

Pat suddenly raised his hands to his mouth as if in prayer, made some thoughtful sounds and said, "Right, I've got it."

"What?" Aden said, leaning forward in disbelief. "What do you mean, you've got it?"

"It goes like this. Pearl's father murdered her mother as he just couldn't live with her moaning anymore. You know what women are like, right?"

Aden slumped back in his chair and rolled his eyes.

"He was so worried that his daughter would find out, he put her in a pea green boat with an owl and a pussycat and set her off sailing on the high seas. He couldn't live with himself after what he'd done so went to visit Davy Jones's locker and didn't come back." Pat thought for a moment. "Pearl is seeing the French advisor. Her boyfriend couldn't take it, got really upset and came all the way to England, shot someone and had so much to drink he couldn't stand properly, lost his balance and fell in front a train. Happens every day on the tube, doesn't it?"

Suddenly the laughter stopped.

"Oh Pat, ya blethering eejit, I've gone and put my daft big foot in my mouth again." Pat slapped his forehead with his palm. "It was your colleague he shot and I was insensitive. I am sorry."

Pat cupped the sides of his head with his hands and raised his eyes to the ceiling. "I get kinda carried away, so I do, and my mouth just runs on and on with itself and I can't stop, I just can't stop – look it's doing it again, so it is."

Pat clasped his hands together, stood up straight and took a deep breath. "Right, time to get serious."

He looked at the board, mumbled something under his breath and made a humming sound. The rest of the team all looked at each other and shared various expressions.

"Right, I've really got it."

The team looked up.

"I reckon this Pearl gal is still hung up about the death of her parents and is trying to get to the bottom of what happened, hence her meeting with the French minister."

"Finally serious," Aden said as he sat up in the chair. "And now we're on the case and finding out things that people might not want us to find out, they send someone to kill us." Aden added.

Pat shrugged his shoulders. "Maybe."

"Pearl's company supplies technology to the French government, many governments in fact," Aden said.

Pat shrugged again. "Okay – unless it's a cover. To get up close."

Aden got up and moved forward. He stabbed his finger against the board. "And what about this body?"

"Dougie Malone. Little shit from Belfast. I don't think this is anything to do with the IRA. I think he was a gun for hire. Many of the old guys are these days, putting their hard-earned skills to good use."

Aden took a step back and pondered for a moment.

"Maybe Pearl knows we're on to her. Maybe she hired those goons to come after me and Caren. If that's the case I wonder what she's planning." Aden cupped his chin in his hand, thought for a moment and prodded the board. "She is the key. She's the one we need to go after."

Pat nodded.

The door opened and Caren walked in.

"You two got to know each other yet?"

"Well, no, not really, but we have come up with some ideas about this case."

"Interesting ..." Caren said as she sat down. "Tell me more."

Chapter 14

Ready

Meanwhile, in a distant land, Pearl stood on a beach looking out to sea. Her bare feet sank into the soft sand. Her white gown loosely fluttered in the breeze revealing part of her flesh beneath.

She closed her eyes and ran her right hand through her hair. Her left hand swung by her side clutching a radio.

With her eyes still closed, she tilted her face upwards. The heat of the sun warmed her and the gentle breeze massaged her skin.

The radio buzzed into life. "Pearl, are you there?" a man's voice asked.

She raised the radio to her mouth. "Yes, go ahead."

"We're ready."

"Okay, I'll be up in a moment."

Pearl lowered the radio and smiled. She looked up. Her eyes followed the towering cliff walls from the beach towards the highest point, on top of which was the old monastery she had renovated.

She often imagined the Shaolin monks going about their business and what a peaceful and uncomplicated life they must have led. They had left many years ago, and these days the locals considered the place to be haunted, which helped maintain her cover.

***

In a control room within the monastery, a man sat with a radio in his hand. He was watching a screen showing the output of a video camera from the beach below. He pressed a few buttons and zoomed. He zoomed in further and his pulse started to race. As the breeze caught Pearl's gown her upper thigh was exposed. He nudged the camera upwards. He could see part of her breast. He felt something stir.

***

Pearl felt a shiver through her spine, as though someone was staring at her. She looked round, but there was no one there. She looked up. She saw the video camera pointing at her. She snapped her head away and turned towards an opening in the cliff.

Inside, she walked up to an elevator and pressed a button. The lift went 'ping' and the door opened. She stepped inside and pressed another button. As the door closed, she couldn't help thinking this was one of the best modernisations she'd added – much easier than the original four hundred and twenty three steps down to the beach.

Chapter 15

The Green Cupboard

Aden pulled the BMW into a parking space and turned off the engine. He looked all around.

"Wow, you live here?" Pat gasped.

"Yep," Aden replied.

"Looks swanky," Pat said looking at the building.

Aden looked around, "Yeah, I guess so."

"No white van this time," Pat said.

"No, doesn't look like it. Come on."

Aden's flat was on the ground floor of a three-storey town house – four storeys if you counted the basement flat below. As they walked up the steps, Pat craned his neck to see if he could see in through the large windows of the basement.

Aden examined the lock. No sign of tampering.

"Look okay?" Pat asked.

"Yes, seems fine."

He unlocked the door and walked in.

Pat looked up. The hallway was large with a distinctive smell of bleach that tickled his nose. The stairs up to the other floors were on the left with a back door fire escape to the rear.

"This yours?" Pat said, pointing to the door on their right.

Aden nodded and examined the lock. He ran his hand up

against the edge of the door from top to bottom.

"Look okay?" Pat asked.

"No damage," Aden replied.

He inserted the key in the lock and turned. He fiddled with it, moving it slightly from side to side.

Aden could feel Pat's eyes burrowing into the back of his head.

"The lock's playing up. Has been for ages, I just keep forgetting to get it fixed."

It finally clicked into place and Aden slowly opened the door and peered around the edge. Pat held the main front door open in case they needed to make a quick getaway.

"Look okay?"

Aden turned his head, "Is your needle stuck?" He looked around. "Yes. it seems fine. Come in."

Pat shrugged his shoulders and closed the main entrance door. He followed Aden into the flat.

"Home sweet home," Aden said as he took off his leather jacket, threw it on the arm of the sofa and sat down. He rubbed his eyes and yawned.

"Don't you mean home home?" Pat said.

"What?"

"Home home – there's nothing sweet about this!" Pat joked.

Aden rolled his eyes.

"It's a bit sparse, isn't it. I was expecting some kind of posh bachelor pad."

Aden looked around as if nothing was wrong. "I like to live simple."

"My friend, there is simple and there is worn out seventies' minimalism – just look at that telly and the table!" Pat said, pointing with exaggerated disgust.

Aden looked at the television, then at Pat. "I rarely watch TV so don't need anything special." He thought to himself for a moment. "I can't actually remember when I last turned it on."

He looked at the table and back at Pat. "This table has been in the family for years. Just a hand-me-down really." Aden picked up a magazine lying on it. "It does its job," and he dropped the magazine back down again.

"And look at that sofa!" Pat sat down and sank amongst the worn out springs. He looked over with a 'told you so' expression on his face.

Aden gave an exaggerated smile. "It helps if you sit this end."

As Pat sank further into the frame, he realised his mobile phone had slipped out of his pocket. He struggled to sit up and put the phone on the coffee table.

"Can I look around?"

"Sure. Knock yourself out," Aden said as he gripped his hands behind his head and stretched.

"You don't have any bars, do you?"

Aden turned his head. He didn't have the foggiest idea what Pat was talking about half the time. "What?"

"Bars. Bars! You've heard about the man that walks into a bar and knocks himself out. A metal bar!"

Aden shook his head, closed his eyes and rested his head back into the sofa.

Pat, with his hands in his pockets, wandered around the flat. It was a spacious room with nice tall ceilings but it was so empty. "You could hold an Irish dance in here, so you could."

Aden didn't respond.

As well as the sofa, coffee table and the television, there was a tattered armchair which looked almost pre-war, and a bookcase with a few books but mostly scraps of paper, envelopes, mobile phone box, charger and all manner of other odds and ends. There was nothing hanging on any of the walls, except for a mirror on the wall behind him. Pat turned round, looked at himself and adjusted his hair.

"I need to buy meself a comb, just look at the state of me. You'd think I'd crawled through a hedge backwards."

Again, Aden didn't respond.

"How much time you here?" Pat asked.

"What do you mean?" Aden replied with his eyes still closed.

"How much time do you spend here – at home home?"

"Oh, I see. Erm, hardly any at all really, always working."

Pat nodded. That made sense.

"You got any food, I'm starving," Pat said, as if he'd just changed the record.

"I don't know actually, you'll have to check in the cupboards." Aden pointed. "Kitchen."

Pat's gaze followed Aden's finger.

"Now how did I not see that?" Pat smiled to himself.

The kitchen was separated from the living room by a pedestal worktop with a sink. He looked around – microwave, kettle and toaster. Pat nodded as he mentally ticked off his essential kitchen item list – cooker, oven, washing machine and sink.

The cupboards were a sickly green colour to which Pat turned up his nose.

"Now, let's play kitchen lucky dip," he said aloud as he held the handle of the nearest cupboard. "Welcome, Pat, and in tonight's show you have a wonderful opportunity to win some food if you can guess what's in the horrible green cupboards in Aden's flat."

Aden cupped his ears with his hands and kept his eyes firmly closed.

"And here we have cupboard number one. What's your guess, Pat? ... Plates!"

Pat swung open the cupboard door. Inside was some porridge, flour, cornflour and various herbs and spices. The packaging looked old.

"Ahh, tough luck, Pat. For a bonus prize, though, can you guess what year the flour went out of date? ... Now, let me think. Last year?"

He picked up the flour and turned it around until he could see the date.

"Jesus, Mary and Joseph – five years ago. I don't believe it. Surely this thing should be evolving eyes by now," Pat said as he stared with astonishment at the packaging.

He stood back and glanced into the living room. Aden was unresponsive. Pat shrugged his shoulders, put the flour back and closed the door.

"In horrible green cupboard number two we have ..." He thought for a moment. "Plates."

He swung the door open. "Nah, nah. Wrong again, Pat, my lad. Uh oh, what do we have here? This looks promising."

He picked up a can of tomato soup. It had gone off a year ago. A tin of baked beans caught his eye. He picked it up and checked the date.

"Aden?" Pat said, stepping back so he could see him on the sofa.

Aden uncupped one ear, opened his eyes and looked over.

"Your beans are out of date."

"Thanks for letting me know," Aden replied and closed his eyes again.

"In horrible green cupboard number three, we have ... It's got to be plates this time surely."

Pat opened the door. He saw cling film, kitchen roll, some batteries, metal foil and a few other odds and ends. He closed the door and sighed.

"How can anyone not have any plates? It was a sure bet ... You gotta have plates in this one ... And in horrible green cupboard number four, we have ..." Pat swung open the door.

"Oh, bollocks."

Pat's stomach turned over.

He recognised it immediately. He had encountered his fair share of them in his life – the familiar wires linking the explosive to the detonator, the main charge and the digital readout. He blinked and blinked again. The digital readout was counting down – *sixteen, fifteen, fourteen* ...

"BOMB, BOMB, FUCKING BOMB!" Pat yelled at the top of his voice.

Aden had almost dropped off to sleep. He opened his eyes and wondered what type of charade it was this time.

He looked up.

Pat burst from the kitchen. His mad face was pale with a look of terror. "Bomb!"

Aden jolted up and ran towards the door, Pat directly behind him.

Aden fumbled with the lock. "Bloody thing won't turn."

Pat visualised the bomb timer in his mind, counting down.

"Come on, come on, it's gonna go off!"

"Trying. Trying," Aden said frantically as he tried to turn the lock.

Finally – click. The door opened. He felt hands behind push him towards the front door; he turned the latch and yanked the door open – then everything went white.

***

Aden opened his eyes. He could see clouds. He lay in a field with his gran lying next to him.

"What do you see?" she asked.

Aden looked up at the clouds. He squinted and stared. "I see an elephant."

"What else do you see?" she asked.

Aden stared harder. The clouds were changing shape. "It's changed."

"What do you see?" she asked, more determined.

"It's changed into ..." He stared hard. Something flashed across his vision, and then again. Finally he saw it. "A rhinoceros!"

"What did he say?" the woman asked, crouched over

Aden's body on the pavement.

A man knelt at Aden's side. "I think he said rhinoceros ... Hello?" The man waved his hands in front of Aden's eyes again. "You were staring upwards as if you were looking at something. I asked what you were looking at."

Aden turned his head. It wasn't his gran lying next to him, it was someone else. He recognised him – he knew him, but couldn't place the name. Aden was no longer lying in the field. The ground underneath him was hard and uncomfortable.

"Are you okay?" the man asked.

Aden looked upwards to see the face staring down at him, his senses slowly returning.

"I've got a terrible screaming noise in my ears," Aden said.

"It's the alarms," the man replied.

"The what?"

"The car alarms. There was some kind of explosion."

"I can't move my leg!" Aden said.

"We don't want to move you until the ambulance arrives."

"But I can't move my bloody leg!"

"Just wait, the emergency services are on their way."

Aden continued to wriggle.

"Look, your friend is with you."

Aden turned his head to one side. He still couldn't place the name of the person lying beside him. He had a mad-looking face and wild hair.

Aden felt a weight on his body, pressing down. He tried to push against it but it wouldn't budge.

"Pat?" Aden said. He was sure that was his name.

The man lying next to him opened his eyes.

"All right, mucker?"

"I can't move my leg."

"Why not?"

"We were in an explosion."

"That wasn't an explosion – that was a firework compared to some of the stuff I've seen."

Aden tried to move again, the weight still pushing down on him. *Is this what it's like to lose a limb?* Aden thought to himself.

He felt a hand on his shoulder. It was the man crouching over him. "It's your friend. He's lying on top of you."

Aden turned his head. "Pat."

"Yes, mate?"

"Can you get off me, please?"

"I didn't even realise I was on you. Hang on."

Pat groaned and heaved himself off.

Aden shifted his legs and moved his body. It was a welcome feeling. He was grateful to find he was all in one piece.

"Don't move," the man said as he knelt over them.

They both ignored him. Pat was already on his feet. He arched his back and re-styled his wild hair with a quick rake of his fingers.

Aden raised himself onto his knees. He felt bruised – little wonder with Pat's entire weight on him. Pat extended his hand. Aden took it and Pat helped him to his feet. "Thanks."

"Not sure I fancy living in your neighbourhood with this kind of thing going on," Pat said, looking at the building. "And, bugger me, but you're going to need to get the decorators in all right."

Aden blinked and looked at the front of the flat. Smoke was billowing from the windows and the distinctive smell of explosives filled the air. He could hear voices. He looked around and was surprised to see about fifteen people, huddled together, talking and pointing on the other side of the road.

"You shouldn't move. You could be injured," the man who had knelt over him said.

Aden waved away the man's concern. "We're both okay."

The man pointed at Aden's head. "But, you're bleeding."

"You are. You're bleeding." Pat gestured towards his head.

Aden raised his hand, touched his head and examined his fingers. "Thank you, sir. It's nothing serious. We're okay."

He checked his pockets. He thanked his lucky stars he had his wallet and car keys with him. The cars directly outside had had their windows blown in, but a little further up Aden's BMW seemed unscathed.

Aden turned to the man, "Is everyone out of the flats?"

"Er, I think so, yes."

Aden glanced across the road and noticed some familiar faces and a few others he didn't recognise.

"And you've called the Police, yes?"

"Yes, and the ambulance."

"Okay good, they'll manage everything from here."

They could hear sirens in the distance.

"Let's go," Aden said, grabbing Pat's arm.

"Aye," Pat agreed.

"Wait, the ambulance will be here any second."

"We're fine, really we are."

The rest of the crowd looked bewildered as to what was happening.

"I thought they were dead," said one voice.

"I heard it was a gas explosion," said another.

They approached Aden's BMW. Apart from a little dust on the roof, it was undamaged.

"Oh damn."

"What is it?" Pat asked.

"My leather jacket. Caren gave it to me for a birthday present; it was on the sofa."

"Bit brown though, wasn't it?"

"What?"

"If it had been black it would have been worth saving but it was only brown. 'Shit brown' we would have called it at school."

"Damn, I really liked that jacket," Aden muttered as he got inside and slammed the car door.

Pat got in the passenger side.

"Oh, I don't believe it."

"What now?"

"I've just remembered, my mobile was in the inside pocket."

Pat checked his trouser pockets. "Oh feck, mine was on your table."

Pat sighed. "Oh well, we can't go back in, so where we going? Back to base?"

"I thought you were hungry?"

"Aye, I am."

"Well, let's go and get some food," Aden said as he started the engine.

"Aye, that's fine by me. My stomach thinks my throat's been cut."

***

They sat with the engine running at the end of the McDonalds drive-thru queue.

"So tell me a little more about yourself," Aden said, gently dabbing his forehead where he'd got scratched in the fall.

"What's to tell?"

"Where were you born? When did you join the RUC? Anything."

"Well, now then, let's see. I was born in Galway in Southern Ireland to Mummy and Daddy Brogan. Dad legged off and left my mum when I was about six months old. She drank herself to an early grave when I was four and I went to live with Grandma and Grandpa. I lived with them 'til I was about ten, but they just couldn't handle me anymore, so I went to live with Uncle Mickey in Northern Ireland and that's when things really changed."

Aden listened.

"Mickey used to work down at the local pub and his girlfriend Connie used to do cleaning and stuff. School was okay. Rough, but then it was back then. You had to know how to protect yourself, you know."

Aden nodded.

"Things started to get a little shitty when I was about twelve. The pub Mickey was in was rough – local hangout for the IRA. Mickey was involved somehow, don't know how, but one night I had gone to bed, Connie was downstairs and Mickey was at the pub."

Aden gently nudged the car forward in the queue, listening intently.

"I remember I was asleep and having a dream – then a loud noise, banging, screaming and gun fire. The next thing I knew, I came to, turned my head and was staring down the barrel of a gun held by a mean fucker dressed all in black and wearing a balaclava."

Aden inched forward again.

"I seemed to stare down the barrel of his pistol for ages until he said, 'Lucky little shite,' lowered the gun and walked out. I was shitting meself. It was ages 'til I got the balls to go downstairs."

"Hang on." Aden interrupted and turned to the machine.

"Can I take your order?" said the dreary voice.

"Can I have a double cheeseburger, medium fries and a bottle of water please – and ...?" Aden looked at Pat.

"Er ..." Pat thought for a moment, leaned across and said in a raised voice, "I'll have a Big Mac, large fries, onion rings and a Coke."

"Is that everything?" the dreary voice asked.

"No, wait," Pat said, leaving Aden agog at the size of his appetite, "I nearly forgot the chicken nuggets – chicken nuggets."

"Is that one portion of chicken nuggets or a sharebox?"

"How many in a sharebox?"

"Twenty," the voice replied.

Pat deliberated.

You can't seriously eat twenty nuggets, can you? Aden thought.

"Just a portion," Pat replied.

"Okay. Anything else?" the voice asked.

Aden got in first. "No, that's it, thanks."

"Okay, please proceed to the pay booth."

"Talk about an edge-of-the-seat story. Hang on a sec while I pay," Aden said as he moved forward.

The girl in the booth thrust the payment terminal into Aden's hand. He inserted his card and tapped in the pin, handed it back and waited.

She gave the card to him and told him to move along to the next booth.

He nudged forward, stopped, caught the bag that was thrown at him and handed it to Pat.

Within a few seconds Aden had pulled into a space in the car park and turned off the engine.

Pat opened the bag and handed Aden his food, bottle of water and a napkin. He began to tuck in like he hadn't eaten for a week.

"So?" Aden asked as he carefully peeled off the wrapper to the burger.

"Yes, anyway," Pat said, swallowing a mouthful of burger, "I went downstairs. It seemed like ages but it was probably only minutes after it had happened. I hadn't seen anything like that before, so it was like some kind of weird dream. I got down to the hall; the front door had been smashed in and the door to the living room was open, which was unusual because the door was normally closed to keep the heat in. I walked in and there were things strewn everywhere – chair overturned, pictures on the floor, and lying in the middle of it all was Connie. She had her nightgown on which had ridden up around her waist." Pat paused and swallowed hard. "There was a lot of blood. I crouched down beside her and pulled her gown down. I looked at her face. She looked peaceful. That helped. I checked her over and saw she had been shot twice. Once in the heart and once in the stomach."

"Shit, sorry."

Pat shrugged. "Guess they got Mickey after hours at the pub. Dunno why they didn't pop me. S'pose someone up there was looking after me that day for sure."

"So what then?" Aden asked between mouthfuls.

"I went to live with a foster family for a while. Quieter area, school was much less rough, but I couldn't handle it. Got in trouble with school – very rebellious. I guess I couldn't cope with losing mum, dad and now Mickey and Connie as well. Went into an institution for a while, for difficult kids, and then did a spell in the army."

Pat took a long overdue bite of his burger.

"And then the RUC?"

Pat nodded and swallowed. "Aye, army wasn't for me, I had too much of an enquiring mind to be a soldier. Joined the RUC. Plenty of fun moments there, I tell ya – great craic. Moved over to the UK and worked with the anti-terrorist squad – was there for four years."

"You said you guessed they got Mickey. Didn't they find the body?"

"Nope," Pat replied.

"And they never found out what happened?"

"Nope," Pat said.

There was something in the way that Pat replied. It was a little bit too quick, as though there was something more to it. Perhaps it was just difficult to talk about.

"Anyway, what about you?" Pat said, changing the subject.

"Well, childhood was normal, no problems, did quite well at school. I lost my parents when I was fourteen. We were on a skiing holiday. We went every year. I was a bit cocky about my abilities and went off-piste on my own. I didn't realise I was heading into an avalanche zone. Mum and Dad screamed for me to stop and came after me. The next thing I knew, there was a mountain of snow falling behind me and suddenly Mum and Dad were gone."

Pat frowned. "Oh, Jesus."

"It was so bizarre. Everything was normal and suddenly everything was completely different. A guy from the embassy came to see me and explained what would happen. Went back home on the plane and went through social services for a while. Lived with foster parents and the like but they couldn't handle me. 'Good boy gone bad,' they said but, shit, I'd just lost my parents. My ... my continuity had gone, you know."

Pat nodded.

"I started to wonder what was the point of it all. I felt guilty – that was the problem. It was all my fault. If I hadn't gone off-piste, it wouldn't have happened."

"Ahh, you can't beat yourself up. These things happen. It was an accident."

"Not many kids get their parents killed."

Pat listened.

"Then one day, I woke up and felt different. Less angry. I'd got myself into a real mess and wanted to do something to make a difference. I started to wonder where I could put things right that were wrong."

"So you decided to become a copper?"

Aden nodded. "I was very lucky. There was this guy at the assessment centre who could see past my difficult years and believed in me. I found the tests easy, was very fit and sailed through. I went to Hendon, joined the Met and ended up working in Special Operations where I was introduced to the SIA and that's how I joined."

"And I understand that there is a little something between you and the boss lady, eh?"

"Water under the bridge."

"You were married though, right?"

"Technically, still am. We're separated."

"Any chance you'll get back together again?"

"Nah, marriage and the job don't mix."

"Did you live together?"

"For a while yes," Aden replied.

"Not in your place though?"

"No, I lived at Caren's."

"But you kept your flat?"

"It was handy. If I was on a job working odd hours I could go back to mine, plus I enjoyed having a little bolt hole. Basically I think we just preferred living on our own. You married?" Aden asked.

As Pat shoved a few chips in his mouth, he raised his left hand and revealed his finger. "No ring there, never was and never will be."

"No one at all?"

"There have been a few sweethearts but nothing too serious. I guess my heart is just in my job."

They continued to eat, watching people and cars come and go.

"Can you swim?" Aden asked.

"No. Can't swim. Nearly drowned in a river when I was a kid. Bloody terrified of water. You?"

"Yes. I just took to it when I was a child. I was even in the school team. I could have swum for the county and turned professional, but I wasn't that interested in it."

"So you're a good swimmer?"

"Yes," Aden said, nodding.

"Maybe you were a mermaid in a former life."

"Merman," Aden insisted.

"Do they even have such a thing?"

"Of course, how else do you think mermaids have merb-abies?"

"Doh, I am an eejit," Pat joked as he took a mouthful of burger. "Of all the questions you could ask, what made you come up with that?"

"'Cos I said water under the bridge earlier."

"Ahh ..." Pat said.

They sat again, looking out of the window, watching the world go by and other people sitting in their cars, just like them, shovelling processed food down their throats.

Aden polished off the last few chips and crumpled up the packaging. He wiped his mouth with a napkin and un-screwed the top of the water bottle.

"I loved my flat."

"Ahh, bollocks, you said yourself, you're hardly ever there."

"True, but it was always somewhere to return to. It was

reassuring, especially after all those years of being passed around, being someone else's responsibility."

"Well, look at it this way. It's an opportunity to redecorate and make it into a proper home with some nice colours, pictures on the walls and some modern furniture."

Aden nodded.

"Bloody close though, eh!"

"Yep, thank God you were hungry."

"Aye, always been one for my food. As my grandma used to say, you can't do anything on an empty stomach."

Aden drained the last few drops of water from the bottle and happened to glance in the rear-view mirror.

"In fact my stomach has got me out of a fair few scrapes. There was this one time ..."

Aden held his hand out, Pat stopped.

"IC1 male approaching from behind," Aden said as he watched the man walk towards the rear of the car. He was ducking as though he was trying to peer inside, his hand concealed in his jacket pocket.

"What's happening?" Pat asked, craning his head to try and see in the wing mirror.

"Not sure. He's definitely coming this way."

The man appeared at Aden's door. He rapped on the glass.

Aden looked at Pat. Pat shrugged his shoulders. Aden lowered the window slightly.

"All right?" the man asked.

"Yeah, you?" Aden replied.

"Yeah."

Aden wondered where this was going.

"You leaving?"

"What?"

"Are you leaving?"

"Not yet."

"Oh."

"Why?"

"There are no parking spaces left."

"Oh, right." Aden glanced around. "Just you is it?"

"No, I've got my two girls and two of their friends in the car."

"All right, give us a minute."

"Great, thank you. I appreciate that," the man smiled and began to turn.

"Actually, hang on," Aden said, grabbing the empty food packaging from Pat. "Can you drop this in the bin for us and we'll get a move on."

"Er, yeah, sure."

Aden handed him the rubbish and nodded. The man smiled again and walked off towards the nearest bin.

"Nothing like getting the public to do your dirty work," Pat joked.

Aden grinned and reached to start the engine. "Sorry if I was a bit off when I first learned I was going to be teamed up with you."

"Ahh, never mind, I'd be pissed off if I was to be teamed up with me too."

Aden smiled and looked at him.

"Ahh, up your arse. Let's go."

Chapter 16

Orders from Above

Chief Inspector William Headley stormed into Caren's office.

"Hello, sir, is everything okay?"

"Not really. A bomb went off at Aden's flat about half an hour ago."

Caren went deathly white.

"It's okay," William said as he held out his hand to calm her. "We have eye witness reports that Aden and Pat got out okay and drove off. We've been trying to call them but their phones are off. We've just located Aden's car near McDonalds in Shadwell."

The colour came back to her cheeks a little. "Thank God."

"I presume you haven't heard anything from Aden or Pat so far?"

"No, nothing, I'll call him right away." Caren picked up her phone. "Damn, you said their phones were off."

"Exactly. Either they've turned them off or they lost them in the explosion."

Caren placed her phone back down on the desk.

"Let me know when they've been in touch."

"Yes, sir, of course, sir."

The Chief Inspector could see she looked troubled.

"Don't worry, I am sure they're both fine."

"Thank you, sir."

As he turned to leave, he paused. "By the way, the Home Secretary has asked me to keep him appraised on the status of this investigation, so make sure you do the same with me."

"Er, yes, of course, sir, but I didn't realise this was such a high profile case."

"Well, a known assassin turning up in London and two attacks on our officers tends to raise the profile somewhat. Keep me updated."

Caren nodded as William closed the door behind him.

"Bloody hell," Caren said aloud as she stared at the desk. She grabbed her car keys and went to stand but put them down again. It would take her ages to get across to Shadwell at this time of day and they might have left by the time she got there. She slumped in her chair. All she could do was wait.

Chapter 17

Launch

Pearl tossed a leaf-green scarf around her neck and stood in front of the full length mirror.

It went with her other earth shades, khaki trousers and a beige blouse. She smiled. She looked great and she felt great.

As she left her room and walked up the wooden panelled hallway she felt a pang of excitement. She had waited a long time for this day to come.

Towards the end of the corridor was a room with two large doors. When she reached them, she grasped the ornamental handles and pushed.

The space was originally an old chapel, since converted into the main computer operations room. With wood panelling everywhere, it hummed with the sound of computers.

At one end above a fireplace were a number of screens showing various images and graphs. In the middle was a bank of eight desks. Seven very focussed operators didn't even acknowledge she had entered.

To her left was a desk overlooking the team of operators, at which a man sat. He was oblivious to her entering the room. He sat back in the chair, eyes closed, with his hands behind his head and his feet up on the corner of the desk.

He opened his eyes and jumped up.

"Sorry, Pearl, I was just ..."

"Are we ready?"

"Er, yes, we are, we are ready. I await your command," Morgan said as he hurried to his seat at the eighth desk.

Pearl sat down and looked at the team in front of her.

Morgan was a bit of an enigma to her. He was socially awkward and seemed to lack common sense at times, but he more than made up for this with a brilliant technical mind and in-depth knowledge of network protocols, which had been invaluable to her. But something had changed.

In all this time he had been dedicated and committed, but lately there was a sense that greed was driving him. She also suspected he had a crush on her. It was understandable, living and working in such close confinement for such a length of time, especially due to the need for security and lack of contact with the outside world. She had felt herself being watched on the cameras. Was he in love with her? Is this why his mood had changed so much lately?

"Okay, everybody, listen up."

The clattering of keys stopped and everyone looked over.

Pearl couldn't have wished for a more loyal and hard working group of people; amazing considering the nature of the work they were involved in. Not often does a programmer get offered a top secret job working out of an old monastery at the top of a mountain. It takes a special kind of software engineer.

Her team sat eagerly awaiting what she was about to say.

"I have long waited for this moment. You have performed your jobs admirably. I am proud. Finally, there will be no more secrets, no more lies, no more cover-ups – we will know everything!"

She took a deep breath and thrust her finger towards Morgan.

"Launch!"

Morgan straightened the keyboard in front of him and started to type. With his finger poised over the return key, he looked at Pearl.

Pearl nodded confidently.

Morgan tapped the key.

It was done.

Morgan stared at the cursor flashing on his screen. Meanwhile, around the world, hundreds of thousands of networked devices all began to obey their pre-programmed instructions.

Pearl spun a full circle in her chair and looked upon her team with admiration.

It was an international mix of experts. She had run a competition online for an exclusive job with eight positions. They had to break a code she had personally written. She had never expected it to be such a success, with news spreading like wildfire within developer blogs and forums. She'd had to work hard to keep a lid on the real purpose of the project, but thankfully the competition was a tremendous success and, after the intensive and personal interview stage, she had found eight first class people.

Morgan, Pierre, Dominic, Natasha, Milo, Elene, Kris and – she smiled – Sinead.

She spun around again.

"Status report?"

Morgan tapped the keyboard and a series of numbers were displayed on screen.

"Yes, it is well underway."

Pearl brought her hands together against her mouth and smiled. She continued to spin in her chair.

Morgan glanced but quickly looked away when their eyes met.

Pearl brought her chair to an abrupt halt.

"How many connections?"

Morgan tapped another command into the computer.

"Just over two hundred million."

"Spectacular!" Pearl replied. "Space available?"

"We started with one petabyte and we have just over 950 terabytes remaining."

"Stupendous!"

She stood up and pushed her chair under her desk. "I'll be with my horses. Let me have an update every half hour."

Morgan nodded and watched Pearl leave the room.

He looked around at the rest of the team. They were all deeply involved with their work. He looked at the clock in the bottom right hand corner of his screen and started to count down. As soon as one minute had elapsed, he quietly stood up and sneaked out of the room.

He didn't realise Sinead had watched him leave.

Chapter 18

Reunion

"Where have you been? I was worried sick!" Caren said as she rushed up to Aden and hugged him.

"Whoa!" Aden said, struggling to remain upright. "I'm fine. We're fine."

"How ya doin'?" Pat said as he closed the door to Caren's office and grabbed a chair.

"So what happened? Why didn't you call me?" Caren snapped.

"Sorry, we lost our phones in the explosion."

"But what happened?" Caren said, pushing him away and thumping his shoulder.

"Ouch, careful. I am rather bruised, you know."

Caren bit her lip.

Aden sat down and leant forward in the chair. "We went to my flat. I was lounging on the sofa while Pat searched the kitchen cupboards for food ..."

"Aye, and you wouldn't believe what I found," Pat interrupted. "Food that had gone out of date years ago – I don't know how your man survives!"

Aden frowned and turned back to Caren.

"A bomb?" Caren said, propping herself against the edge of the desk.

"Yes, a bomb," Aden said.

"Oh yes, and a bomb," Pat said, sitting back.

"Was there anything about the bomb that stood out?"

"Yes, it exploded," Pat quipped, scratching his head.

"Yes, apart from that. Anything about how it looked, the way it was put together – I dunno, the type of explosive they used. You must have seen loads of devices during your time in the RUC, Pat."

"Well, now you mention it, yes, there has been something bothering me."

"Which is?" Caren said, gesturing with open hands.

"Well, it was a very wee bomb."

"Wee?" Caren quizzed.

"Wee – small – it was a very small bomb and also the explosive was very weak."

"Weak? How could you tell?"

"The effect of the explosion and the smell, as though they'd diluted it. More whoosh, less boom."

"That's interesting," Caren said.

"Could it be they were just trying to minimise collateral damage?" Aden suggested.

Pat thought for a moment and rubbed his chin. "I dunno. I've yet to encounter a considerate bomber, if you know what I mean."

"But they were obviously trying to kill you," Caren said.

"Well, that's the thing. I don't think they were. There wasn't enough explosive to kill us. It was almost ..."

"Almost what?" Caren asked, picking up a pen from the desk and playing with it between her fingers.

"Well, almost as if they were trying to warn us."

"Perhaps that's what this is all about – warning us off the case," Aden said, sitting upright. "Think about it. They could have mounted a more effective attack the other night and they could have used a bigger bomb – if they had wanted to kill us. Maybe it was just a warning."

Caren pushed herself back from the desk. "So, what now? Suggestions?"

"We need to find out more about Pearl," Aden said.

Pat nodded.

"Yes, I agree. Her company is registered in Paris so start there and see where it takes you," Caren said.

Aden nodded.

"Make sure you get a couple of replacement phones before you leave."

"I've already got my old personal one from my desk drawer," Aden replied, lifting it from his pocket.

"Just get issued with company kit."

Aden nodded and Pat opened the door.

"In the meantime, I'd better give the Chief Inspector the update he wanted. Have a safe trip."

Chapter 19

A New Consultant

"Yes, Jenny?" Greg Willis said as he picked up the phone.

"Deputy Prime Minister, I have a caller on the line. Something about arranging a consultant. Is this an IT issue – shall I transfer him to IT?"

"Er, no," Greg replied decisively. "I'll take it. Put it through."

Greg listened: there was silence on the line. He spoke. "Hello?"

"Hello. Is this Greg Willis, the Deputy Prime Minister?" The man spoke with a French accent.

"Yes, it is. How can I help you?"

"We have found a new consultant for the joint-EU project," the man said.

Greg shifted his weight in his chair.

"We shall proceed?" the man asked.

"Oh, yes, please. Definitely proceed," Greg said excitedly.

"Okay," the man replied.

"Wait – before you go ..."

"Yes, there is something else?"

"We've been working on that other information you needed."

"And?" the man said.

"You'll need to follow things up from your end."

For a moment there was silence. "Very good," the man said. "I will look into it personally."

The caller was gone.

Chapter 20

Bonne Arrivée

"Let's get that one," Pat said, pointing at the picture on the wall.

"A Mercedes?"

"Yep, always wanted to drive one, never have."

"The boss is going to love that."

Pat winked and smiled.

"Celle-là, s'il vous plait," Aden said, pointing at the picture on the wall.

The lady behind the car rental desk confirmed the choice and began processing the paperwork.

Aden glanced at the clock on the wall. It was just after ten in the morning. *Is that all?* he thought as he stifled a yawn. It had been a very early start.

He looked round at the mounting queue behind him.

"Monsieur?"

Aden nodded and put his credit card in the machine.

The woman pressed a few buttons and in a moment the transaction was complete. Aden took the keys and the various bits of paper that were handed to him. "La voiture se trouve vingt metres au gauche."

"Merci. Au revoir," Aden said, and Pat turned to the door. "I think she said it was down here," Aden said, leading them both through the line of hire cars.

"What's the best car you've ever driven?" Pat asked.

"Best car? That would probably be the Audi R8 I drove last year."

"Wow, you had an R8. How come?"

"It was on a job. I was a successful drug dealer and needed a car that would look the part. Four weeks I was driving it round and round London. It's amazing it wasn't scratched to bits."

Aden scanned the cars in front looking for a gold Mercedes. "And you?"

"BMW M3. We ran it as an intercept car in Northern Ireland. Damn, that thing could move."

Pat could see the car up ahead.

"Press the button, press the button," Pat said.

"Yes, yes, I was going to."

Aden pressed the button on the remote control and a few cars in front of them a gold Mercedes AMG chirped. Pat ran on ahead. By the time Aden caught up with him, Pat was running his hand down the lines of the car.

"Beautiful, bloody beautiful. I'll drive."

"Can you drive?"

"Of course I can drive. I've been driving since I was ten," Pat replied proudly.

"Okay, hotel first," Aden said as he tossed him the key.

"Aye, aye, right you are, sir." Pat caught the key and in a flash was sitting in the driver's seat, measuring up the inside.

Aden got in. It was a nice car. It oozed quality, even if it was a rental. "Good choice."

"Aye, indeed, it's a corker."

Pat started the engine, adjusted the seat, fiddled with a few buttons and gently pulled away.

As they sat in traffic on the way to the hotel, Aden thought about some of the stories Pat had told him.

"You're very quiet there, partner."

"Just thinking."

"Penny for 'em."

"I was thinking about your uncle and his girlfriend, actually, and how awful it must have been."

"Aye, I try not to dwell on the past. Brings you down, so it does. Enjoy the moment, I say."

Aden nodded and looked at the sat nav display.

In this traffic he suspected the journey might be a little longer than the forty-five minutes it predicted.

Chapter 21

The Lead

"I don't know, Mum, it might be another couple of weeks," Caren said, holding the phone to her ear. "I told you, there was a water leak. The decorators are in sorting it all out ... I know I'm in the top floor flat, the water tanks are in the roof," Caren sighed.

There was a knock at the door.

"Sorry, Mum, I've got to go. Someone needs to see me. I really appreciate you letting me stay ... Yes, yes. I'll be home about seven. Thanks. Bye."

Caren looked up to see Josh from the Technical Operations department waving through the window.

"Come in," she said and beckoned him with her hand.

"Sorry to disturb you, ma'am." Josh entered the room sheepishly.

"That's okay," she said, sitting back in her chair. "What is it?"

"We've been running those facial recognition checks on that photo," Josh said nervously.

"And?"

"We've got something on the woman."

Josh approached the desk and handed Caren a printout.

"We turned up an ID card from the Sorbonne. It was registered with her local Gendarmerie for some public order offence after a party."

"Thanks, Josh, very helpful."

"No problem. If we turn up anything else, we'll let you know."

Caren nodded while studying the information in front of her. She picked up her mobile phone to send a text message.

Chapter 22

The Message

"Bonjour," Aden said as he approached the hotel receptionist.

"Bonjour, monsieur," she said, looking at Aden, "Monsieur," looking at Pat.

"We have a reservation. Jenkins and O'Reilly," Aden said.

"Ah, oui, two rooms, one night. Please complete this registration card."

Aden grabbed the pen and hurriedly filled out the card. "Here you go."

"Merci, monsieur," the receptionist said and handed them two keycards.

"Merci," Aden said, accepting one.

"Thanks," said Pat, taking the other.

As they walked across reception towards the elevators they heard a phone beep.

Pat checked his mobile. "I think that was you?"

"Was it? I'll have to change this default tone." Aden reached into his pocket and read the message:

`Pearl was Wilson in 99 Sorbet`

"Is that from wifey?" Pat asked.

"Er, yes, I don't quite understand it though."

"What does it say?" Pat asked, trying to look at the screen.

"Well, I'm guessing Pearl went under her mother's surname in 1999, but Sorbet?"

Pat reached out his hand. Aden gave him the phone.

"Sorbet. Sorbet? I know what this is, it's bloody autocorrect. She means Sorbonne." Pat handed the phone back with an extra big grin.

"Of course, yes. Well done."

"That's okay. I've sent my own fair share of mistyped texts in the past."

As Aden jabbed the lift button, Pat chatted away.

"There was this girl I was seeing, Lorraine. Lovely gal, she really liked me, but she was a bit clingy and lacking in confidence. It wasn't that serious, but I liked her. So, I was busy on a job and trying to concentrate and she sent me a text saying it was going to be her birthday and she wanted to see me on her special day."

At that moment the lift arrived. They walked in and Aden punched number seven.

"Anyway, I wanted to go and I also wanted to say that I liked her, you know, to try to help her with her confidence, so I sent her a text back saying, 'I really like you, I want to get you a present, see you later'. I got on with the job and heard another text come in. I was too busy to read it but another text came in, then another. I turned my phone off in the end."

Aden listened politely as he watched the floor numbers change.

"At the end of the day, I clocked off and turned my phone

back on. I had like twelve messages from Lorraine. Twelve! I couldn't work out what the hell she was going on about."

The elevator pinged and the door opened. They were in rooms 712 and 713. Aden walked out of the lift and turned right.

"She was saying stuff like: wow, this is great – she didn't realise I felt the same way – we have to get married first so can she start making arrangements – can she tell her mum – I should ask her dad's permission, blah, blah, blah."

As Aden counted up the room numbers, he wondered if there would ever be an end to this story.

"I was like, what the hell, she's gone in the head – effin' married? This bloody bird's a nutter."

Aden saw the rooms ahead of them.

"I sent a text back saying I'm not sure I'm ready for that type of commitment right now and maybe we could discuss it again in the future, and I got a text back from her saying she was very confused and what about the baby?"

They had reached their rooms.

"I was ready to bang my head against the wall. I'd not even got it in her hole; how the bejeezus could I have got her knocked up?"

Aden stood patiently with his key in his hand and again wondered if this story was ever going to end.

"So I sent a text back to her suggesting perhaps we shouldn't see each other for a while, and that was it. I didn't hear from her again."

"I'm sorry to hear that," Aden said, thinking it was finally the end of the tale. He was about to turn and unlock his door.

"No, wait," Pat gestured. "The next day I just couldn't get my head around what was going on so I was reading back through the texts. It turns out, instead of saying, 'I want to get you a present', I'd said, 'I want to get you pregnant' – bloody autocorrect, see!"

Aden thought about it for a second and started to laugh. "Poor girl."

"Aye. Poor little Lorraine. I did like her. Just not enough to have a little snapper with her. Anyways, what's the plan?"

"Right, thirty minutes." Aden checked his watch. "We'll get freshened up and head on to the Sorbonne – that's our lead."

"Right you are. See you in a while, crocodile."

Aden pushed open his door and tossed his bag on the bed.

Meanwhile, in the hotel lobby, a man in wire-rimmed glasses raised a mobile phone to his ear.

Chapter 23

The Melody

Pearl had three horses, Onyx Wildflower, Peppermint Seafoam and Emerald Princess. She loved them all; they were her best friends.

She rubbed her cheek against Emerald's head and closed her eyes. She began to hum a melody. The horse gently pushed against her and blew through its nose.

As she hummed, her mind travelled back through time with vivid pictures forming of her mother and her father. She focused on one event in particular. She could see it clearly.

It was her tenth birthday tomorrow and she could tell her parents were up to something. They were behaving oddly and for some reason she was told she couldn't go into the barn.

She sat in her bedroom looking at the barn. She was excited and mystified. She had never been told not to go into the barn before. In fact she hardly went into the barn anyway. It was just a glorified shed, full of her father's fishing gear and a half-repaired boat.

Her inquisitive mind could take no more. She sat looking out of the window until an hour after her parents had gone to bed.

They must be asleep by now, she thought.

She had seen her father go to the barn last thing that night, which was something he never did.

What's in there? she kept thinking to herself.

She opened a drawer in her bedside cabinet and pulled out a torch. She tiptoed from her bedroom, through the living room, out of the front door and outside.

In her nightdress and slippers, she stood outside the barn, her heart beating like a drum. She struggled with the latch, trying to remain as quiet as possible, and opened the door enough so she could squeeze inside. She turned on the torch. The amber glow was faint, but it helped her see a little better. Inside was dark. She was worried and apprehensive yet her curiosity kept her going. She pulled the door closed behind her and listened.

Suddenly the excitement turned to fear. She could hear breathing. Whatever it was, it was bigger than she was, much bigger. Fixed to the spot and unable to move, she nervously raised the torch. She moved the beam slowly around the barn. She could make out the boat, but what were the other shadows? At first she thought she could see a snake but it was a coil of rope. She could see a shark, but it was just the tip of a paddle. She heard it again, breathing. Her pulse raced, her stomach was in knots. She moved the torch further to her right, higher and higher – and then her fears turned to elation.

"A horse!"

***

It was just before sunrise when Pearl's parents found her in the barn. She lay on an old tarpaulin in the part-repaired boat, asleep.

"She must have been up most of the night," her father whispered as he picked up her floppy body.

"Put her back to bed. She can get another few hours' sleep."

***

When Pearl awoke in bed, she didn't know if what she had seen had been real or not.

She hurried out of her bedroom to find her mother and father sitting at the table drinking tea.

"Happy birthday, Pearl," her mother said.

"Happy birthday, my little jewel," her father said.

Pearl rubbed her eyes. "I had the most amazing dream. I dreamt I had a horse."

"Really?"

"It was so real. You'd hidden it in the barn and I stayed up all night."

"What an amazing dream. Shall we go and have a look to see if it was real?"

"Yes, yes, let's!" Pearl said, jumping up and down.

Her mother and father walked either side of Pearl, holding her hands as she skipped her way to the barn. Her father unbolted the door and opened it very slightly. "Go on, then."

Pearl looked up beaming and rushed inside.

She looked around. A partly-repaired boat, fishing equipment, pots, boxes, bits of wood, rope, but no horse.

Her mother and father entered.

Pearl sighed and lowered her shoulders in disappointment. "But it was so real."

"Dreams can be like that sometimes, almost real."

Pearl flung herself at her mother and threw her arms tightly around her.

"Don't be upset," her mother said. "Shall we show you your real present?"

Pearl looked up. As tear followed tear down her cheeks, she reluctantly nodded.

"Come on."

They held her hands again and strolled to the house but, instead of going to the front, they led her towards the rear.

"Where are we going?" Pearl asked.

"To find your present," her mother replied.

As they walked around the back of the house, Pearl stopped in her tracks and screamed with excitement.

"A horse! So, it wasn't a dream after all?" This time tears of happiness were running down Pearl's face.

"No, it wasn't a dream," her father said, kneeling in front of her. "Just remember, don't go looking for something until it's ready to be found – be patient and you will be rewarded."

"Okay. I'll remember. Does it have a name?"

"No, he doesn't have a name yet."

"What can I call him?" Pearl asked, looking eagerly at her mother and father.

"Whatever you like; he's your horse."

Pearl thought for a moment.

She remembered a poem about a mermaid. In the story,

the mermaid cried out of happiness and her tears formed a cascade down her cheeks. As Pearl wiped away her own tears, she came up with the first part of its name.

She thought a bit longer. There was a story her father used to tell her when she was younger, 'The Tale of the Kingfisher'. It had been passed down through the family and his description of the majestic kingfisher had always beguiled her.

"I've got it," Pearl said and looked up. "Cascade Kingfisher," she announced proudly.

"What a beautiful name," her mother said.

"Very appropriate," her father added.

As Pearl continued to hum her melody and reminisce on her happy thoughts, she had no idea that someone was approaching from behind.

Morgan had been watching her from outside the stable. He stepped towards her quietly. He held something in his right hand.

Unsettled, the horse snorted.

"What's up, my beauty? What's the matter?"

Chapter 24

La Sorbonne

They were back on the road. This time it was Aden driving the gold Mercedes with the sat nav programmed for the Sorbonne.

"ETA 20 minutes, or in this traffic more like an hour," Pat said, playing with the route planner.

Pat could see that Aden kept glancing in the rear-view mirror.

"Problem?" he asked, leaning back with his right arm hanging out of the window.

"Not sure. There's a black Citroen behind. It's been on our tail since the hotel. That's five turns now and it's still behind."

"Could just be coincidence. This would be a main route from the hotel."

"True, could be."

Aden followed the sat nav's instructions whilst negotiating the Paris traffic.

"And I thought London was bad," Pat said as he reached forward to check something on the screen.

A taxi whizzed by with just millimetres to spare.

"Bugger me, did you see that?"

"That could've taken your arm off."

Pat nodded and rubbed his arm, appreciating it still being part of his body.

Aden looked back in the rear-view mirror. He couldn't see the black Citroen anymore. He alternated between mirrors.

"Has it gone?" Pat asked.

"Not sure."

As it poked its nose out of the traffic behind, he saw it again. "No, still there. It's behind a van. Not a lot I can do to lose it in this traffic," Aden said, stamping hard on the brake as the traffic light in front of them turned red. He jabbed the sat nav and zoomed out. "Look at the map. If I take the next right, then left, then left, then right, that'll put us back en route. Let's see what happens – hopefully he won't notice."

The lights changed to green. Aden didn't budge. After a moment the sound of horns erupted from behind them. He waited and waited – "Now," he said. He let out the clutch, yanked the steering wheel hard right and raced up the road.

Aden checked the rear-view mirror. Two cars managed to make it through before the lights changed. He eased off the accelerator and slowed down.

"Gone?"

"Yep, didn't make it through in time."

"Good. Sorbonne here we come," Pat said, relaxing into his seat.

Aden continued. The sat nav re-plotted the route.

"So what's the plan?" Pat asked.

"We'll find the main admin office, go in and find the records room, set off a fire alarm, photograph the information we need and get out."

"So basically walk into one of the most well-known universities in the world, cause a commotion and sneak out again."

Aden chuckled, "Yep."

"Love it!" Pat said, rubbing his hands together.

***

Aden slowed down as he approached the Universities of the Sorbonne.

"Jesus, Mary and Joseph! Would you just look at this place."

"It is rather grand, isn't it?" Aden said, admiring the building.

"Grand? Are you sure we didn't take a wrong turn and end up at the Louvre or something?"

"Nope, sure. Been here since 1253 apparently."

"How do you know that?"

"I Googled it before we left the hotel."

"Hmm, amazing," Pat said. "Which building do we want?"

"The Office of Administration," Aden said. "I Googled that too. Not sure which one it is though."

Aden saw a parking space. "I'll park here. We can walk the rest of the way."

He pulled the car into the space and they got out.

Pat arched his back. "This is nothing like the schools I went to, that's for sure."

In front of them was a central building, dominant and large.

"Yes, looks promising," Aden said.

People hustled around, professor-types, teacher-types, student-types, clutching folders and books to their chests, shoulder bags and satchels stuffed full of literature and notes. Voices chattered in a foreign tongue.

They walked confidently together towards the main building, strode up the steps and inside. They were greeted by the distinctive echoed tones of a large stone building – whispering voices, clattering heels on a stone floor and Pat exclaiming, "Fuck me, get a look at this!"

Inside the door on the right-hand side was a map. They scanned the list of departments.

"There – Salle des Dossiers, Hall of Records," Aden whispered to Pat.

They walked up the beautiful stone staircase which led to the first floor, following the directions they had seen on the map, towards the Hall of Records.

They reached the room at the end of a long hallway. "Ready?" Aden asked. Pat nodded.

"Thirty seconds and hit the alarm," Aden said. Pat nodded again.

Aden grabbed the handle and opened the door.

He was not quite sure what to expect from a room named the Hall of Records, but he certainly didn't expect this. It was incredibly ornate with detailed stonework and embellishments that wouldn't look out of place in a stately home.

There were dozens of filing cabinets all around the edge of the room and in front of him were four desks. Brass lamps with green cowlings gave off an eerie golden light. It was as if he had gone back in time. At one of the desks sat a young woman.

Pat peeked in. He was about to walk back to the fire alarm he had noticed earlier, but instead followed Aden into the room.

"Bonjour, messieurs, je peux vous aider?" she asked.

Aden turned. He hadn't realised Pat had followed him into the room. He furrowed his brow. Pat shook his head and nodded towards the desk.

Aden stepped forward. He could see the woman more clearly in the amber light of the lamp. It seemed to him that every French woman he had ever clapped eyes on was beautiful. Her black hair framed her soft angelic face. Her dark brown eyes smouldered. His eyes traced the seductive curve of her lips.

"Monsieur?"

Aden smiled. "Désolé de vous déranger, je cherche la Salle des Dossiers," Aden said, aiming for something along the lines of, "Sorry to trouble you, I'm looking for the Hall of Records."

"Monsieur, your French is very good. This is the Hall of Records, how can I help you?"

Aden looked from side to side and said, "You are all alone?"

"Yes, my colleagues take an early lunch; it is just me. What can I do for you?"

Pat stepped forward. "Well, hello, darling, we wanted to enquire about our daughter coming to study here."

At first the woman was confused. "Our daughter?" she said. "Pardon, perhaps my English not so good. You need the Department of Registration, Département de l'Enregistrement, on the ground floor."

Pat stood closer. She instinctively moved her chair backwards slightly. He picked up a stapler from her desk.

"Monsieur, que faites-vous?"

Pat threw the stapler to Aden. Her eyes followed it travelling through the air and, before she realised it, Pat had swiftly brought his open hand down against her neck. The woman went limp and slid from the chair onto the floor.

"She's got great legs, look."

"Pat! This wasn't the plan."

"It's only her," he said, pointing at the floor. "Better than all the commotion of setting off the alarms."

Aden threw the stapler at Pat. He caught it and replaced it on the desk.

"Help me get her in the chair," Pat said.

Aden helped pick her up and ease her back into the chair. Pat folded the woman's arms onto the desk and laid her head gently down on them.

"Sleepy, sleepy." He gently brushed her hair.

Aden rushed over to the filing cabinets and inspected them. "They're all by year. This should be quite easy," he said as he counted down and found ninety-nine. He tried to open it, but it wouldn't budge.

"Keys?" Aden called over.

Pat checked the woman's waist and looked on the desk. Nothing. He opened a drawer, opened another and found a set of keys.

"Here," he said, tossing them over.

Aden caught them and hastily searched for the appropriate key. He noticed each one had a small engraving – 02, 01, 00, 99.

"Got it. Go keep a look out," Aden said.

Pat nodded.

"Sorry about that, my dear," Pat said as he gave one final stroke of the receptionist's hair and hurried towards the door.

Aden rifled through the contents of the drawer. "Bingo." He found a file called 'Pearl Wilson'. This was definitely Pearl; she had hardly changed. He pulled out his phone and took photos of the individual pages.

He glanced round. "Everything okay?"

"Yes, all clear," Pat replied, peeking out of the door and down the hallway.

Aden continued to review the paperwork. There was something about a computer offence and something about Église de la Sagesse which he understood to be Church of Wisdom. He found an email address and a postal address which he guessed were probably out of date.

"Aha." He found a mobile telephone number.

"Aden."

He wasn't listening – too engrossed in what he'd found.

"ADEN!"

"Yes?"

"It's not clear anymore."

"Nearly finished."

"Three girls approaching," Pat called out as he saw three young women walk up the steps at the far end of the hall. It was no coincidence that there were four desks in the room.

"Nearly there, stall them," Aden whispered loudly whilst continuing to race through the pages in the file. *I don't want to leave anything behind.*

"Stall them. Stall them, he says," Pat muttered to himself – then he thought of a plan.

He rushed out of the room towards them. Part way along the corridor there were three steps that split the hall into a semi-second level. As he approached he could see the girls were walking quite slowly. One of them was showing the other two something on her mobile phone.

He approached the top of the steps: *Ahh, bugger it – here goes.*

He deliberately missed the first step, tumbled and fell. He made it as dramatic as he could and finished with a nice roll, hitting his heels as hard as he could into the stone floor for extra effect. The thump echoed around down the passageway.

"Oh, mon Dieu, vous allez bien?" one of the girls asked as all three of them rushed forward to his aid. They had all crouched down, concern on their faces, attempting to help Pat to his feet.

"Merci, merci," Pat said, becoming as heavy as he could. He wondered how Aden was getting on.

"Il est si lourd, je ne peux pas le bouger," one of the girls said. Pat was oblivious.

"Avez-vous besoin d'une ambulance?" asked another girl.

He wasn't quite sure what she'd said but he thought he recognised the word 'ambulance'.

"No ambulance, no ambulance, très bon, très bon," Pat said repeatedly.

Aden appeared. "Il y a un problème?"

"Cet homme est tombé, il pourrait être blessé."

Pat pushed the girls aside, stood up and dusted himself off. "Très bon, très bon. Merci, au revoir," he said as he walked off towards the steps down to the entrance.

The girls looked at each other in amazement and whispered under their breath. Aden shrugged his shoulders, smiled and followed his partner along the corridor. The girls stared for a moment, giggling, spoke rapidly and carried on walking towards the end of the hallway.

"Nice decoy."

"Thanks – banged my bloody knee though. That floor was really hard!"

"It did the trick. Right, let's get back to the hotel and review this information. We've got to get a lead on Pearl."

***

Pat plotted a course on the sat nav back to the hotel and Aden followed the directions.

All of a sudden, in his rear-view mirror a familiar vehicle came into sight.

"I don't believe it, that bloody Citroen is back."

"Same one?"

"I think so. Got a partial on the plate and I'm sure it's the same one ... Think of somewhere famous in Paris."

"Eiffel Tower?"

"Too close, something else."

"Sacré Coeur?"

"Yep, that'll do, tap it in."

Pat quickly tapped in a route to the Sacré Coeur.

Aden turned right. The black Citroen turned directly after them.

"Yep, definitely following us."

Aden changed down a gear and jabbed the accelerator. The engine responded immediately. He planned on putting some distance between them.

"Third left up ahead, then change lanes," Pat said, reading the sat nav.

"Got it," Aden replied.

Cars honked their horns disapprovingly as he careered the Mercedes through the Parisian traffic.

"After the left turn, you want to go immediately right."

"Right, okay."

Aden didn't take his eyes off the road as he concentrated on every potential obstacle in front of him.

"Is it still there?" Pat asked, craning his neck to see in the mirror.

Aden glanced behind. He couldn't see the black Citroen. He looked forward and back again. There it was, flicking in and out of view as it attempted to follow in his wake.

Aden looked for a gap through the opposing traffic and snapped the wheel to the left. Pat reached out and hung onto the dashboard as the car veered sharply. Aden accelerated and snatched the wheel to the right. He switched lanes, aimed for a clear gap and jabbed the accelerator again.

"Stay on this road for four kilometres. The Boulevard de Sebastopol."

"Got it."

Aden kept his foot on the accelerator. His pulse raced. It was dual lane all the way. He weaved left and right, slowed, accelerated, braked and accelerated hard again through the traffic. He kept glancing behind. The black Citroen was still there but he had put some good distance between them.

"Okay, left turn just up there," Pat said.

A car pulled out of a side road in front of them. Aden braked hard. They were both thrust forward. Aden hammered the horn with his fist. The driver in front waved his arms. Aden flashed the lights of the Mercedes, ordering him to move. The driver shook his fist and stuck his ground. A gap opened up. Aden yanked the wheel, floored the accelerator and sped on through it.

"Okay, where is this turning?" Aden asked without taking his eyes off the road.

"Two hundred metres, closing fast – second left."

"Yep. Got it."

The commotion behind had caused a natural snarl-up in the traffic. Aden couldn't see the black Citroen.

"No sign of it. Turning – now!"

Aden yanked the wheel left and put his foot down.

"Right in 300 metres," Pat said, sitting forward, scanning the sat nav.

"Okay."

Aden raced along the route as Pat instructed. "Turning – now!" He snatched the wheel hard right.

"Okay, one kilometre to the Sacré Coeur. In 500 metres turn right, then left, then right, then right, then right."

"Right, left, right, right, right," Aden repeated.

He took the turns rapidly, wrenching hard on the wheel. The road narrowed in front of them.

Aden slammed on the brakes. "Damn, this is a lot of people."

As they got nearer the Sacré Coeur, so the tourists became more numerous, as did the tourist shops and cafés. Aden jabbed the horn and edged forward. The tourists moved slowly. He nervously checked the rear-view mirror.

"Any sign?" Pat asked.

"No, all clear," Aden said, gripping the wheel tightly. "Come on – move!"

Aden hit the horn again and nudged forward.

"Maybe we should get out here?" Pat suggested.

A gap opened up. Aden sped through and slowed again. "Give it another thirty seconds. Let's see how we get on."

"Right just here," Pat said, pointing to the road. "Café on the corner."

"Got it," Aden replied.

He nudged forward again, accelerated and took the turn. He slammed hard on the brakes.

The Basilica of the Sacré Coeur filled the skyline in front of them. The road was narrow with more tourist shops and cafés. A crowd of tourists milled around. Aden hammered the horn.

Meanwhile, behind them, a black Citroen approached a narrowing in the road.

"Come on. Come on, bloody move," Aden snapped.

They stared at him in defiance, waving their arms. Aden revved and inched the car forward. They began to separate and he forced his way through.

"Last right, follow the road round to the front of the building."

Aden checked the map. "Okay, that's where we'll abandon the car."

He slowed down until he reached the top of the slope. He

checked all was clear, tugged the wheel to the right and sped around the grand building. Meandering tourists leapt out of the way with shouts in various languages.

"Okay, bail in five seconds."

Aden counted down and brought the car to a standstill in front of the basilica. He turned off the engine, left the keys in the ignition and opened the door. Pat got out, opened the back door and removed both their bags from the rear seat. He threw Aden his bag over the top of the car.

"Good idea not to leave this stuff at the hotel, they'll probably be waiting for us," Aden said as he caught it and put the straps over his shoulder.

Pat held his bag tightly, closed the door and ran round the front of the car.

"Down the steps," Aden said, leading the way.

Pat followed closely behind and, weaving their way between the gaps in the crowds, they ran down the steps.

They were almost at the bottom of the first set of steps when a black Citroen pulled up alongside the gold Mercedes. A man with wire-rimmed glasses got out of the car and rushed to the edge. He looked down to see the two men running across the Rue de Cardinal and on to a further set of steps.

The driver got out and stood beside him.

"Et maintenant?" the driver asked.

"Rien, on sait ce qu'ils vont faire," the man said, removing his glasses and wiping them with a handkerchief from his pocket. "Allons-y." He replaced his glasses and got back in the car.

The driver got in too, started the engine and pulled away.

Chapter 25

The Fright

Emerald Princess tossed her head backwards and snorted.

Pearl recoiled and looked round just as Morgan reached out.

"Oh, my God, you scared the life out of me!"

"Sorry, Pearl, you left your radio inside and I couldn't contact you." Morgan handed her the radio.

"There was no need to creep up on me. You gave me a real fright."

"Sorry. I didn't mean to."

"Is everything all right?"

"Yes, everything's fine. All processing well, one hundred and fifty terabytes received, still flooding in," Morgan stated.

Pearl tried to steady her breathing. "Thank you."

Morgan stood in silence a little longer than was comfortable.

"Is there anything else?"

"No, that's it." He turned and left.

Pearl placed a comforting hand on Emerald Princess's nose and stroked it lovingly. She heard a neighing nearby.

"It's okay, my darlings, it'll be your turn next."

Chapter 26

A Bold Move

Pat toyed with the menu in his hands and eagerly looked around to see what the other diners were having, while Aden sucked lemonade through a straw.

"You okay translating the menu?" Aden asked, raising his voice a little over the noisy restaurant chatter.

"Don't understand a bloody word, it's all foreign." Pat tossed the menu onto the table. "What are you having?"

"A Croque Monsieur."

"If it's good enough for you, then it's good enough for me." Pat held his glass of coke and looked out of the window.

"You are ready to order?" the waitress asked.

"Croque Monsieur, s'il vous plait," Aden replied. The waitress scribbled on her pad.

"Monsieur?"

"I'll have what he's having," Pat said.

The waitress looked confused. "Monsieur?"

"Yes, that's it, a Monsieur please – thank you," Pat said, wagging his finger jokingly.

The waitress scribbled something onto her pad and walked off towards the kitchen.

"So where did you learn French?" Pat asked.

"For a job last year – part of an Anglo-French operation. I can just about get by."

"Sounds good to me."

"If I don't use it for a while I get rusty, but being back amongst the French it just seems to come back to me – although I understand more than I can say."

"Aye, use it or lose it," Pat said. "Good one?"

"Good what?" Aden replied.

"Was it a good operation?"

"Oh right, erm ..." Aden said as he rested on an elbow. "It didn't go as well as expected. Bloody French bureaucracy," he added, suddenly remembering where he was and lowering his voice a little. "So much red tape. Basically, big mysterious gangster fellow – The Raven – strong connections with the French Government, big business and banks. We suspected he was trying to buy ministers in our UK Government and people high up in big business too – trying to control the economy and even countries. Not only that, but laundering money for illegal arms sales and then siphoning it off through other services, making it look legitimate when it was all really as dodgy as hell."

"So what happened?"

"Red tape – we needed more information from the French Government but they closed ranks, as if they'd found something they didn't want us to see."

"Or were too embarrassed to share," Pat said.

"Yeah, probably."

"What did you say his name was – The Raven?" Pat asked.

"Yes, that's what they call him. It's like a codename. We

have no idea what he looks like or sounds like."

"He doesn't have a fluffy white cat, does he?" Pat grinned.

"A cat?" Aden said. "I don't understand."

"The Raven. He sounds like a James Bond character. I could just imagine him sitting with a fluffy white cat on his lap," Pat said, his grin waning.

"Oh, I see. Anyway, we need to come up with a plan."

Pat nodded as he took a sip of coke.

Aden reached into his bag, pulled out a small netbook computer and turned it on. He removed the cover from his mobile phone, pulled out the memory card and pushed it into the small slot on the side of the computer.

Pat pulled his chair closer to Aden. They had chosen a table near a wall at the back of the café, a place where they knew they wouldn't be overlooked. Within a few seconds they were viewing the first picture from the Sorbonne.

"General admin stuff by the looks of it," Aden said as he flicked through the images. He zoomed in to read the text more clearly.

"Look here. It's a registration form from 1998. It has her contact details and look – a mobile number."

"That was years ago, it'll be out of date by now," Pat said.

"I don't know. I'm still using the same number on my personal phone and I've had that since 1996. It could be a lead."

Aden picked up his mobile and went to dial .

Pat reached out and grabbed his arm. "Wait, what are you doing?"

"I'm going to phone her."

"What? What do you mean you're going to phone her?"

"Why not? We need the break, time's short, we're being followed. Seize the day, my friend, seize the day."

"Bet it doesn't work," Pat said.

Aden dialled the number – "Here goes!"

Chapter 27

The Unexpected Call

Pearl walked up the wooden passageway towards her room. As she approached she was certain she could hear her mobile phone ring.

She opened the door and ran in.

She had forgotten where she'd put it. She turned her head, listened and ran towards the dressing table. She put the radio down and picked up the phone.

"Hello?"

"Hello, is that Pearl?"

"Yes, who's this?"

"Oh, hi, you don't know me but my name is Miles Jenkins. I am a Marine Biologist."

Pearl listened.

"I realise this call is out of the blue but I wonder if we could meet."

"Meet? Why? I don't know who you are."

"I appreciate that, and I apologise for the unexpected nature of this call, but I have something of your mother's for you."

"My mother's? You have something of my mother's, how?"

"I'd rather not go into it over the phone, this line is insecure. But let's just say it's your namesake and I would like you to be reunited with it."

Pearl paused and thought for a moment. She had some very important things going on in her life right now. She couldn't afford to take any risks. It was true, this call was out of the blue, but curiosity got the better of her.

"Okay, where?"

"I'm easy, at your convenience. I want you to feel comfortable and safe."

"How about the Oko Restaurant in Macau, tomorrow 9pm."

Aden looked at his watch and did a quick bit of flight arithmetic.

"Okay, Oko Restaurant, see you at 9pm. If there are any problems, we have each other's numbers."

"Okay. Bye," Pearl said, hanging up the phone.

She put the mobile down on the dressing table and stared at it.

He has something of my mother's for me. My namesake?

The only thing Pearl could think of was her mother's pearl necklace her father had made for their wedding day. It was the most beautiful necklace she had ever seen. Could it be this man had her mother's necklace? But where did he get it from? And how did it come to be in his possession? He said he was a marine biologist and so was her mother. She thought of the words he'd used. 'The line is insecure; I want you to feel comfortable and safe' – if anything, he sounded like the police.

Pearl was so taken aback by the call, she'd forgotten to ask where he'd got her number. It was all so sudden and unexpected. She picked up the phone, ready to call back and tell him the meeting was off, but decided against it. There was something very intriguing about this.

Swapping her phone from hand to hand, she walked over to her desk and sat down. She leant back in the chair, stared at the walls and pondered for a moment.

Her room was very ornate with typical Chinese splendour. The dark red wood panels that lined the space were embellished with gold and split the room into four parts. There was the bedroom, bathroom, dressing area and a work area where she sat now. Above her desk on the wall was an antique sword with a curved blade and a detailed handle.

She put the phone down on the desk. Her gut told her it would be okay. She decided to go ahead.

She reached for the computer mouse and clicked. The screen came to life. She clicked on an instant messenger application and double clicked on Sinead's name. She typed, 'Hiya' and hit the return key.

After a moment a response came back: 'Hi, you okay?'

'Yes, fine. Come and see me.'

'Okay, give me 5 mins and I'll be there ☺'

Pearl closed the chat window, checked her email and checked on the status of the running program. She smiled and watched the digits on the display continue to update.

***

Sinead got up from her terminal and walked over to the door.

"Where are you off to?" Morgan snapped.

"Pearl asked to see me."

"She didn't mention it to me."

Sinead shrugged her shoulders and opened the door.

"Well, don't be long, I might need you. This is an important time."

Sinead rolled her eyes and closed the door behind her.

Morgan sat back in his chair and counted down from one minute. He glanced around the room. Pierre looked up, smiled and put his head down again. The other members of the team carried on working, concentrating intensely and tapping on their keyboards.

Morgan stood up, grabbed his mobile phone and left the room. He walked to the end of the corridor, turned a corner and checked everything was clear.

He dialled a number. It rang.

"Yes?" said a man with a French accent.

***

There was a knock on the door.

"Come in," Pearl said.

Sinead walked in and saw Pearl standing near the desk. "Everything all right? You seem tense."

"I just had a bizarre phone call."

"How so?"

"Completely out of the blue, a man called and said his name is Miles Jenkins. Apparently he is a marine biologist and has something of my mother's. He wants to meet."

"Really?" Sinead stepped closer.

"Yes, really," Pearl said.

"What did you say?"

"I said, yes. I'm meeting him tomorrow night in Macau."

"Do you think that's a good idea?"

"I don't know. I won't know unless I go."

"Do you want me to come with you?"

Pearl smiled. "No, thanks, I'll go on my own. I don't want it to distract us from the project."

"Okay."

There was another knock on the door and Morgan walked in.

"Morgan. The idea is to knock and wait to be invited in!"

"Er, sorry, Pearl, I, er, just wanted to, er, let you know we've reached a landmark."

"Could it be that we have exceeded 350GB downloaded by any chance?"

"Er, yes – but how did you know?"

"Because I just checked the status for myself," she snapped, pointing at the display on her monitor.

"Oh, right. I just thought you'd want to know."

"Next time, update me on the radio."

Morgan nodded and lowered his head slightly.

"Is there anything else?"

He looked at them both and hesitated. "No." He very slowly pulled the door closed, still peering around the edge.

Pearl touched Sinead's arm and her hand began to move upwards gradually to her shoulder. As Morgan closed the door completely, they embraced.

Morgan huffed, chewed his lip and muttered something under his breath as he stormed back to the control room.

Chapter 28

A Parisian Lunch

"You cheeky bastard. I can't believe you did that!" Pat said with his hands either side of his face. "Well? What did she say?"

"She's happy to meet me tomorrow night, 9pm."

"Wow." Pat was impressed. "And that's here, in Paris?"

"Er, no. Macau."

"Macau? Isn't that in China?"

"Yes, that's right."

"China!"

"Yes," Aden smiled. He knew what Pat was getting at. "Don't worry, we should get there in time."

"Are you really sure about this? And you said you had something of her mother's? What was that about?"

"Yes, it'll be fine. I know what I'm doing – and yes, I have something of her mother's. I figured it would help get a meeting with her. All she knows is that I'm a marine biologist like her mother and I have something of hers she might want."

"But what?"

"A necklace."

"Sweet Jesus – how the hell did you get her mother's necklace?"

"This old man gave it to me when I went out to the island. He asked me to swear that I would return it to her. I thought it would help me get to meet her and, as it turns out, it worked a treat."

Pat sat upright in his chair. He put an open palm to his forehead.

Their lunch arrived.

"Merci," Aden said as the waitress placed the plate down in front of him.

"Cheers," Pat said as he received his.

"Well, eat up, Pat, we have a long journey ahead of us."

"Yes, we do."

"Thank heavens we don't need to go back to the hotel."

Pat swallowed hard. "Er, yes, now, about that ..."

Chapter 29

The Inspector's Update

Caren drummed her fingers on her desk.

What were the boys up to and how were they getting on? There was only one way to find out. She picked up her phone and dialled. After a moment it connected.

"Hiya, how are you?" Aden said.

"I'm fine, but more importantly, how are you getting on?"

"Thanks for the text. We went to the place you suggested and we're following a lead. We've just got to get there by tomorrow night."

"Where's that?" Caren asked.

"Macau."

"Macau? But that's in China. How are you going to get there in time?"

"Well, that is something we're just deliberating."

"What's the lead?"

"Someone who might know something."

"Who?"

"Well, they've tried to keep their identity a secret so I'll tell you after tomorrow."

"Oh, okay. I hope it goes well. The Chief Inspector wants me to keep him updated so I'll let him know. Good luck."

"Thanks. I'll call you when we get there."

"Okay, bye."

Caren hung up and dialled internally. "Hello, sir, I've got an update for you on the case."

"Tell me in person," the Chief Inspector said.

"Yes, sir, I'll be right up."

Chapter 30

A Calculated Risk

"It's a calculated risk but it's our only choice," Aden said as they walked back in the direction of the Mercedes at the top of the hill in front of the Sacré Coeur.

"Aye, I know."

"I doubt they'd be waiting for us at the car because there'd be no guarantee we'd return to it."

"Aye, I know."

"Getting the metro back to the hotel, then to the station to get a train all the way to the airport is just going to eat up too much time."

"Aye, I know."

"We'd miss the flight!"

"Aye, I know."

"The car's our only choice." Aden looked round.

Pat gave a cheeky smile. "Aye, I know."

"Okay, here goes," Aden said as they walked up the steps against the throng of tourists.

"Handy cover, this," Pat said as they pushed their way through.

Aden nodded.

They watched and checked every face. They didn't know what their pursuers looked like but they could judge body language and behaviour. Tourists of all nationalities, walked, mingled, laughed, spoke, took photos of each other, but thankfully nothing looked untoward.

They approached the top of the steps.

"It's still here, then," Pat said.

Aden walked around to the driver's side and looked in. The keys were still in the ignition.

"This wouldn't have lasted two minutes in London. It would either be nicked or towed." Pat examined the inside. "I doubt they would have booby-trapped it, there'd be no point."

Aden grabbed the release catch on the boot and paused. "Well, there's one way to find out."

He flicked the catch. The boot opened.

It was empty.

"All clear."

"Phew. Thank heavens," Pat said as he threw his bag inside. "I'll just have a quick shufty underneath," he added, dropping to the ground.

Pat got up and ran his hand around the edges of the wheel arch and exposed parts of the body.

"No bugs or trackers. All clear."

"Good," Aden said.

"But, wait, I did find this," Pat said.

Aden walked around the passenger side. "What?"

"This," Pat said, holding up his mucky black hands. "Dirt … and lots of it."

Aden wrinkled his nose in playful disgust and pulled a water bottle from the side pocket of his bag. He took off the lid and poured it over Pat's hands.

"Cheers, big ears," he said, rubbing his hands together vigorously.

Aden put the bottle back in his bag, dropped it into the boot and closed the lid. "Come on," he said, getting into the driver's seat.

Pat got in, fastened his seatbelt and rubbed his hands on his trousers. "You realise something though."

"What's that?"

"Well, if they're not waiting for us here, they'll probably be waiting at the hotel."

"Yes, that's what I'm worried about," Aden said, starting the engine.

Chapter 31

The Passport

"I can't believe we're doing this," Aden said, locking the car.

"I'm sorry, I'm sorry," Pat said as they walked along the pavement towards the hotel.

"Of all the things you could forget. Clothes, no, phone, no, bloody passport, yes!"

"I said I'm sorry," Pat said and shrugged his shoulders. "How do you want to play this?"

"Well, we still don't know who these people are or what they want."

"But we have to assume they're dangerous," Pat said.

"Exactly. For all we know, these are Pearl's men who want us dead so we can't get close to her."

Pat thought for a moment. "You know, something doesn't quite add up to me."

"What's that?"

"Why Pearl would agree to meet with you tomorrow if she wants you dead."

"What?" Aden said in disbelief. "Because she's not meeting me, she's meeting Miles Jenkins. She doesn't know it's me!"

Pat slapped his forehead. "Doh, what an eejit I am."

Aden shook his head, walked a little further, slowed down and stopped. "We have to assume they're watching the hotel." He paused for a moment, remembering the layout. "We could try going through the back way, maybe through the kitchens and up a service elevator?"

"Or what about the brazen way?" Pat suggested.

"Brazen, is that some kind of Irish thing?"

"Yep, it means having the balls to walk in through reception, up to the room and back out again."

"But they might be watching."

"But you'll be watching my back."

"We don't know how many of them there are or what their intentions are."

"I know, but as you said – there's only one way to find out." Pat grinned and, pulling his shoulders back, he strode off towards the hotel.

Aden shook his head and looked around. He couldn't help thinking this was a risky strategy.

It was a busy road, with parked cars and a line of trees. *The ideal cover*, he thought to himself. He stopped behind a tree, waited and watched.

He saw Pat reach the hotel and disappear into the reception.

On the opposite side of the road two men got out of a black car, buttoned their jackets and dodged the traffic to cross the road. A third man sat in the driver's seat and appeared to make a call on his mobile.

If someone was going to try anything, this could well be it. Aden had no time to waste; he had to help his colleague.

***

Pat strode through the main foyer of the hotel. There were small tables provided for guests and a number of them were occupied. Pat quickly observed a man reading a paper, two ladies in business attire engrossed in discussion, and a man and a woman probably having an affair.

He walked past reception, smiled at one of the young ladies on duty and veered right towards the lifts. He looked round and noticed two smartly dressed men walk into the hotel.

Now that's a coincidence, Pat thought to himself and pressed the button to call the lift.

He stood motionless and watched the men as they walked through the foyer. They looked around and finally looked in his direction.

Pat turned as, *ping*, one of the lifts had arrived. There was a young man and woman already inside.

"Going up?" Pat gestured with his hand.

"Yes, we go up," the young man replied in broken English.

The men were heading straight towards Pat. He had no choice. He stepped into the lift and promptly pressed the button for his floor. As he turned he could see the two men rush forward. The door closed with a satisfying thud and they started to move upwards.

Pat exhaled deeply. "Well, bugger me that was close."

He turned his head, remembering he wasn't alone. The man and woman looked away and chatted to themselves in French.

"Pardon," he said.

A troubling thought entered his mind. There were two people already in the lift and he had boarded on the ground floor. But how did they get into the lift? They were already inside, waiting – waiting for him. Trained assassins who didn't look like assassins to prevent suspicion, travelling as a couple so they wouldn't look out of place.

He clenched his fists ready for action.

***

Aden rushed into the foyer of the hotel.

He saw the two men disappear into one of the lifts.

"Damn," he said under his breath as he charged through reception towards them. He could see both lifts were going up; he had no choice but to use the stairs.

He rushed forward, shoved the door open and began to run up. He counted the floors.

First floor, six to go …

***

Pat watched the display – *second floor*.

He looked down at the control panel. There was a button for car park. They'd come from the basement. They weren't assassins after all.

Pat's hands relaxed and he watched the counter rise – *third floor* – but there were two men after him and they were probably in the other lift by now. He had to assume they knew what floor he was staying on. They were probably watching the hotel when he and Aden were here earlier or they could have checked with reception.

Fourth floor … Ping.

Pat was jolted from his thoughts as the lift stopped.

"Pardon, monsieur," the man said, trying to get past.

"Aye, right you are," Pat said, stepping aside.

"Merci," said the man.

"Merci," said the woman.

Pat nodded and stabbed the button until the doors closed.

He was hoping he'd arrive at his floor before the other lift but he wasn't sure he'd make it.

Fifth floor …

"You stupid bastard – so much for the brazen method!"

He could picture it. The doors would open and one of the men would be standing directly in front of him. The man would be holding a silenced pistol pointed straight at him. He would hear the 'pfft, pfft' of two shots to the chest – and he'd slump to the floor.

Sixth floor.

As he lay dying, he'd hear the final 'pfft' to the head. And then nothing. *Goodnight Irene – it was a great craic!*

Seventh floor.

Ping!

He held his breath. The doors opened.

He was pleasantly surprised – no gunman.

He poked his head out of the lift, looked left and right, nothing. He stepped out of the lift and looked at the display above the other lift doors: *sixth floor*.

His instinct told him to run but there was no time – the lift went *ping* and the doors opened.

He heard voices, talking in French. Pat stood steadfast in the centre of the corridor, arms to his sides, fists clenched and poised for action.

The men walked out of the lift, turned to face him and stopped in their tracks.

Pat stared.

The two men stared back.

The door behind swung open and Aden appeared, panting but also ready for action. He drew a deep breath and stepped squarely into the corridor.

The men looked at them both. One of them shrugged his shoulders, uttered something in French and edged forward.

"Pardon, monsieur," he said as he brushed past Pat. The other man followed. They continued to talk in French.

"Quelle situation étrange! Cet homme avait un visage fou et en plus vous avez vu ses cheveux sauvages."

"Oui, oui, c'était bizarre."

"De toute façon, vous êtes sûr que vous avez bien préparé votre discours pour le séminaire cet après-midi?"

Pat turned to Aden and raised his hands. "What the hell was that?"

Aden exhaled sharply. "I guess we got the wrong end of the stick."

"That was mad," Pat said.

"I think they reckon you are too."

"What?"

"Oh, just something they said."

Pat was none the wiser.

"One of them is speaking at a seminar this afternoon."

"How do you know?"

"Because it was what they were talking about."

"Oh, right."

"Haven't you got a passport to find? We've got a flight to catch."

Pat took the keycard from his pocket and they walked off in the direction of his room.

Chapter 32

A Higher Level

"Okay, so to re-cap." The Chief Inspector sat forward in his chair. "Initially the only lead we had was that Pearl's company is registered in Paris. But then Tech discovered she had studied at the Sorbonne."

Caren nodded as the Chief Inspector continued. "Our officers managed to obtain information from the Sorbonne that has led us to a lead in Macau and they intend to travel there to investigate further."

"Yes, that's right. It sounded a very positive lead."

The Chief Inspector raised his hand, rubbed his chin and thought for a moment. "Okay. Good move. Keep me posted."

"Yes, sir," Caren said, stood up and left.

As she closed the door, William noticed the time: 13:55. He picked up the phone and dialled.

"Rod Jennings," a voice answered.

"Hi, Rod, it's William."

"William, what gives?" Rod replied.

"I just wanted to give you an update on that case as you requested."

"Fire away," Rod said directly.

"Our two officers are in Paris. They obtained some infor-mation from the Sorbonne where Pearl studied in ninety-nine and they've got a solid lead in Macau."

"And where are they now?"

"At the hotel, I believe, shortly to leave for the airport."

"Thanks, I'll let Greg know."

The Chief Inspector thought he had misheard him. "Greg? The Deputy Prime Minister?"

"Yes. He has asked me to keep him appraised of the situation at all times."

"Oh, right, of course. Okay, Rod, I'll speak to you soon."

William hung up and sat back in his chair.

Now that was interesting ...

***

At the Cabinet Office in Whitehall, a phone rang.

"Yes?"

"Deputy Prime Minister, I have the Home Office for you."

"Thank you, Jenny. Put it through."

"Deputy Prime Minister, its Rod from the Home Office."

"Ahh, Rod, I've been waiting for your call."

Greg listened.

"Thank you. Keep me posted."

He placed the phone down and picked up his mobile. He had a message to send.

Chapter 33

Destination Charles de Gaulle

"How long?" Aden asked as Pat consulted the sat nav.

"Half hour. Just keep following the A1, E19, Autoroute du Nord."

Aden chuckled.

"What?"

"It's so funny listening to you speak French with your accent."

"Wee wee, miss yur, oovray la fennetree sill voo plaice, to be sure, to be sure."

Aden laughed and casually glanced in his rear-view mirror. "Uh oh – tail's back."

"Ahh, bollocks," Pat said, craning his neck to look out of the passenger mirror. "Black Citroen by any chance?"

"Yep, that's the one," Aden said.

"What a surprise. I guess they were waiting at the hotel after all."

"We don't need this right now," Aden said, switching lanes.

"If we come off anywhere it's going to put us loads behind. We might not make the flight."

"We'd better not come off then," Aden said, edging into the middle lane. He pulled forward and slotted the Merc neatly between two cars.

The driver sounded his horn. Aden waved an apology.

"Is it definitely the same one?" Pat asked.

"Yep, definitely."

"Ahh, shite."

Chapter 34

A Coded Message

The Deputy Prime Minister, Greg Willis, tapped a very simple message into his mobile phone.

```
p in mfm nxt flt cdg
```

He waited a moment until it had gone and deleted it permanently.

***

In the black Citroen something beeped.

The man in wire-rimmed glasses pulled out his phone, read the message and put it back in his pocket.

"Plus lentement, s'il vous plaît. Nous savons déjà qu'ils vont à l'aéroport."

The driver nodded and pulled out of the fast lane.

Chapter 35

Missing Tail

Pat watched Aden stare in the rear-view mirror. "Don't forget we're travelling forward."

"What?" Aden said.

"You need to look out of the front window from time to time."

"It's gone."

"Really?"

"Yes, really, it's really gone."

"That's weird."

"Yes, that's exactly what I thought."

Chapter 36

The Long Flight

Pat sat forward playing with his ticket. "Did you know the route before we booked?"

"I had an idea although I didn't expect the extra flight to Frankfurt," Aden replied.

"Paris to Frankfurt, one hour twenty," Pat said. "Frankfurt to Shanghai, ten effin' hours and fifty-five minutes," he moaned.

"Shanghai to Macau, two hours and forty-five minutes. And that doesn't take into account the layovers of one hour forty-five minutes in Frankfurt and three hours forty-five minutes in Shanghai. I've been working it out. It's a grand total of fourteen pissing hours and fifty-five bloody minutes flying time," Pat complained, waving the ticket around.

"What's the matter? Don't you like flying?"

"Let me tell you – I'm the fella who's only flown from Belfast to Heathrow. It took just over an hour and even then I was twiddling me thumbs, grinding me teeth and biting me nails. What the feck am I going to do for fourteen fecking hours and fifty-five minutes stuck in a metal tin can hurtling through the sky at five hundred miles an hour!"

Pat shook his head, stared at his ticket and muttered something under his breath.

"If God had wanted us to fly he would have given us all parachutes – just in case – you know! What's a layover anyway?"

"It's just the waiting time between flights," Aden said.

"So what's the difference between a stopover and a layover?"

"A stopover is part of the overall itinerary, where a layover is a short period of time between two flights."

"And, final question, Mr Frequent Flyer Man, what's the difference between a layover and a legover?"

"Ahh, well, whilst the layover is a short period of time between two connecting flights, a legover is a connection between two people and, instead of a short period of time, in your case, it's a short something else."

"Ya cheeky gobshite. Get away with ya. I'm hung like a donkey."

"Sure that's not an ass?" Aden smirked.

Before Pat could reply they heard an announcement.

"Come on, that's us," Aden said, rising to his feet. "You could browse through the in-flight magazine, read a book or watch a film," he suggested as they walked towards the departure gate.

"Or," Pat said as though he'd thought of the idea of the century, "I could catch up on my sleep."

"Lucky you."

"Why, can't you sleep on flights?"

"Nope."

"You're going to be knackered."

"Not to worry, I'll sleep during the layovers."

"Sure you don't mean legovers?"

"Nope, I never fall asleep during those connections." Aden looked round. "Sure you're not thinking of yourself?"

"Come 'ere, ya bloody shite!"

Chapter 37

Arrival in Macau

Pearl felt a little weary as she walked through the busy Arrivals lounge at Macau International Airport. It had been a long day and she hadn't got much sleep the night before. Everything seemed to be happening all at once; the progress with the project, the chance telephone call, this meeting with Miles Jenkins and the thought of being reunited with her mother's necklace.

She looked around. Could this mysterious man be here already? Perhaps he had the advantage; perhaps he knew what she looked like? She had worked hard over the years to try and retain her mystery and not put too much personal information on the internet for others to find. She believed she had succeeded so far.

She had Googled Miles Jenkins, but she hadn't found much – some research papers and a biography, but little more than that. No pictures. She was definitely at a disadvantage.

She passed through the crowded lounge and made for the exit. She stepped outside into the warm, humid air and hailed a taxi to the Oko Restaurant.

***

Aden entered the bustling Arrivals area and yawned.

"Told you you'd be knackered," Pat said.

"How are your nails?" Aden asked.

Pat raised his hands and wiggled his fingers. "All present and correct. And I even managed to catch up on my sleep too. I just don't fancy doing that again in a hurry."

"So how are you getting home?"

"Ahh, shite!"

Aden looked around.

"You think she'll be here?" Pat asked.

"No. I'm pretty sure she'd go directly to the restaurant. She has the disadvantage; she doesn't know what I look like."

Aden had thought Pearl would choose a place relatively close to where she lived, which at least gave him some idea she was located in this part of the world. The choice of this meeting point was very clever, implying she could have flown in from potentially anywhere, or come from Macau itself. But Aden had a plan to find out exactly where she had come from.

They stood outside in the muggy evening air of Macau. There was a short queue for taxis.

Aden got out his phone. "Get us a taxi. I'm just going to ask Caren to look for a lead on this location where we think Pearl is based."

Pat nodded and joined the queue.

Aden dialled. In just a few moments, Caren answered.

"Hiya, good flight?"

"Long and tiring, but we've just arrived."

"Pat okay?"

"Yeah, he's fine. We're about to follow up this lead but I've had a thought. Can you check on something for me?"

"Of course," Caren replied.

"You remember that printout you showed me about the Church of Wisdom?"

"Yes, I remember."

"At the top was a logo. Can you get the boys in Tech to run it through image recognition software and see if they can track it down to a building that actually exists, especially in this part of the world?"

"Yes, sure, I'll get them right on to it," Caren replied.

"Okay, thanks."

Aden looked round and saw Pat had hailed a taxi and was waving to get his attention.

"Sorry, got to go, I'll call you later."

"Okay, bye." Caren hung up.

Aden ran over to the taxi.

Chapter 38

Leverage

Greg Willis drummed his fingers on the table and sighed as he read the text message.

`call me ASAP`

He selected a recently used number and dialled. The call was answered.

"It's me," Greg said.

"We need you to do something," the man with a French accent replied.

"Oh, yes?" Greg said, and listened intently to the instructions given to him. "Okay," he sighed finally. "I'll get it done."

Greg hung up and thought about what had been asked of him – *in case we need a bargaining chip*, he recalled.

He called another number.

Chapter 39

An Uncomfortable Feeling

Caren rifled through the paperwork in the trays on her desk.

"It's definitely here somewhere," she said out loud.

She pushed her mobile phone to one side and picked up a stack of files from the top tray. She began sifting through them looking for the background information on Pearl.

"Oh, this is taking too long," she said, growing impatient.

She moved the files to the side of her desk to access her computer keyboard. She tapped a few keys until the document with the logo appeared on her screen. She attached it to an email, wrote a brief message and sent it off. Hopefully it wouldn't be too long before Tech were able to get back to her.

Caren's stomach rumbled, reminding her how hungry she was. She grabbed her purse, stood up and was about to walk out of the office when she remembered the cheque she needed to pay in. She opened her drawer, pulled out the paying-in book and left.

Everyone was on the phone with the exception of Steph.

"I am just going to pop out for a bit to get some lunch and pay a cheque in. You can forward any calls to my mobile."

"Okay, Ma'am," Steph said and smiled.

Caren walked to the end of the corridor, down the stairs and out of the main door. She turned left to walk the short distance to the bank at the end of the road.

The street was bustling as usual. The smell of vehicle fumes filled the air. She heard a horn to her right and looked round to see a cyclist have a lucky escape. He rode off with a raised arm and an extended finger.

She held the paying-in book in her hand and pulled back a few pages to look at the cheque inside. It was a fifty-pound win on the Premium Bonds. She'd had just over 11,000 of her hard-earned pounds invested in Premium Bonds for years and she'd not won a thing. Then, out of the blue, a win. It was only small, but still, she could buy a few things with that.

A shiver ran down her spine. She felt uncomfortable, as though someone was staring at her. Instinctively she looked around. There were other people walking along the pavement, rows of parked cars, cars driving past, but nothing seemingly out of place. She carried on walking, attempting to turn her thoughts back to what she might buy, when she felt the shiver again. She stopped and turned.

Using all of her years' experience as a trained officer, she watched and waited, but still nothing.

She was being paranoid. It was probably the investigation and the attack on her flat playing tricks with her mind. She wasn't being followed; she was just being silly. She carried on walking briskly towards the bank.

She wasn't into shoes or even clothes for that matter. Her life was the job so most of her clothes were work clothes and even her shoes tended to be flats. She was a practical girl at heart so her thoughts turned to something else she might need at home. Her flat was going to be off limits for at least another couple of weeks, as it had become a crime scene and she would need to get the insurance finalised before she could at last get the decorators in.

She looked round and noticed a white van come to a halt. She had noticed it before. It had been parked further down the street, but it had moved and was double-parked with its indicators flashing. She waited a moment. It could just be a delivery van but why had no one got out? A worrying thought hit her: *it was a white van that had been parked outside Aden's flat that night.*

Caren's stomach turned over. Her intuition was rarely wrong. She went to reach for her bag. She had left it in the office. She reached into her pocket. No phone; she'd left it on her desk. All she had with her was her purse and her paying-in book.

She weighed up her options. She was closer to the bank than she was to the office and the van was between her and the office. The bank would be a secure building. It was the best choice.

She carried on walking as fast as she could without actually breaking into a run. She could see the bank up ahead, nestled between a newsagents and a sandwich shop. She glanced over her shoulder; the van was on the move and was catching up with her. It was now or never. She started to run.

Within a moment the van was alongside. She heard the screech of brakes and saw the sliding door open. Two men dressed in black with balaclavas jumped out and ran towards her.

There was a row of parked cars in between them and her. She stopped, sidestepped and dashed towards the bank. One of the men had gone around the back of a car which put more distance between her and him, but the other was almost upon her.

The man reached to grab her. She ducked and his hand brushed her shoulder. She began to sprint. Her heart was racing. Every sense was attuned as adrenalin coursed through her veins. Sounds all around her were amplified. She could hear the heavy footsteps of the men behind.

The bank was just fifteen metres away. She was almost there.

She felt a sudden pressure on her shoulder and a force pulling her backwards. One of the men had grabbed her. She did her best to pull herself away but his grip was firm. He lunged forward, put his arm around her chest from behind and wrestled her to a stop. He shoved his other hand over her mouth.

Caren tried to break free but it was no use; he was too strong. Her purse and paying-in book fell to the floor. She struggled to breathe. His hand smelled musty, like an old attic.

He dragged her towards the van. Her heels scraped on the floor, her screams muffled by his hand. As she was dragged nearer the edge of the pavement, she could see a fifty-pound Premium Bond cheque flutter into the road.

Chapter 40

A Short Taxi Ride

Aden and Pat sat in a bright yellow taxi with their bags in between them on the back seat.

"Hold tight," Pat said. "I think we're in the Macau rally."

The driver said something and craned his neck round to look at them. He swerved.

"Whoa, eyes on the road, pal."

The driver cackled and said something in the local language. They looked at each other and shrugged their shoulders.

"Wifey all right?"

"Yeah, she's fine."

"Are you sure? Your face says different," Pat said.

"Oh, it's just that after the phone call I had a funny feeling in the pit of my stomach. You know, when something doesn't feel right: like a feeling of foreboding."

"Aye, I know that feeling all right."

"I'm sure it's nothing."

"What shall I do while you're at the restaurant?" Pat asked.

"I doubt very much Pearl would have a bodyguard. This is something she would have to do on her own, but you could keep an eye out. She doesn't know what you look like either so just enjoy the evening and have a bite to eat on another table."

Pat rubbed his stomach at the thought of food. "Sounds good to me."

The driver swerved to avoid a collision.

"That is, of course ..." Aden said.

"That is what?"

"That is providing we make it there alive."

Pat nodded and crossed his heart.

Chapter 41

A Friendly Face

Caren continued to struggle. It was no use.

Out of the corner of her eye she could see the van. The other man had already jumped inside and was holding the sliding door open.

"Come on, come on. Get her in."

God knows what fate awaited her.

Through teary eyes she instinctively looked up. Over the top of the parked cars she saw a man walk out of the sandwich shop. She recognised the familiar bulk as a fellow officer. Sam had been a police constable she had worked with on a job and he had recently been promoted and transferred to the SIA. He was deep in conversation on his phone and carried a sandwich neatly wrapped in a brown bag.

"Sam!" The scream was stifled and barely distinguishable. "Sam!" Indistinguishable again. She strained her head from side to side and the man struggled to restrain her. Left, right, left, right and upwards. The man's hand slipped from her face and in that split second she screamed: "SAM!"

The man slammed his hand hard over her mouth. The force was shocking and for a second she was disorientated. She began to kick, her legs flailing, desperately trying to make contact with his leg.

"Argh. Fucking bitch!" the man shouted as the heel of her shoe slammed into his shin. He threw her to the ground.

"OY!" Sam had heard his name and had seen what was happening. He had leapt into action and was tearing around the parked cars.

"Come on, let's get out of here," the man in the van shouted.

"But what about the woman?"

"Forget it. We can't afford to get caught. We'll try again."

The man looked down at Caren. She was on her knees trying to get to her feet. He looked at Sam and back down at Caren.

"Lucky bitch!" he said as he lunged forward and struck her on the side of her face.

He vaulted into the van. The door slammed shut and it sped off with a plume of smoke and squealing tyres.

Sam rushed to her side. "Ma'am? Caren? Are you okay?"

She felt dazed yet everything was coming back to her.

"Sam! Have they gone?"

"Yes, ma'am," Sam said as he took her arm and helped her to her feet. "Who were they?" he asked.

"I don't know. I was on my way to the bank when they jumped me."

"Okay, ma'am, let's get you back to the office."

Chapter 42

The Meeting

Pearl walked into the Oko Restaurant and made her way over to a table in the corner. The restaurant was essentially a giant wooden hut with bamboo walls, bamboo ceiling, bamboo floor and even the chairs were made of bamboo. She looked around. There were a few diners, locals and a few other nationalities, but definitely no Miles Jenkins, Marine Biologist.

She walked over to a table in the corner and sat down. The chair creaked slightly as she settled into it. The restaurant was very cosy with subdued lighting and dark red material draped from various bamboo supports. Plants grew from floor to ceiling. She smiled. She loved it here. She always had.

"Ah, Miss Pearl, how are you today?" The manager, a short, squat, homely fellow with rosy cheeks, rushed over to see her.

"Hello, Bumbum. I'm fine thank you, how are you?" She smiled whenever she said his name.

"I keep well, Miss Pearl. You been asked for drink?"

"No, not yet."

"My staff! I sack them all if they were not my family."

Pearl chuckled. "It's okay, I'm not in a hurry."

"You be alone or meet somebody?"

"Er, meeting someone."

"Ooh ..." Bumbum gave a cheeky little grin.

"Oh no, it's not like that. It's ..." She had to think for a moment. "It's just someone through work."

"Oh, I see, I see. Well, you have nice evening, Miss Pearl, I send Simmy to get your drink."

Bumbum hurried over to a young man standing on the other side of the restaurant. He slapped the man across the head and pointed to Pearl's table. The young man ducked to avoid a further slap and hurried over.

"Sorry to keep you waiting, Miss Pearl, what drink would you like?"

"That's okay, Simmy. Can I have ..." Pearl rested her hand on her chin and looked into the air for inspiration. "Can I have an iced tea, please?"

"Certainly, Miss Pearl, coming right up."

She watched Simmy rush off towards the bar. It was so obvious he had been to school in the UK for a year. The western influence in the way he spoke was very clear – unlike his father.

Simmy spoke to his brother, Sammy, who managed the bar. Sammy waved. Pearl waved back. She had been coming here for years. She adored just sitting and observing the family work, play and fall out with each other. It was like watching a real-life soap opera complete with melodrama, fun and sometimes sadness.

There was Bumbum on front of house, his wife, Magdola, who worked in the kitchen, their two sons, Simmy and Sammy, and their daughter, Bambi, who also waited on the tables.

Pearl escaped in her thoughts for a moment. This had been the first restaurant she had come to – in fact the first place she had visited at all when she arrived in Macau. She'd just got off the flight and had said to the taxi driver, "Take me to a nice restaurant in Macau," and he had brought her here.

As soon as she arrived she knew there was some kind of special event happening. It turned out it was Bumbum's mother's 100th birthday. Luo had travelled all the way from the provinces where she had lived all her life for this special celebration. It was the first time she had ever set foot in Macau, even though her son had been running the restaurant for years.

Pearl had been welcomed to join in the celebration as if she had been family herself, until things took an upsetting turn.

"There you are, Miss Pearl, iced tea." Simmy placed the glass on the table in front of her, complete with a little red umbrella poking out of the top.

"Thank you, Simmy," Pearl said. "Are you well?"

"Yes, very well, thank you, Miss Pearl. Are you ready to eat? If so I will send Bambi over to take your order."

"Not yet, I am waiting for someone."

"Ooh ..." Simmy said, playfully.

" No, no, not like that. A work colleague."

"Oh, okay." Simmy winked. "I tell Bambi to come later."

"Thank you." Pearl raised her glass and sipped. She put it back down on the table as she savoured the flavour of the iced tea on her tongue. She watched Simmy go back to the bar and start talking to his brother. It was obviously a fairly playful conversation from the way Sammy kept flicking a damp tea towel at Simmy's rear.

Pearl returned to her thoughts about their first meeting.

She could tell something had happened. Where there had been laughter there were now cries of despair. The family were huddled round one corner of the room where the birthday girl had been sitting. Pearl had rushed over and seen Luo in the arms of Bumbum. He seemed completely lost and powerless, tears streaming down his face, looking around for someone to help.

Luo was clutching her chest. Pearl suspected it was a heart attack and began to administer emergency CPR. "Call an ambulance!" she shouted, and half the family suddenly pulled out their phones. Pearl continued tirelessly pushing down on Luo's chest for ten minutes until the ambulance arrived.

Unfortunately Luo died three days later, but it was three extra days thanks to Pearl's quick reactions.

Bumbum had said she was the 'extender of life', giving him three more days with his mother he would not have been able to have. Since then Pearl had been welcomed into the heart of the family.

A clatter from the kitchen brought her back to reality. For a moment she had almost forgotten why she was here.

She toyed with her glass and thought about this Miles Jenkins person. There were a lot of questions going through her mind.

Out of the corner of her eye, something attracted her attention.

She only had a slight view of the entrance to the restaurant but she could see a taxi had pulled up outside. She could see a man get out and pay the driver through the window. *Could this be Miles Jenkins?* she thought to herself.

As the man turned towards the restaurant she thought she could see someone else get out of the other side of the car but she couldn't be sure.

Aden walked into the restaurant and looked around.

He noticed her. He raised his hand and waved.

She nodded.

She could see Bumbum walk over and talk to him. Aden pointed towards Pearl. Bumbum nodded and brought him over.

"Miss Pearl, your work colleague is here. Sir, you sit."

"Thank you," Aden said and smiled.

"I get waiter to take your drink order."

"Thanks," Aden said and Bumbum walked away.

Pearl noticed another man walk into the restaurant and sit at one of the tables near the door. He looked over, looked all around, pulled his phone out of his pocket and stared at it. He shifted his position a few times until he was comfortable and looked over again.

Pearl was pleasantly surprised by Miles Jenkins. There was a certain air about him. He seemed charming and had a lovely smile that made his eyes light up. It made her feel comfortable.

"Work colleague?" Aden said, sitting down.

"They asked who I was meeting and it was the first thing that came to mind."

Aden couldn't believe for one moment this woman in front of him had arranged for hit men to try and kill him –

but guarded he would try to remain.

"Thank you for meeting me."

"That's okay. Can I see your passport?"

"Er, yes, of course."

Aden pulled his passport out of his inside jacket pocket and handed it to her across the table.

Her hands were delicate and her skin was pale like porcelain. She opened the passport, turned it on its side to match the picture of the man sitting opposite her and read the details.

Aden looked at her face. She was a very beautiful woman, confident too, but with a certain softness about her. He had always had a thing for confident women, probably why he had fallen for Caren. In the brief moment of their meeting he could tell that, behind her exterior shell, there was a gentle centre with a very warm heart.

"You like drink, sir?" Simmy asked.

"Water, with a dash of lemon please."

"Yes, sir, coming right up," Simmy said and walked off towards the bar.

"Okay?" Aden asked.

"Yes." She handed the passport back to him. "I just wanted to check you are who you say you are, Miles Jenkins."

Aden replaced the passport in his jacket pocket.

"You realise your call was unexpected, to say the least?" Pearl said.

He smiled. She liked his smile. "Yes, I understand. Well, if there is anything I can do to allay your fears?"

"Where are you from?"

"London."

"What do you do for a living?"

"I'm a marine biologist."

"How old are you?"

"Thirty-nine – you've just seen my date of birth in the passport."

"Just checking," Pearl said. "Who do you work for?"

"I'm independent."

"Who have you worked for?"

"Various companies and organisations, project based work. I've also given talks."

Pearl pondered her next question as Simmy arrived with Aden's drink.

"Thank you," Aden said.

He had tried to be non-specific whilst keeping his answers as realistic as possible. He did work independently most of the time, until Pat came along. He also had worked with various companies through the line of his work and other law enforcement organisations. It was true that he had given talks to trainee officers on career opportunities in the SIA. *Keep it as real as possible,* he thought.

"Did you know my mother?"

"No."

"But you said you have something of hers?"

"Yes."

"Where did you get it from?"

"I was recently working in Polynesia and I had the opportunity to visit Tikehau."

But that's my home, she wanted to say, but held back. Charming as he was, she was still unsure of him.

"It's a place I've always wanted to visit. Being so isolated and so far out into the Pacific Ocean and with such a fascinating reef – which seems to be regenerating, albeit slowly. Regenerating all the same."

As he spoke, she listened but, in the back of her mind, she couldn't help the memories start flooding back.

"And whilst I was there on Tikehau I met Monsieur Aguillard."

"Stop!" Pearl sat upright in her chair. "Monsieur Aguillard, he is still alive?"

"Yes, he's very frail but he's definitely got all his faculties."

"He was like a grandfather to me when I was growing up," Pearl said.

Aden watched tears begin to well up in her eyes. He couldn't believe she'd had anything to do with the attacks or the tail. Here she was, sitting in front of him. He felt he had stirred genuine emotions in this woman. She wasn't a killer, he was sure of that.

"What did he say and why did he talk about me?"

"Well," Aden said, resting his elbows on the table, "I wanted to know more about the history of the island and it was recommended I speak to Monsieur Aguillard. I sat with him for some time and he told me about what the island was like and how things had changed when the French Navy carried out experiments. He spoke fondly of your mother and father; told me how they'd died, leaving you all alone. You'd got off the island by boat and …"

Pearl grabbed a napkin off the table and lowered her head. She dabbed the corner of her eyes.

"I'm sorry."

"No, it's okay – just fond but painful memories."

"I understand."

"So ..." She composed herself "You said you have something for me?"

"Yes. Monsieur Aguillard had been looking after it."

Pearl watched as Aden put his hand in his pocket. She was excited, nervous and apprehensive all at the same time. So many feelings and emotions all stirred up; it had taken her completely by surprise.

Aden held a black necklace box in his hand.

"Oh, my God. I can't believe this is happening," Pearl said as she looked at the box and then up at his face. There was that smile again.

She reached out and took the box, placing it in front of her on the table.

She hesitated and opened the lid.

"It's my mother's pearl necklace," Pearl said with an emotional crackle in her voice. "Dad made this for her. It's so incredibly precious. Thank you," she sobbed.

"You're welcome."

Pearl stared at the necklace in front of her. It obviously conjured up some very lovely yet very painful memories. She reached for the napkin, lowered her head and dabbed her eyes once again.

Aden watched her. It was a very touching moment. Rarely did his actions cause such joy – usually very much the opposite. She was very beautiful. The photo he had seen really hadn't done her justice.

He saw her look at the box and then inspect it more closely.

"What's this?" Pearl said as she reached inside.

A knot tightened in Aden's stomach – *what had she found?*

Pearl pulled it from the box and held it in front of her.

Aden blushed. "Sorry, that's mine. I bought it from a young boy when I was in Tikehau." He reached across, took the bracelet he'd intended to give to Caren and put it in his pocket.

She stared at the box for a moment, lost in thought.

"There is just one thing I don't understand," Pearl said, looking up. "Why would Monsieur Aguillard give the necklace to you to give to me? You don't know me, or where I live. I could have been anywhere in the world."

Aden was suddenly snapped back to reality. "Er, that's a good question actually."

"Yes, isn't it?" Pearl said, waiting for an answer.

"I told him I travel a lot all around the world."

Pearl interrupted, "But Monisieur Aguillard doesn't know where I live."

"You're right, he had no idea. I said I travelled a lot, plus I'd told him the nature of my job and, as it was the same as your mother's, I think he just thought I would be able to find you. Perhaps a little like when you tell someone you come from London and they say, 'I know some people in London, maybe you know them.'"

Pearl watched Aden very carefully. She glanced back over towards the man sitting on his own near the door. She noticed him look over and quickly look away.

"And who is the man at the front of the restaurant?"

Aden glanced round to where Pat was sitting and looked

back at Pearl. "Who? That guy over there on his own?"

"Yes, you came in a taxi together."

Aden was impressed. She didn't miss a thing.

"He's a colleague. We're in this part of the world together and he said he'd keep himself to himself while we met."

Bambi appeared from behind Aden's shoulder. "Hello, Miss Pearl, you eating with us today?" She looked at Aden. "Sir?"

"Er ... yes, if that's okay, I am rather hungry. I've not eaten since the flight," Aden said.

"Pearl?" Bambi said.

Pearl stared at the man opposite her and back towards the front of the restaurant.

"What about your friend?" she asked.

"As I mentioned, he said he'd keep himself to himself."

Something didn't feel quite right.

"Actually, Bambi, I can't quite decide what I am going to have, can you give us another five minutes, please?"

"Sure thing, Miss Pearl." Bambi smiled and walked away.

Aden looked confused.

"I have one more question for you."

"Sure, fire away."

"How did you get my number?"

Aden had mentally prepared for every conceivable question. About his reason for being in Tikehau, meeting Monsieur Aguillard, even down to facts relating to marine biology. But he hadn't quite been prepared for such a simple and obvious question.

Keep it real, he thought to himself, *keep it real.*

"The Sorbonne," he said. "They had your mobile number

on record as a way of getting in touch with you."

"But why would the Sorbonne give the number to you? They wouldn't share any personal information like that."

"Well, I had your mother's necklace I desperately wanted to get back to you. I said how important it was and really laid it on thick about how much it would mean to you to be reunited with it."

Pearl nodded. That was plausible, possible even.

"Although – more to the point – how did you know I went to the Sorbonne?"

As hard as he tried to think, Aden couldn't come up with a logical answer. He felt a wave of disappointment run through him. His expression said it all.

Pearl leant forward. Her face said it all too.

"I don't know who you really are, or why you've come, but I thank you for returning my mother's necklace to me. Now I think I should leave," Pearl said as she pushed her chair back.

Aden raised his hand. "No, wait, please. I'll explain everything."

She looked at him with cautious eyes. Although her instincts had been right, there was still something oddly trustworthy about this man.

Aden sighed and took a sip of his drink before resting his glass carefully back down on the table.

"My name is Aden Fitch. I am with the Special Intelligence Agency in London. Over there is my colleague, Pat Brogan, and we are involved in a rather baffling case."

"The Special Intelligence Agency? I've never heard of that," Pearl said.

"We don't advertise ourselves like some of the other services. We had a tip-off a known assassin called Mykola Liski had flown into London. We were tailing him. He got wind that something was up, shot one of my team and when we chased him into the tube there was an incident on the platform and he fell in front of a train."

Aden could see Pearl was listening intently. Yet there was no reaction when he had mentioned the assassin's name.

"The weird thing is this assassin met with a certain French minister on exactly the same day as you did and that's how you got onto our radar."

Pearl was concerned at the mention of her name but listened to what he was saying.

"We investigated further but there was an attack on my superior's house and a bomb had been planted in my flat. Thanks to Pat we managed to escape just before it blew up."

"But what were you doing at the Sorbonne?" Pearl asked.

"Following your meeting with the French minister we found out who you were and that your company was located in Paris. Whilst we were there, we got another lead from a photo of an old blog post while you were at the Sorbonne."

"Ahh, I see. I should never have posted that blog."

"You deleted it afterwards."

"Obviously not quickly enough," Pearl said. "So, you've found me, now what?"

"Well, you were our only lead to connect this together. We suspected you of ordering the hit men, the bomb and the tails in Paris. But now I've met you, I don't think that is the case."

"It isn't," Pearl said.

"I didn't think so."

Suddenly, something registered in her mind.

"Hang on – did you say someone was tailing you in Paris?"

"Yes, that's right."

Aden watched Pearl slump back in her seat. It was as though all of the earlier joy had been taken out of her.

"If you didn't order the tail it must be someone else – perhaps someone trying to find out how much we know?" Aden said.

"No, not you – me!" Pearl snapped.

"What do you mean?" Aden didn't quite understand.

"It's me they're trying to get to, through you, and I fear you may have led them to me."

"But I don't understand, what has this got to do with you?"

"You're the police, I can't talk to you."

Pearl stood to leave. Aden reached out for her arm. She pulled it away.

"Look, I want to help," Aden said. "I've been attacked, followed, shot at and nearly blown up. As far as I'm concerned, you've had absolutely nothing to do with it but I really desperately want to find out who is behind all this."

Pearl stood and looked at Aden very carefully.

She had worked so hard for what she believed in and kept it a secret for all these years. She certainly didn't want to throw it all away at the last moment. A little voice in her head told her it would be okay but her logical mind said this was a policeman and he had already lied to her once. He could be lying now.

"I'm sorry, I'm leaving," Pearl said. She picked up her bag, put the necklace box inside and closed the clasp. "Thank you, Aden, for your kindness in returning my mother's necklace. I do appreciate it, more than you'll ever know. Good evening."

He stood, smiled and nodded. He watched as she said goodbye to the man in charge and left.

Pat looked over and held up his hands. Aden beckoned him over.

"So what happened?" Pat said as he sat down.

"She's a clever girl."

"A looker too."

"She rumbled me."

"So you told her who you really are?"

"Yes, she clocked you as well – as I say, she's a clever girl."

"So what did you say?"

"I told her what had happened to us and she said they're trying to get to her through us."

Pat scratched his head. "Through us?"

"I think you were right all along," Aden said. "You did say there wasn't enough explosive in that bomb to kill us."

Pat nodded. "Clever bastards."

"Yep," Aden said.

"We need to find out what's going on. We've got to find out where she's going," Pat said hurriedly as he stood to follow Pearl.

"No, it's all right, I've got that covered," Aden said as he gestured his colleague to sit.

"How?" Pat said, sitting back down.

"I had Tech fit a tracking device into the necklace box I gave her. We can track it by satellite."

Aden grabbed his phone, pressed a few buttons and showed Pat a map of the city with a flashing red dot.

Pat examined the screen. "She's on her way to the airport."

"Yes. And, if I'm not mistaken, I believe she'll be on the last flight out of Macau to ..." Aden said as he displayed the live airport departures from Macau on his phone, "... here," and he showed the phone to Pat.

"Bloody Shanghai, we've just come from there!"

"We'll fly in the morning."

"So that means we'll be doing a sleepover."

"Yep. You're getting the hang of this."

"In that case," Pat said, rubbing his hands together in excitement, "whilst we're here ..."

"Let me guess ..."

"Let's get something to eat!"

Aden raised his hand and Bambi came hurrying over.

Chapter 43

The Short Flight

Pearl walked up the aisle of the short-hop scheduled flight to Shanghai, found her seat and sat down next to the window.

She opened her bag and pulled out the necklace box.

Her mother's necklace ... She held it in her hands. She felt the curvature of the pearls between her fingers. She caressed the shape of each individual jewel. She smiled. She remembered Aden call it 'her namesake' on the phone and she had been right; it was her mother's necklace. It brought back such warm and stirring memories, memories she had not allowed herself to think about for many years.

She felt a tear in the corner of her eye. She wiped it away, put the necklace back in the box and closed her bag.

Had Aden led them to her?

She leant on the armrest and pulled herself up so that she could see over the top of the seat and look around. The flight was half-full and was scheduled to take off any moment. There was a real mixed bag of travellers, as you would expect on an internal flight in China. There were a group of old ladies, probably going home after a day trip or special event, a number of teenage backpackers, and a few businessmen who most likely took this flight as part of their daily commute. The only other person was the man in wire-rimmed glasses sitting in the row opposite her, but he looked harmless enough.

Pearl decided not to worry, but to sit back and relax. She could think about what to do next when she got back to the monastery.

Chapter 44

The Sleepover

"Where is she now?" Pat asked as they sat in the hotel lounge, drinking beer.

"Looks like she's well on her way to Shanghai," Aden said, showing Pat the phone.

"You were right," Pat said. He strained to see the map.

Suddenly the phone rang in Aden's hand.

"I think like wifey wants ya," Pat said, recognising Caren's name on the display.

"Hiya," Aden said and smiled.

"Now, don't worry," a male voice replied at the other end of the line.

Aden sat bolt upright in his seat.

"Who is this?"

"Aden, it's William."

Aden's stomach twisted into a tight knot. "Chief Inspector. Is everything okay?"

"Everything is fine."

"Where's Caren?"

"She's been taken to hospital ..." the Chief Inspector began.

"Hospital?" Aden butted in.

"Aden, listen. Earlier this afternoon Caren was walking

up the road and two men assaulted her. It appears they tried to kidnap her but thankfully an officer was nearby and managed to intervene."

"What's going on?" Pat asked.

"It's Caren, she's been attacked."

"Is she okay?" Pat said.

"Aden, are you still there?"

"Yes, sir, sorry, sir, just a little bit shocked."

"I understand. She's at the hospital being treated for a cut on the side of her face but, apart from being a little shaken, she's fine."

"Who's with her?"

"Do you know Sam Chester?"

"Big Sam, yeah, I know him. That's good. Thank you."

"No problem, I'll call you with any further updates."

"Thank you." Something troubled him. "One thing, sir …"

"Yes?"

"Why are you calling me on Caren's phone?"

"She left it on her desk when she went out. She's at the hospital and I'm in her office."

"Ah, I see."

"Now, how are you getting on?"

"We're in Macau at the moment. We followed up the lead."

"And … who is the lead?" William asked.

"Well, believe it or not, it was Pearl," Aden said.

"What? You met with Pearl, the key suspect in this case?"

"Yes, that's right."

"But Caren didn't mention this."

"She didn't know. It was a judgement call I had to make, sir. I needed to strike while the iron was hot, but now there are a number of things that don't add up."

"Such as?" William asked.

"Well, having met her, I'd bet my reputation on the fact she's got nothing to do with the attacks on us."

"How so?"

"She's just not the type, Guv; it's not her thing."

"And is that it – a gut feeling?"

"No, not only that. She thinks we are being followed to lead them to her."

"Why?"

"She didn't say, but that could explain why the attacks have failed, like the bomb with not enough explosive to kill us," Aden said.

"Interesting theory."

"And there's one more thing that doesn't add up, sir."

"What's that?"

"When we were driving to the airport in Paris yesterday we had a tail who seemed determined not to lose us, then, all of a sudden, it vanished."

"What time was that?" William asked.

Aden thought for a moment, "It was nearly 3pm our time so it would have been 2pm your time, sir."

"Interesting," William said – something was beginning to dawn on him. "So what's your next move?"

"Whilst Pearl may not have been behind what's going on, I think she's still a key part in all this, so I've planted a tracker and we're going to catch up with her in Shanghai tomorrow."

"Okay. You boys had better get some sleep. I'll put Caren in a safe house for tonight – don't worry, we'll look after her.

"Thank you, sir. Good night."

William hung up and put Caren's phone down on the desk. He swung around in her chair. Something didn't feel quite right.

Chapter 45

The Hospital

Sam Chester sat in the hospital waiting room reading a copy of *Top Gear* magazine.

"Sam," Caren said as she appeared out of a small side room.

"Ma'am." He dropped the magazine down on the chair beside him and stood up. "How are you? Is everything okay?"

"Yes, I'm fine, just a bit of a cut," Caren said, pointing to a dressing on the corner of her eye. "Thankfully no stitches."

"Well, that's good news."

"Can we go back to the office?"

"Yes, certainly, ma'am."

Sam led the way to an unmarked car in the car park outside.

"I hear you're working on a mysterious case at the moment," Sam said.

"Oh, yes, how much have you heard?"

"I know it's related to the death of that assassin on the tube and that it's all hush-hush, need-to-know stuff."

"Yes, that's right," Caren nodded. "Given we have hardly any leads and not much information to go on – yes, I guess you could say it's mysterious."

She looked at Sam as he towered above her. She could tell he wasn't trying to get information out of her. He was just making conversation.

"Well, here we are." Sam opened the doors to the unmarked Volvo Estate.

They both got in and Sam pulled away, navigating the winding turns of the car park towards the exit.

"Any time today," Sam said, drumming his fingers on the steering wheel as he waited for a suitable gap in the traffic to pull out. "Ah, thank you." Sam raised a hand to the man who let him go.

As he pulled out, he failed to notice the white van pulling into the line of traffic three cars behind the kindly driver.

"Dammit! I was going to ram it at the gates," the driver of the white van said, hitting the dashboard with his fist.

"We'll box it in further on," the other man said.

Up ahead was a set of traffic lights that seemed to favour red more than green.

The van nudged forward and two of the cars in front turned left into the hospital car park, leaving one other car between them and the Volvo.

Sam stabbed the brakes and came to a stop behind a black cab. "Bloody lights," he said as he craned his neck to see which lane of traffic had the next turn.

"NOW!" the man shouted to the driver in the white van.

Sam sighed, "At this rate it's going to take ..."

There was a massive jolt from behind.

Caren stared in disbelief as the Volvo shunted forward into the back of the black cab. She was thrown forwards and backwards then forwards again in her seat. She was dazed for the second time that day.

She looked at the back window of the cab and could see a man in a suit, madly waving his fist and pointing at his watch. She raised her hands in a gesture of helplessness.

"What the hell?" Sam said, rubbing the back of his neck. He checked the rear-view mirror, "Looks like a van's gone into the back of the car behind."

Caren turned, wide-eyed and full of fear.

"What colour van?"

"It's ..." Sam realised her point. "White!"

Caren looked up. The man in the black cab was frantically trying to get her attention and pointing behind them. Two men had jumped out of the van – one of them had something in his hands.

Sam turned the key to re-start the engine. No luck.

"Sam, we need to get out of here!"

"Trying, ma'am, trying," Sam said, turning the key again. The engine turned over but wouldn't start.

The cab driver had got out and was assessing the damage to the back of his car, beckoning Sam to get out and look.

"Get back in, get back in!" Caren shouted. "Sam, they're coming."

Boom! The back window exploded under the force of a blow from a large hammer.

Sam ducked in his seat and kept turning the key – still the car wouldn't start.

With the window gone, they could hear the commotion outside – screams, two men shouting and the sound of the car's engine, finally revving to life.

Sam engaged reverse and stamped on the accelerator.

The car jolted backwards by about a foot.

Boom! The passenger side back window exploded.

Caren covered her head. She could hear a man shouting, "Get out, get out!"

She looked up. The driver of the cab's expression had changed. A man in a balaclava rushed up to him waving a hammer. The cabbie raised his arms to block the attack but it was no use. He fell to the ground.

Boom! Caren's window smashed and she was showered with tiny fragments of glass. "Sam!" she screamed.

Sam slammed the car into first and stamped on the accelerator. The force of the impact was enough to shunt the cab forwards.

Caren looked out of the corner of her eye and saw hands reaching towards her.

Sam yanked the wheel hard in reverse and they jolted backwards. As the car moved the man jumped out of the way.

"Quickly, Sam, quickly!" Caren screamed.

The other man ran forward and, with one powerful swing of the hammer, the windscreen shattered.

Blindly, Sam turned the wheel in the opposite direction and accelerated forward. He heard a thump and a shout as the man attempting to reach Caren was knocked off his feet. They mounted the pavement.

The hammer came crashing down through the front window. Blow after blow. It got stuck. The man pulled and twisted until it came free with a huge piece of windscreen attached. As the man struggled to remove the glass from it, Sam could see once again.

"One more!" Sam said, jerking backwards into the car behind.

He rammed into first gear and mounted the pavement again. The man trying to reach Caren jumped and rolled out of the way whilst the other struck wildly with the hammer. Sam covered his face as his door window smashed.

"Hang on," he said as he steered carefully around the cab on the pavement and back into the road. He pressed a button on the dashboard to sound the siren and raced back to base.

Chapter 46

Change of Plans

"Hello?" Greg Willis answered his phone.

"The information has proved most helpful," said the man with the French accent.

"So you will be able to proceed to the next stage then?"

"Yes."

"In that case, I presume I can cancel those other arrangements I'd made?" Greg asked.

"That is correct. It is no longer necessary," the man said.

"Okay, I'll sort it out."

The man hung up.

Greg looked up another number to dial.

Chapter 47

A Strong Drink

Caren sat in the Chief Inspector's office, feeling shaky and vulnerable.

"Can I get you anything?" William asked.

"A strong drink would be nice."

William nodded and went over to a large bookcase against the wall. He opened one of the cupboards, poured a neat whisky and handed it to her.

He sat on the edge of the desk in front of her. "I presume it was the same van?"

"It was a white van with two men in balaclavas," she said as she sipped her drink. She held it with both hands and closed her eyes, shivering as she swallowed.

"They obviously want you badly to try twice in the same day and in a public place with such a flagrant use of force."

Caren nodded. "I just wish I knew why."

"Me too, Caren, me too," the Chief Inspector said, standing up. "One moment."

Caren looked round to see Superintendent Lawrence Alberforth at the office door.

"William. Do you have a moment?" the Superintendent asked.

"Yes, sir," William said. He walked over to the door and out into the corridor.

Lawrence Alberforth was a formidable man. He hadn't reached his position by just being good at his job. His look, manner, everything about him, was fearsome. Caren turned back round and stared into her drink. She listened. She could just about make out some of the words: 'Pearl', 'officers', 'China', and the word that alarmed her most of all, 'suspend'.

"I understand, yes, sir, yes, sir," William said, before returning to his office and closing his door.

"May I ask what that was all about?" Caren asked.

William sat back down on the edge of the desk. He looked worried.

"The Superintendent has just asked us to suspend the operation and recall our officers back home."

Caren sat bolt upright, nearly spilling her drink. "Suspend the operation? But – but, that doesn't make sense, sir."

"No," William said. "That's exactly what I thought."

"The assassin, the attack, the bomb, and now they're trying to kidnap me," Caren said, her face glowing red. "We've got to keep going ..."

"Hang on, Caren – hang on," William interrupted. He stood up, walked over to the bookcase and poured himself a glass of whisky. He took a sip and paced.

Caren could see he was deep in thought and it was never a good idea to interrupt the Chief Inspector's thought process.

"I know there's a lot to this, Caren, many unanswered questions. And incidentally I, too, want to get to the bottom of it, but there is one thing in particular that hasn't felt quite right all along." William paused and took a sip of whisky as though he was adding the final touches to what he was going to say.

"Which is, sir?" Caren asked.

William slammed his glass down heavily on the bookcase. "Never mind, an order is an order."

"What?" Caren gasped.

"If we didn't obey orders, Caren, things would be in chaos."

Caren couldn't believe her ears. "But we can't just let it go."

"Caren," William said standing over her, "if you have any future in this department, it will be because you can obey orders. Do – you – understand?" His voice boomed.

She couldn't fathom what was going on. Neither could she fathom what the Chief Inspector was doing with his hand – why he was waving it around in front of her like that.

"Now, where are you staying?"

"Er ... at my mum's."

"Come on, then, I'll take you home."

Chapter 48

The Chief Inspector

Caren pulled the car door shut.

"Sir, I don't understand."

William didn't respond, but turned off his mobile phone and gestured to her to do the same.

She opened her bag and rummaged inside. She found her personal mobile, purse, lipstick, mirror and finally her work mobile. She turned it off.

"Okay, let's go on a drive," William said as he started the engine.

"But where?"

William turned his head to face her. "A drive," he said firmly.

He pulled away and out of the car park.

Caren looked out of the window and watched the world go by until, without warning, William changed direction and disappeared into an underground car park.

"But where are we going, sir?"

"You'll see."

Caren was starting to get worried. There had been some very strange things going on: she'd almost been kidnapped twice and now her own boss was acting weird – *surely William couldn't be involved in it all?*

She looked around. The underground car park was dark and foreboding – not a sign of anyone else. They were heading for what seemed like the furthest corner – well away from the entrance.

Why had he brought her here?

What were his intentions?

William pulled into a space and turned off the engine.

Caren felt an uncontrollable sense of panic. In waves, it engulfed her. She couldn't believe William was involved. She had only one chance; she had to get away.

She yanked at the door handle and pushed the door. She tried to get out but she couldn't move. The seatbelt – she stabbed at the button but she couldn't get the belt undone – then, *click*. She threw the belt off and tried to get out. Before she could move, she felt a firm hand grab at her arm.

Chapter 49

The Game Plan

"What are you doing?" William asked, placing a comforting hand on her arm.

"You're involved," Caren said, still panicking.

"No, I am not. I've come down here so we're away from prying eyes and ears."

Caren turned. "What?"

"I was trying to give you a signal in my office."

"What signal?" Caren said.

William waved his hands at her.

"Ahh, so that's what you were doing!" Caren realised, as things started to make a little more sense.

"I agree with you, there are some bizarre goings-on and I think someone on the inside is working against us," William said.

"You do?" Caren felt a sudden flood of relief. She closed the car door and turned to face William. "Who?"

"Obviously we need to work together on this. Absolute secrecy – understand?" William said.

"Yes, sir, of course, sir."

"The Deputy Prime Minister, Greg Willis," William said assuredly.

"No way!"

"Yes," William confirmed.

"But how?"

"Well, I had been requested by Lawrence to update the Home Office on every step of the case."

"Not unusual in cases of national security," Caren added.

"Exactly, but Rod, my contact at the Home Office, happened to let slip the other day that he was going to update the DPM."

"The Deputy Prime Minister! But why?"

"That's what I thought. It just doesn't add up. He asked to be updated and has taken a very personal interest in this case."

Caren shook her head. "We know there's an increasing rift between the DPM and the PM, so maybe Greg wants to turn this into some kind of public relations exercise, to taint the PM's good name."

"I did wonder myself, but I'm not sure. I think there's more to it than that. We know they have disagreements with education, the NHS and most notably Europe, and ..."

Caren cut in. "When I am Prime Minister ..."

"Pardon?"

Caren remembered something that had stuck in her mind from the recent televised debate. "During the televised debate – right at the end when Greg was getting really angry, he said, 'When I am Prime Minister'."

"You're right, he did." William pondered. "I wonder what he was getting at?"

"Killing the PM?" Caren suggested.

"I can't believe that," William said, shaking his head.

"The assassin was due to meet with the PM," Caren added.

"True, but there's nothing to link them together. And it still doesn't explain the French minister and this Pearl woman. Where do they all fit into this?"

Caren sighed. "I guess we'll never find out."

"Why do you say that?" William asked.

"Because the Superintendent has shut down the operation."

"Over my dead body," William said defiantly.

Caren was taken aback.

"I suspect Lawrence has been asked to drop the case because either the Home Office or Greg Willis himself has asked him to. There are so many unanswered questions, I'll be damned if we're giving up now."

Caren smiled. She was seeing a side to her boss she'd never noticed before.

"We need to find out how this Pearl woman fits in," William said, then remembered Caren wasn't completely up to speed. "You know Aden said he was following up a lead in Macau?"

Caren nodded.

"It was Pearl. Aden met with Pearl."

"Really? But he didn't say."

"I know. I think he was just being cautious," William continued. "His gut feeling is that she didn't have anything to do with any of these attacks, but she is still somehow key to the investigation."

"But ..." Caren was confused. "If that's the case, who arranged the attack, the bomb and who the hell is trying to kidnap me?"

William thought about the update to the Home Office,

the timing of the call and the tail breaking off in Paris. He decided to keep that little bit of information to himself.

"Well, obviously we're going to have to be careful. I can't be seen to ignore an order from above, and neither can you. We have our positions to think about."

Caren nodded.

"Why don't you take a holiday? I understand it's always been your intention to visit China and it just so happens that your husband is out there as well."

"Why, sir, that's a great idea. Yes, I have always wanted to see China and it would be nice to catch up properly with Aden."

"Of course, you'll have to decide what to do with Pat."

"I think it would be a good opportunity to get to know him better, sir."

"I like your thinking, Caren," William said with a smile. "Now, if we're quick we should be able to swing by your place with enough time to pick up some clothes. Then I'll take you to Heathrow."

"Are you sure, sir?"

"Absolutely. After what's happened to you today, I don't want to let you out of my sight."

Caren gave a huge smile and nodded. She buckled her seatbelt as William started the engine and pulled out of the car park.

Chapter 50

A Comfortable Bed

Pearl yawned as she walked through the corridors of the monastery towards her room. It was late and she was tired.

She imagined the Shaolin Monks who used to live there, whose temple they now inhabited. She had researched what had happened to them after finding out about the place. They had lived and prayed there for thousands of years and then, for seemingly no reason, they all committed ritual suicide. Since then a legend had grown of evil spirits lurking there who must have caused the monks to take their own lives. The place had been deserted. Spiritually fenced off from society, it was ideal. No one would ever come near the place now. She had invested a great deal of money and resources into the monastery to create a safe haven for herself and her team so she could complete her life's ambition.

Pearl turned a corner into another corridor.

With her back to the camera she didn't see it turn to face in her direction.

Morgan sat hunched over his desk, watching the feeds from the cameras.

"Soon it will be time," he said aloud to himself.

***

Pearl walked into her room and up to her desk. A small lamp cast a warm glow throughout. She tapped a few keys on the keyboard and the screen sprang to life. She had been wondering what the status was on the journey back and now she knew. She wasn't disappointed either. She smiled and felt a jolt of excitement. It wouldn't be long now.

She took off her jacket, hung it in the wardrobe and walked over to the dressing table. She opened her bag and pulled out the necklace. Holding it in front of her, she smiled. She still couldn't believe she had finally been reunited with her mother's pearls.

She felt a shiver run through her and looked over her shoulder. It was as though someone was in the room with her. She looked back at the necklace and, for a giddying moment, she could feel her mother's presence. She snapped her head as though shaking silly thoughts from within.

Set on the corner of the dressing table was a female bust she had nicknamed Samantha. Upon its head was a black rimmed hat. Pearl opened the clasp and fastened the necklace around the bust's neck. She stood back and smiled. "There you go – pretty as a picture."

"Hello," said a voice from behind.

Pearl turned on her heels in surprise to see a lithe figure move beneath the sheets. "I didn't see you there. You startled me!"

"Sorry," Sinead said. She rubbed her eyes and stretched. "So, how did it go?"

Pearl sat down on the side of the bed and placed her hand on Sinead's arm.

"Well. It was a bit weird actually. It turns out Miles

Jenkins isn't a marine biologist after all. He's some kind of policeman named Aden who works for the Secret Intelligence Agency or some such organisation."

"What?" Sinead said, resting on her elbow.

"Apparently he is investigating some terrorist attacks and he thinks I am connected with them," Pearl said in disbelief.

Sinead sat up. The sheet dropped to her waist. "He thinks you're a terrorist?"

"Yes. Well, no. He did at first but now he has met me he doesn't think I am."

"So what does he think you are now?"

"I don't know, I left. He said he was followed when he was in Paris and I have a horrible feeling they're trying to get to me through him."

Sinead looked confused.

Pearl stood up. "I wasn't followed. I'm sure I wasn't followed. I was very careful – very careful." She paced around the bed. "I thought I had everything under control, but for the first time in years, I am worried. And scared."

Sinead leant forward and pulled Pearl closer to her.

"I'm sure you're worrying over nothing. No one knows what you've been doing here – how could they? You have a really good team; honest, trustworthy and reliable. Things will be fine I am sure."

In that moment, Morgan appeared in Pearl's mind. Sinead's words echoed: *honest, trustworthy and reliable.* Pearl had handpicked her team and vetted them to the nth degree. She was sure they were all of those things and more: dedicated, committed and dependable.

"Okay?" Sinead said, breaking Pearl from her thoughts.

Pearl smiled. "Yes, okay, I'm sure you're right."

"Now come to bed," Sinead said, and playfully traced rings around her bare breasts.

Chapter 51

Illumination

A man wearing wire-rimmed glasses stood beside a hire car, with a mobile phone to his ear. In the distance he could see the twinkling lights of an illuminated monastery.

"I've found it."

"And you're sure she is there?" said a voice on the other end of the line.

"Yes, she is there."

"And it is the place?"

"Yes, as expected."

"Very good. Our waiting will soon be at an end," the voice said, with a menacing tone.

"Oui, monsieur, it will."

The man hung up, put the phone in his pocket, got into the car and drove back to the nearest town.

Chapter 52

High Speed Packing

"Just here, sir, on the right," Caren said as they approached her flat.

William pulled his car into the kerb and killed the engine. He opened the door.

"Where are you going?" Caren asked.

"I am coming in with you."

"You don't have to do that sir, I'll be fine."

"They could be watching us right now and we need to make the flight. Please be as quick as you can."

"Yes, sir, I'll be quick. You stay here and keep watch," Caren said, jumping out of the car. She flew up the steps and rushed inside.

William pressed the button to lock the doors, watched and waited.

Caren knew that being a woman and being asked to pack quickly was a paradoxical juxtaposition of evolutionary conditioning, to coin a phrase, which made her smile – but she would do her best.

As she rushed in and opened the door, a feeling of dread engulfed her. Not only was this the first time she had been back since the attack, but there was a chance they could be waiting for her again.

Having entered the flat, she moved quietly, even though if anyone was there they would already have been alerted to her presence.

She put her head around the kitchen door and looked in. Everything appeared as it always did, with the exception of the pan on the hob. It had thankfully been extinguished, although the unmistakable smell of burnt chilli still lingered.

Caren reached through the doorway and grabbed a knife from a drawer. Holding it firmly in her hand, she inched her way further into the flat.

***

William craned his neck to look around. So far, everything seemed clear, but if someone was waiting, would they strike straight away or would they wait until she came back out?

Out of the corner of the rear-view mirror he noticed a man walking along the pavement. William moved his head to get a better look. As the man got closer, William could see he had a bag over his shoulder. It was a worn, brown leather satchel. The man walked confidently with a spring in his step. He was walking in the direction of the flat.

William didn't carry a firearm but at that moment he wished he did. He watched the man get closer and closer, his eyes fixed on the satchel around the man's neck. He could see there was a bulge in the bag and, whatever it was, it was long and round. William hurriedly planned how he might react. Did the man even know he was in the car or had he just seen Caren run up the steps and go into her flat? If the man didn't know he was there, it gave him the upper hand. He could jump out behind the kidnapper and foil his plan. He had to be quick though. It would only take the man a second to grab the gun from his bag and he was determined to keep Caren safe.

William shrank down in his seat until he had as much of his body in the footwell as possible. He reached up, stretched and adjusted the rear-view mirror so he could still see the man's whereabouts. He was just two cars behind. He watched. One car behind. He watched, heart racing. The man was level with the car.

William didn't move a muscle in the hope that he wouldn't be seen and thankfully he wasn't. The stranger sailed past without a care in the world, right past Caren's flat and off down the road.

"William, you bloody fool," he said as he straightened himself back up in the seat.

He wiped a bead of nervous sweat from his brow and chuckled at his own stupidity. As he adjusted the rear-view mirror back into position, the chuckle turned to shock. A bolt of fear shot through his bones – a white van had just rolled slowly into view.

***

Why is the bedroom door closed? Caren thought to herself.

She never closed the doors in her flat; it shut things off and she didn't like that. She wanted everything to be accessible. She distinctly remembered it being open when she was last there. It could have been Scene of Crime Officers, but surely they would have left everything exactly as they found it – there could be only one explanation …

There's someone in there!

She slowly approached the door with the knife gripped firmly in her hand. She gently placed her ear against the door and listened. She could hear nothing from the other side. That didn't prove anything. They could be very quiet; they could be on the other side of the room. They would know she was inside. It was just a waiting game. They could be poised there, ready to strike.

She realised her heart was beating wildly and her breathing was too loud. She steadied herself and took a deep breath. In a moment she was calmer.

It was her or them.

She gripped the door handle and, with the knife at the ready, she flung it open.

With the memory of the attack clear in her mind and two attempts to kidnap her in one day, she was red with rage as she rushed in. Lashing wildly with the knife, she gradually realised there was no one there. She stopped, calmed her breathing and walked back out into the hall. She checked the bathroom and finally the living room – all clear.

Caren let out a big sigh of relief and put the knife on the mantelpiece. The room looked bizarrely foreign to her as she surveyed the damage for the first time since it had all happened.

Not only was there plaster all over the floor, but also silvery-grey dust graced every other surface where Scene of Crime officers had obviously brushed the place for prints. Bullet holes riddled the ceiling and wall near the library and white tape traced the outline of the body that had lain on her floor.

She shivered as she recalled the events of that night; then snapped back to the present and reminded herself she had some very hasty packing to do.

***

William didn't dare blink as he watched the white van. It had come to a stop and was double-parked about thirty feet behind. No one had got out and he was certain the engine was still running.

He strained to see into the dark cab, but it was no use. There was too much reflection on the windscreen and too much distance between them.

He continued to watch and hoped Caren would be out soon.

A worrying thought came to his mind. *Is there a back way into the building?*

***

Caren had snatched a bag and was frantically shoving everything inside that she would need for an unscheduled trip to China, for an unknown period of time and with an unfamiliar climate. T-shirts, thin jumper, thick jumper, pants, socks, jeans, woolly hat, scarf and gloves. She opened the wardrobe, pulled out a pair of trainers, put them in a shoe bag and stuffed that inside. She rushed over to the dressing table and emptied her make-up bag. *Take only what's essential*, she thought to herself as she put in foundation, mascara, lipstick and blusher.

She looked around and was about to leave when she remembered the coat on the back of the bedroom door. She put it on and ran into the bathroom.

She opened the bathroom cabinet and picked up a wash bag. She checked it was empty and put in her shampoo, make-up remover, toothbrush, toothpaste, brush, comb, tweezers, nail-clippers – she stopped herself. *Only what is essential.* She pulled out the comb, tweezers and nail-clippers, put in a razor and zipped it shut. She rammed it into the top of her bag. *Done.* If she'd forgotten anything she could buy it when she arrived. *It's not as if they won't have shops.*

With one last look around the flat, partly to check there was nothing else she needed and partly to say goodbye for a while, she straightened her coat, put her bag over her shoulder and picked up her handbag. *I'm ready*, she thought to herself and grabbed the handle to the front door. She was about to open it when she heard something.

Oh no, there's someone coming up the stairs!

***

William blinked. It was almost as if his eyes were drying out, he had been staring so intently.

He had decided that, even if there was a back way into the flat, there was little he could do. Caren had closed the door behind her and as far as he was concerned, whoever was in the white van didn't know he was waiting in the car.

He continued to watch, the van's engine idling – waiting.

He looked at his phone. He wasn't sure who he could trust. He needed a plan.

***

Caren listened carefully to the footsteps coming up the stairs. She had the advantage. She would be on a landing with a firm footing and a heavy bag. She could rush out and knock them backwards before they even had a chance to register what had happened.

She needed to choose her moment perfectly. She waited, counted down from three and flung open the door.

"Caren!" shouted the ashen–faced woman from flat number two.

Caren stood stock-still and lowered the bag. "Sorry Mrs Lazenby."

"You scared the life out of me, dear. Is everything all right?"

"Yes, sorry, I am in a hurry to catch a flight."

"Oh, I see, going anywhere nice?"

"China."

"Oh, China, it's so lovely there. I spent a whole year there in 1969. It was probably the best year of my life. I remember ..."

"I am so sorry to interrupt you, Mrs Lazenby, but there's a car waiting outside to take me to the airport."

"Oh, I'm sorry, dear, it's just that when I start I just can't ..."

Caren interrupted. "Was there a reason for coming up?"

"Oh, yes, I took in a parcel for you, dear," Mrs Lazenby said as she handed her the box.

Caren took it. Something rattled inside.

"Is it anything interesting, dear?" she asked.

Caren stared at the box, remembered the bomb in Aden's flat and felt her stomach tighten.

***

William was attempting to form a plan of action. It had to be one that wouldn't result in him being shot and Caren being abducted by the kidnappers in the white van.

He could pull out of the space and reverse up in front of them so they couldn't move the van. Or he could ram them, but then they wouldn't have a car to drive away in. As he played it through in his head, he could imagine the scenario – the kidnappers jumping out of their van and riddling the car with bullet holes. Alternatively, he could climb over to the passenger door, get out and crouch behind the parked cars to approach the van from the side. But then the kidnappers would open their door and riddle *him* with bullet holes. Either way he played it, it didn't end well.

He needed to think of something.

***

"Caren, dear, what is it?" Mrs Lazenby asked.

"Mrs Lazenby, I want you to go back to your flat now. Lock the door and go into the bathroom and wait there for ten minutes."

"What? But I don't need the bathroom."

"Mrs Lazenby! Do it now!" Caren ordered.

"I really don't know what's got into you. I'm going back to my flat," Mrs Lazenby said, shaking her head as she disappeared downstairs.

As soon as Caren heard Mrs Lazenby's door slam shut, she very carefully bent down and put the box on the floor. She dropped her bags and knelt to inspect the package further. Caren dug her nails underneath the tape and slowly peeled it back to free the edges of the box.

She remembered Pat's words about the other bomb, 'more whoosh, less bang', although at this distance she was still convinced more whoosh would kill her.

As the lid came free, she looked inside.

"Oh, you muppet!" Caren said with a sigh of relief. She glanced at the label. The package was from Boots. "It's just my make-up," she added aloud.

She took a moment to compose herself and tossed the box into the flat. She closed the door and locked it. Picking up her bags, she raced down the stairs.

***

Something caught William's attention up ahead. The door swung open and Caren appeared. She stood at the top of the steps and smiled. She skipped down and towards the car. She looked through the windscreen and noticed the expression on William's face. She looked up and spotted the double-parked white van. She froze to the spot in fear.

The white van beeped its horn – a long, drawn-out, single tone that seemed to resonate to her very core.

William heard it and craned his neck to look behind. He expected to see the kidnappers, armed with guns or at least hammers, rush forward to bludgeon Caren to death.

Caren couldn't move. She stared in disbelief – for the third time in one day, luck was really not on her side.

She heard a shout. She looked to her left. The front door to a flat opened three houses up. A man appeared and closed the door behind him. He rushed down the steps, across the pavement and into the road. He jumped into the van. The door slammed shut, the engine revved and the driver drove off.

Caren looked at William through the windscreen. She could see him return the look. They just gazed at each other until William waved her to get a move on.

Caren flung open the car door. "That was tense."

"You're telling me. Now, come on," William gestured.

Caren flung her bag onto the back seat and got in. William engaged first gear and sped off. Caren had a flight to make.

Chapter 53

A Simple Transaction

Morgan was still hunched over his desk. He stared transfixed at the numbers on the screen, his mind struggling to grasp the sheer quantity of data they were capturing.

His phone rang. He answered.

"Hello, Morgan, do you know who this is?" a voice asked.

Morgan sat bolt upright in his chair. He knew this moment would come.

"Er, yes ... I know who this is. You are – the Raven?"

"Yes, I am," the voice said with an ominous tone.

Morgan held the phone tightly to his ear. He struggled to control an involuntary shudder.

"Morgan, have you thought more about our offer?" the voice asked.

"Yes," Morgan said confidently, "and I am willing to do business, but on my terms."

"That is most understandable considering the circumstances," the voice said, the sentence drawn out, cold and intimidating.

"When I have the data, I will bring it to you in ..." Morgan quickly thought of a place. "Bangkok."

"Is that where you are now?" the voice asked.

"As I told the other man, I am not willing to reveal my

location – my terms, remember?" Morgan said firmly, impressed with his own negotiating skills.

"Very well. This is a simple transaction. You give us what we want and we give you everything you asked for."

"Everything?" Morgan said, his confident tone wilting slightly.

"Everything," the voice said. "You are collecting the data now?"

"Yes, as we speak."

"And when is it due to be finished?"

Morgan checked his screen. "The current estimate is 4pm tomorrow."

"That is Bangkok time?" the voice probed.

"No …" Morgan stopped and kicked himself. He had nearly revealed his location. He realised he was hunched over the desk again. He had to take back control of the conversation. "I have your number. When the data has been received, I'll contact you to make the trade."

"Very well, Morgan," the voice said. "This is a very important mission – don't let me down."

"I won't," Morgan said, "I won't."

"Oh, and Morgan?" the voice rasped.

"Yes?"

"There is a slight change of plan."

"What do you mean?"

"You'll need to clean up before we arrive."

"Clean up? I don't understand."

"I mean you need to kill everyone."

"But … but …"

"You need to protect yourself, Morgan."

"Protect myself, why?"

"You don't want anyone telling the police about what you've done. You could go to prison. You don't want to go to prison do you, Morgan?"

"No, I don't."

"Well, you'll need to clean up before we get there."

"But, that wasn't the plan."

"If there is one thing I have learned in business, Morgan, it is that you need to adapt to survive. You need to make tough decisions and often those decisions are hard, but they need to be made, Morgan." The man drew a throaty breath. "You can adapt, can't you, Morgan?"

"Yes, I can."

"Then, tomorrow, you will be a very rich man."

Morgan struggled to contain his excitement. "Okay," he said, playing it cool.

"Very well. Until I receive your call, goodbye, Morgan," the voice said and the speaker hung up.

Morgan sat back in his chair and smiled. *A very rich man.*

He leaned forward and tapped a few keys. On the screen appeared pre-recorded video footage from the beach. With his eyes he traced the contours of Pearl's body, from her ankles, up past her calves to her thighs. Though she was mostly obscured by her gown, he continued upwards to her cleavage and zoomed in.

He touched himself. A wave of emotion ran through him. A tear formed in the corner of his eye. He wiped it away. Before another surge of emotion had the chance to surface, he stabbed at the keyboard and the picture was gone.

Chapter 54

Departures

"You're going to have to be quick to make this flight," William said as they approached the Departures entrance at Heathrow airport. "I'll just stop and you can jump out, okay?"

"Yes, that's fine. Thank you, sir," Caren said.

"Here we are," William said, pulling up to the kerb.

"Thanks, sir."

"No problem. Just look after yourself and say hello to Pat and Aden when you see them."

"Will do," Caren said, smiling.

She got out of the car and opened the back door to retrieve her bag.

"Be careful," William said.

Caren nodded. "Goodbye, sir."

"Goodbye, Caren."

Caren slammed the door and William watched her walk away.

The word 'goodbye' reverberated in his head as he felt a knot tighten in his stomach. He had an uneasy feeling that it was final.

Chapter 55

LHR to PVG

Caren found her seat on the plane and sat down. She caught her breath and watched the other passengers organise themselves. Her bag was safely secured in the overhead locker and she cradled her handbag in her lap.

"You'll need to put your bag under the seat in front of you."

"Pardon?" Caren replied to the lady sitting to her side.

"Your bag, they'll ask you to put it under the seat," the lady said.

"Oh, yes, of course. I will. In a moment."

Caren opened her handbag and rummaged inside. She remembered she had powered off her work phone and given it to William. She still had her personal phone though. She recalled Aden saying he had his personal phone with him too. They'd both had their phones for years. They'd often used them when they first started seeing each other, in the hope their communication would be more private and off the record than on their work ones.

She toyed with the idea of sending Aden a text but realised it was too late and he would probably be asleep. She had a better idea – she'd surprise him at the other end.

Chapter 56

The Ruffled Sheets

Pearl opened her eyes, turned her head and stroked the bed beside her. There was a ruffled patch of sheet where Sinead had lain the night before.

Pearl had tried hard to keep their relationship secret but she was aware that everyone knew about it. There was little chance of keeping anything quiet when they had all lived together in such close confinement for so long. She was discreet by nature though and that is how she wanted to keep her private life.

She raised her hands behind her head, stretched and sighed gently. She smiled when she thought of Sinead – the feel of her soft skin, her smell, her taste.

Pearl's thoughts flashed back to her time at the Sorbonne and her encounters with other girls. She thought of Jana with whom she'd had her first experience. With her long dark hair, Pearl had seen a mirror-image of herself. Her mind had struggled to cope with this concept. It had seemed like she was sleeping with herself and so they had split up.

Then she met Celeste. Celeste was different; short blonde hair, blue eyes, tall, everything as opposite to Jana as could be, but this didn't make Pearl happy either. She felt she was trying too hard. She was not following her heart.

But everything changed when she met Marissa. The experience with her was very different. There was no rush, no pretence. They had become friends and from there things had blossomed. Pearl realised she didn't need to find someone who was the same as her, just someone with whom she felt comfortable. From that moment she became more comfortable with herself.

She smiled and ran a hand across her breasts to her stomach, then lower. She touched herself.

The radio crackled. She sighed.

"Hello, Pearl, are you there?"

It was Morgan. He'd been acting strangely recently, creepy and distracted. But now he sounded different – happy and excited.

Pearl jumped out of bed, ran over to her desk and grabbed the radio. "Yes, Morgan, I'm here."

"Great progress overnight. Just look at your screen."

"Okay, thank you. I will do in a moment," Pearl said.

"Great, see you in a bit."

Pearl put the radio back on the desk and shook her head. It had been a very challenging journey for all of them, cooped up on this island together. Everyone had put in a lot of hard work and effort and perhaps this was the realisation that all that effort had been worthwhile. With the results coming in and visible on screen, their work was almost done.

She sat down at the desk and tapped the keyboard. The screen came to life and she could see the remarkable progress that had been made overnight. She felt a wave of excitement rush through her. Her fingers tightened. She clenched her fists, raised her hands over her head and stretched upwards. Soon she would know the truth.

Chapter 57

The Hire Car

With a strange feeling of déjà vu, Aden and Pat walked across the car park of the car rental office in Shanghai.

"I can't believe this was the only car they had available," Pat said.

"I know. No button to press this time," Aden said, holding the key.

"I've got a strong suspicion I am going to be very disappointed." Pat stared ahead trying to find their car. "What's it called again?"

"I dunno, I can't read Chinese," Aden said, waving the paperwork.

"There it is." Aden pointed.

"What is it?" Pat asked.

Aden shrugged his shoulders. "I don't know – never seen one before."

"Told you I'd be disappointed," Pat sighed. He ran his fingers along the bulbous bodywork and pretended to cry. "It's just not the same ..."

Aden put the key in the lock and tried to turn it. It wouldn't budge. He tried and tried and finally, *clunk*. He opened the door, got in and reached across to open Pat's side.

"Jesus, it's a bit small, isn't it?" Pat said as he squeezed himself inside and examined the interior of the car. "It's like something from the 1950s."

"It probably is."

Pat ran his hands across the dashboard. There was a deep trough in the middle. "I wonder what's lurking in there?"

"It'll do," Aden said as he started the engine.

Pat made a sound of disgust and sat back in the seat.

Aden revved the engine and tried to put it in gear. Clunk. Grind. Crunch.

"I'll name that tune in three," Pat said.

Aden finally found first gear and tried to pull away. "It's gutless," he said as he slowly released the clutch, hoping it would eventually bite. It stalled.

"Want me to drive?" Pat quipped.

"Bear with me," Aden said, re-starting the engine.

He tried again. The car jerked forward. "Right, got it."

Aden pulled his phone out of his pocket and handed it to Pat. He watched the glowing red light flash showing Pearl's position.

"Okay, driver," Pat said, "if you would like to exit the car park and take a right, proceed down the road for approximately a quarter of a mile and then turn left."

Aden nodded and jerkily pulled away.

"And then, driver ..."

***

"We're almost there," Pat said.

"Are you sure? It doesn't look right," Aden said. "It looks more like a farming community."

"Maybe she works on a farm."

Aden shook his head. "No, doesn't seem the type."

"Okay ..." Pat pointed. "That building – shed, barn – whatever it is."

Aden nodded, drove up and came to a stop.

"This can't be right," he said, getting out of the car.

Aden stood in front of the barn with his hands on his hips and looked around. They were surrounded by fields in every direction, little shacks and farm buildings, sheds and, in front of them, a wooden barn.

"We going in?" Pat asked, handing Aden his phone.

Aden checked the screen and looked up at the barn. "Yes. This is where it says."

He followed Pat around the other side of the barn where there were two large doors fastened with a tatty piece of rope.

"Ready?" Pat asked.

Aden nodded.

Pat unhooked the rope and opened one of the doors. He peered inside. "Nothing."

Aden walked in and looked around. *Nothing.*

It was a very simple wooden barn. Against one of the walls were a number of bales of hay.

"Maybe there's some kind of bunker underground?" Pat said, stamping the floor.

Aden noticed something black on the ground. He walked over to inspect it. As he approached he recognised it immediately. *The necklace box.* He picked it up.

"What's that?" Pat asked.

"The tracker," Aden said.

"Great. Did she rumble that too?"

Aden inspected the case and the false bottom covered in velvet was still intact. "No, I don't think so."

"Maybe she dropped it," Pat said.

"Or, maybe she was being thorough."

"Clever girl," Pat muttered under his breath. "So what now?"

"Open the other door, would you?" Aden said as he noticed something else.

Pat walked over and opened the other door so that the barn was flooded with light.

"Car tracks," Pat said.

"Exactly. She must have got a taxi from the airport. She obviously kept a car here so she could use it to throw anyone off her trail."

"And I wonder where she went in it?" Pat said.

"I've no idea." Aden was filled with disappointment. He sat down on one of the bales of hay.

Pat walked over and perched down next to him. He leaned back against the barn wall, folded his arms and looked out through the doors at the farmland beyond.

Aden toyed with the tracker in his hand. They sat in silence for a while.

"We have nothing to go on," Aden said.

"Aye."

"Nothing at all," Aden said.

"Aye."

Aden sighed.

"Well, the trick is to not give up," Pat said.

Aden looked at him. "But we've got nothing to go on."

"You know what I like to do in situations like this?"

Aden shook his head.

"Ask the universe."

"What?"

"The universe – that massive thing all around us, black and cold – the universe."

"I know what it is, I'm just not sure what you mean by 'ask the universe'."

"Well, I'm not a religious man, at least not anymore, not since – well, whenever – but I believe that there must be some kind of higher power out there somewhere and that it lives in the universe."

"Right?"

"So, if you want something badly, really badly enough, if you ask the universe, really nicely, you'll be rewarded with what you want."

"And you think that really works?" Aden said.

"Yes, of course. It's worked for me in the past," Pat said excitedly. "For loads of things. Go on, ask the universe." Pat nudged him with his elbow.

Aden felt silly.

"No, really, go on."

"What do I say?"

"Something like: Dear universe, please can you give us a lead on the case we're working on so that we know the location of Pearl?"

Aden shook his head in disbelief.

"Come on."

Aden sat upright, feeling embarrassed. "Dear universe - I feel a right dick!"

"Come on. We need the break," Pat said, nudging him again.

Aden looked upwards. "Dear universe, please can you give us a lead on the case we're currently working on by helping us find where Pearl is located?"

"There you go."

Aden waited. "And?"

"You can't rush it. When it's going to happen, it'll happen."

Aden shook his head, put the tracker in his pocket and cradled his phone in his hands. He sat back against the wall and quietly and patiently observed the fields.

Chapter 58

The Lead

There was a knock at the door.

Chief Inspector William Headley looked up and waved.

Josh from Technical Operations opened the door and walked in.

"Sorry to trouble you, sir, but I can't find Caren."

"She's on leave."

"I didn't know she was going away," Josh said.

"It was a last minute thing. Is there something I can help you with?"

"Well, it's just that she asked me to look into something."

"What is it?" William asked.

"It's this, sir," Josh said, handing him a piece of paper. "She asked me to run a logo through the computer for a real-world match and I found it. It's a monastery in China, on an island just off the coast of Shanghai."

William studied the print-out and tossed it on top of a pile on his desk. "Leave it with me, Josh."

"It sounded quite important when Caren asked for it, sir."

"As I said, leave it with me. This case has been suspended anyway, so no further action is required," William said stiffly.

"Oh, okay, sir, thank you, sir," Josh said. He nodded diplomatically and left the room.

William watched Josh walk off down the corridor and picked up the piece of paper. He studied it again. It was a photo of a monastery on top of an island peak. Underneath the photo were the geographic coordinates and below that a screenshot of a map with a pinpoint for its location.

He picked up his phone and switched it to camera mode.

Chapter 59

Divine Inspiration

Aden was growing restless. They had to do something; they couldn't sit in the barn all day waiting for the universe to intervene.

Pat sat with his arms folded. He smiled. "As I said, you can't rush these things. All things come to those who wait."

Aden checked the time on his phone. *Five more minutes*, he thought to himself when all of a sudden his phone beeped.

"There you go," Pat said with a nudge, "I bet that's good news."

It was a picture message.

Aden checked it. "I don't believe it."

"What is it?"

"It's a photo of a monastery where Pearl's located with geographic coordinates and a map. It's here in Shanghai."

"There you go, didn't I say it works?" Pat said.

"But ..." Aden was lost for words.

"I don't know how it works, only that it does work."

"I don't believe it." Aden sat, stunned, staring at the picture in front of him.

"Come on, then, we can't sit here all day," Pat said. "Where are we off to?"

"You'll see."

"Why can't you tell me?"

"You'll like this. It's a surprise."

"Suit yourself, but I don't like surprises."

Chapter 60

The Supply Stop

"Stop the car," Aden said. "Pull in here."

Pat swiftly pulled the car into the side of the road. "Why do you want to stop here?"

"We're going shopping."

"What for?" Pat asked.

"You'll see."

Aden jumped out of the car into the hustle and bustle of the high street. He stood in front of a rock-climbing shop and looked through the window.

"I'm not climbing a bloody mountain!" Pat said indignantly. "I don't like heights. Is that where the monastery is – up an effin' mountain? I'm not doing it. I'm not climbing," Pat said, stabbing the air with his finger.

"It's for me, not you. I have a plan."

"I still don't know where this monastery is."

"You'll see."

"I don't like surprises."

Aden needed to reassure his colleague. "I need you to watch my back. The plan is I'm going to climb up to the monastery and sneak in. I'll find out what's going on and decide what to do next. You'll be hanging back, watching me to make sure the coast is clear."

Pat felt a little better. "So I don't need to do any climbing?"

"No, none at all."

"Okay."

"I'm going in to get kitted up with what I need," Aden said, looking around. "See down there ..." He pointed. "There's a camera shop. Can you go and buy a pair of 10 by 50 binoculars?"

"Yep, okay. I'll meet you back here, yes?" Pat said.

"Yes, I'll be in here."

Pat nodded and strolled off towards the camera shop.

The door to the climbing shop was open. Aden walked in.

"Herro, sir, you Engrish?" the cheery shopkeeper asked.

"Yes, I am. How could you tell?" Aden replied.

"Your dress, sir, the way you dress."

"Oh, I see," Aden said. "I'm going to be doing some climbing nearby and need the whole kit: boots, harness, two lengths of rope, quickdraws, carabiners, pitons, hammer, cams and chocs."

"Yes, yes." The man smiled and gestured around his shop. "We have everything you need."

***

Pat mumbled something under his breath as he walked into the shop. A young man was standing behind the counter and the shop was full of camera equipment, everything you could ever imagine or ever need.

"All right?" Pat said as he approached the counter.

The man stared.

"I'm after a pair of binoculars," Pat said.

The man behind the counter shrugged his shoulders.

"Can – you – understand – me?" Pat said slowly.

The man behind the counter shook his head and shrugged his shoulders.

"Oh, bollocks, this ain't gonna be easy," Pat said. "Did you understand that?"

The man shook his head.

Pat looked all around and noticed a number of pairs of binoculars on a shelf, lined up in differing sizes.

"Those. Those," Pat said, pointing.

The young man nodded, walked over to the shelf and pointed.

"Yes, yes. That's it," Pat said and smiled. *Now we're getting somewhere.*

The man, still pointing, shrugged his shoulders.

"Right, which ones?" Pat said and remembered what Aden had asked for. "I am after 10 by 50."

The man looked at the shelf, looked back at Pat and shrugged.

Pat gestured around the counter and the man nodded, so Pat walked round the back to the shelf where he was standing. Pat looked down. He towered above the man. Pat inspected the binoculars on the shelf and found a pair labelled '10x50'. He grabbed them and handed them to the man, who said something in his native tongue.

Pat nodded, smiled and walked back around the other side of the counter.

The man opened a door behind the counter and disappeared. Pat stood and waited – and waited – and waited.

He fidgeted from one leg to the other, folded his arms and unfolded them.

"If that's the only pair you've got, I'll take those," he said in a raised voice.

The door swung open and the man poked his head through. He looked at Pat, said something, smiled and disappeared again.

"Honestly, I don't want to be a bother. I need to get going. I'll take that pair, it's fine."

All of a sudden the door swung open and the young man reappeared. This time however he was accompanied by his father. The young man stood to one side and grinned as his father spoke.

Pat shrugged his shoulders and pulled a face. He had no idea what the older man had just said.

The man looked at his son and spoke again. The young man shrugged. The older man thought for a moment, picked up the binoculars and put them down again. He swung his arms out to the side.

"I know what you're saying," Pat said. "You haven't got any in stock. It's fine." Pat picked the binoculars up from the counter, held them to his chest and pointed at them.

The man beamed a grin, pointed to the binoculars and then at Pat.

Pat nodded furiously.

The man laughed and turned to his son. The son laughed and turned to Pat. Pat muttered something under his breath and laughed too. The man nodded and held out his hand.

"Hoo-bloody-ray," Pat said. He rummaged in his pockets and pulled out his wallet and passport.

The man pointed to the passport and shook his head.

"You don't need to see that, huh? Okay, I bet you want to see this though," Pat said as he opened his wallet and pulled out a credit card.

The man pointed at the card and nodded. He reached across to one side of the counter, pulled out a card machine and beckoned Pat to put the card inside. The man rang up some numbers and pointed at the machine.

"I have absolutely no idea how much they are but I'll trust ya!" Pat said and smiled. The man gave a beaming smile in return and pointed at the machine. Pat tapped in his pin and the purchase was complete.

The young man rang up the transaction on a separate, very dated, till, handed his father the receipt, who in turn handed Pat both receipts. Both men nodded.

Pat retrieved his card, took the receipts and the binoculars and hurriedly left the shop.

Thank heavens for that, Pat thought to himself as the door closed behind him. *If that was bad for me, God knows how it must be going for Aden, trying to buy all that climbing stuff.*

Pat smirked. He couldn't wait to see Aden struggling with it. With a spring of anticipation in his step he rushed back to the climbing shop.

***

An array of gear was piled on top of the counter.

"You know, I used to crimb when I was younger man," the shopkeeper said. "I crimed K2."

"Really? You climbed K2?" Aden said.

The man nodded and cupped his hands together in front

of him. "Very charrenging, very tough. Trained hard."

"Well, I'm very impressed. Well done you."

"You crimed mountain like K2?"

"Oh, no, too big for me. In the UK we don't really have mountains; they're more like large hills. I mostly climbed crags when I was younger."

The man nodded. Aden wasn't sure if he'd understood everything he had said.

The shopkeeper turned his attention back to the case in hand and began reciting the shopping list under his breath. "Neary finished," he said as he hunted for the last few items.

Aden was standing at the counter doing a quick check of everything that was on his list, when he heard a familiar voice behind him.

"You wouldn't believe the experience I've just had. I've been dying to see how you're coping with it all," Pat said as he strode in.

"Okay, this is everything." The man reappeared. "We soon have you crimbing."

Pat's jaw dropped. "You lucky bastard," he said under his breath.

"What?" Aden turned.

Pat shook his head and walked up to the counter. "Remembered the mule?" he said.

"Mule?"

"Yes, the mule to carry all this."

Aden checked the gear. He took the cams and chocks the man handed him, making sure he had a mix of different sizes, and put them on the counter. That's when he realised he needed something to put it all in.

"Do you have a backpack that I can put this in and also attach the equipment to?"

The man nodded. "Mountaineering backpack you need."

"Yes, please," Aden said.

Pat still couldn't believe Aden's luck; this guy spoke better English than he did.

"This is good one. Many straps. Comes with herremet holder." He studied the kit on the counter and looked as though he had forgotten something. "You need herremet."

Pat looked at Aden. "What the hell is a herremet?"

Aden said the word over a couple of times in his head. "Helmet! Of course, I've forgotten a helmet."

The man disappeared and returned with a bright yellow helmet.

"Thank you," Aden said and smiled.

The man placed the helmet on the pile, double checked everything and totted up the price. He tapped it in on the till and rang it up.

"That is three thousand nine hundred and ninety-four Yuan," the man said proudly and smiled.

Aden lifted the rope bags over his shoulders, picked up the harness and boots and realised he didn't have a free hand.

"You got your wallet handy?"

"Yes," Pat replied.

"Do me a favour and get this, please."

"How much is it?"

"I don't know." Aden thought for a moment. "Er, just under £400 – is that a problem?"

"No, no problem," Pat said as he rummaged in his pockets and pulled out his passport and wallet. He withdrew his credit card, put it in the machine and entered the pin. The man gestured for him to remove it.

"It's okay, I don't need the box for the shoes," Aden said as he tried to push the box on top of the pile and it fell off.

Pat slipped the card back in his wallet and put the wallet down on the counter with his passport. He bent over and picked up the box.

"Pat, give us a hand here, will you?" Aden said.

Pat nodded, opened the backpack and started putting the equipment inside. Aden had picked up as much as he could carry. "You want the helmet in the bag as well?"

"No, it attaches on the back," Aden said, trying to gesture with his head.

The old man who had been watching, rushed forward and connected the straps. "Rike this, rike this," and he showed them excitedly.

Pat nodded, "Yep, I got it."

Aden counted off all the equipment in his mind as they picked it up.

"You have great crimb," the man said, ushering them out of his shop.

"Thank you for your help," Aden said.

They were out on the pavement walking back to the car.

"It was like he was trying to get rid of us," Pat said.

"I think it's just their culture. We'd completed the transaction and he was keen for us to be on our way."

Pat put the bag in the boot and Aden leant forward and dropped in the boots and harness, then laid the rope to one side.

They got in.

"He must think Christmas has come early. I bet he's going to close the shop and go off to the local casino to blow it all and eat sushi off a naked woman's body," Pat said, making himself comfortable in the passenger seat.

"Sushi? You're thinking of the Japanese not the Chinese."

"Oops!"

"Some might call you a racist for saying that," Aden said, smiling.

"I've got an excuse. I'm ignorant," Pat said, putting on his seat belt. He looked around the street and then back at the climbing shop. "Big on climbing over here, are they?" he asked.

"Oh, yes, some of the best climbing in the world is in China."

"Really?"

"Yes. You've heard of K2?"

"Yes, of course."

"And you've heard of Everest."

"Everest is in China? I thought it was in Tibet?"

"Well, it's actually on the border between Nepal and Tibet, but Tibet is a region of China."

Pat shook his head. "I never knew that."

"Well, you did say you were ignorant," Aden smiled.

"Aye, that I did, that I did," Pat nodded.

"Right then, let's go," Aden said, sparking the engine to life.

Chapter 61

The Island

"It's a bloody island!" Pat said in disbelief as the car came rolling to a stop. "You didn't say it was on a bloody island."

"I said it was a surprise," Aden said.

"I hate water. You know I hate water. I am not going," Pat snapped. He slumped in his seat and folded his arms tightly.

"It's okay. I'm going," Aden said. He looked out to sea across to the island. He could clearly see the monastery on top of the craggy, steep cliffs. "I'll take my work phone and leave my personal mobile here. So you can reach me on my new number if you need me – okay?" Aden said.

"Yeah," Pat replied.

"You see all these boats here?" Aden gestured to the quayside as he tossed his personal phone into the glove compartment. "I'm going to ask one of the boatmen to take me over. I'll climb up to the monastery, try to find out what's going on and make a decision as to what to do from there."

"Rather you than me."

"Back in a moment," Aden said, jumping out of the car.

He walked over to the boats on the nearby quayside and waved to Pat to stay with the car.

Pat stretched and sighed, "Bloody island. Bloody water."

He looked around – out to the expanse of water in front of him, across to the boats at the quayside and further up the coast to the left. He glanced around inside the car and noticed Aden's phone on the seat.

I'll leave my personal phone here, he remembered Aden saying.

***

"Excuse me, do you speak English?" Aden said as he approached a fisherman heavily involved with a piece of equipment.

The man swung his head round, shook it and pointed to another boat nearby. Aden nodded and walked towards it. A man appeared to be getting ready to go out to sea.

"Hello, do you speak English?" Aden called over.

The man turned round. "Yes, I speak Engrish," he said, walking round the back of the boat. He was older than Aden. He wore blue denim jeans, a denim jacket and walked with a slight limp. "How I help you?"

"Can you take me to that island?" Aden asked, pointing.

The man shook his head. "Not arrowed."

"I'll pay you, of course." Aden pulled out a handful of notes.

"Not arrowed – spirit of monks forbid it."

Aden needed some leverage. He was pretty sure no one knew about Pearl being on the island. If she was worried people were trying to track her down, she certainly wouldn't advertise her presence.

"I have business on the island," Aden said. "Monk business!" *It was worth a shot.*

The man looked confused. "But you are not monk?"

"No, I am not a monk but I do have business on that island that may help the monks' spirits."

"What business?"

"I can't divulge the nature of my business exactly."

"Then no travel," the man said and turned to walk away.

"Police business," Aden said, pulling out his ID card.

"You are police?" the man said, coming closer to inspect the ID. "You are not Chinese police. No authority."

Aden was starting to lose patience. "I am a special policeman. I have international authority to travel between countries." He stepped forward. "Look, it says it here." Aden pointed to some writing on his ID card, suspecting the man probably couldn't read English, or at least read with much understanding.

The man stared at the card in front of him then looked directly into Aden's eyes. "Okay. For three hundred Yuan I take you," and he held out his hand.

"Agreed," Aden said. He took the man's hand and shook it.

"We go now."

"I need to get some stuff from the car. Can we go in about ten minutes?"

The man checked his watch and seemed concerned about his schedule. "Five minutes – must go in five minutes," he said, tapping his watch.

Aden glanced out to sea. It looked calm and it was a clear day with not a cloud in the sky. He wondered why the urgency.

The boatman obviously picked up on this. "Tide no wait for us."

"Ahh, okay, thanks," Aden said, and ran back to the car.

***

"You got a ride then?" Pat asked, getting out of the car.

"Yeah. Said something about not being allowed and monk spirits but I managed to convince him."

"Money?"

"Yep – that and good story," Aden said. He rushed round to open the boot. "I've only got five minutes – he needs to leave to catch the tide. Can you give me a hand?"

"Yep, sure."

"I need to get changed into looser clothing," Aden said. He reached into the boot and pulled out the clothes he'd bought earlier. "Right, can you take the labels off and attach these – here," Aden said, gesturing to a set of equipment to be attached to one side of the bag.

"Okay," Pat replied.

"And these – here," Aden instructed.

"Yes, okay," Pat replied.

"Oh, and if you can pass the boots. Hurry, we don't have much time," Aden snapped.

"Yes, yes, okay!" Pat snapped back.

"And then attach these – here," Aden said, pointing at various pieces of equipment and the harness.

Pat muttered something under his breath.

"And if you could just make sure everything's securely attached, and check I've got my phone."

This goes here, this goes there, check this – I've got my phone – Aden's words replayed in his mind.

He began ripping off the labels, observing the names as

he did so; quickdraws, carabiners, pitons, cams – names he had never heard of before. *Now, does this go in the bag or on the harness?* And he started attaching everything as best he could remember. He looked at all the equipment and shook his head.

"Do you really need all this stuff?"

"Put it this way, I'd rather have it and not need it than need it and not have it," Aden said as he hurriedly removed his trousers.

"What does this do?" Pat said, holding a cam in his hand.

"It's a cam, or camming device. You place it into a crack or gap in the rock. It has a spring in it that expands to wedge itself into the gap," Aden said, briskly pulling on a pair of baggy trousers.

"And this?" Pat said.

"It's a nut. You wedge them into smaller gaps and cracks. Not as secure as a cam, but sometimes very useful."

Aden crouched down, put on the climbing shoes and tied the laces.

"And these wee things?"

Aden looked up. "They're pitons. You hammer them into the rock, attach a quickdraw and feed the rope through. They anchor you to the rock. That's what I'll be using most of all."

"So that's why you've got so many of them," Pat said. He contemplated for a moment and shuddered. He just couldn't imagine being stuck up a cliff, dangling there, staring down into ... He shuddered again at the thought.

"How high is it anyway?" he asked as he attached the equipment.

Aden glanced over and did a bit of mental reckoning. "Between two hundred and three hundred feet."

"Poke me," Pat said. "Are you mental?"

"It'll be okay."

Pat shook his head and carried on attaching the equipment to the bag. "How long will it take?" he asked.

"About three hours – depending on the quality of the holds."

Pat shook his head again, mumbled, "Jesus, Mary and Joseph!" and handed the bag to his colleague. "There's a lot of weight there."

"Yep, but it'll lighten as I start to use it," Aden said as he put the backpack on. He picked up the rope bags, put them over his shoulder and checked his watch; he was almost out of time.

"Okay, rope, bag, quickdraws, cams ..." Aden said as he went through all the items. "Pitons, chocs and hammer – is that everything?"

Pat looked in the boot, looked back at Aden and shrugged his shoulders. "Yep."

"Great, because I'm out of time." Aden shifted the weight on his back.

"You sure look the part all right – and look at your little booties. Ahh, so cute!" Pat said.

Aden ignored him. "Okay. I'll climb the mountain, get in, snoop around and find out what's going on. If I get into trouble I'll call you."

"Okay, any trouble, you'll call me," Pat said aloud. In the depths of his mind there was something that concerned him about that statement but he couldn't quite put his finger on it.

"I've got to go," Aden said as he straightened the back-pack one last time.

"Okay, take care," Pat said.

"Thanks. Later," Aden said and ran off in the direction of the boat.

"Nutter!" Pat said, shaking his head and got back into the car.

He reached behind and picked up the binoculars from the back seat. He held them to his eyes, moved them around until he brought the island into view and adjusted the focus. He could clearly see the old wooden monastery perched on the top.

"Bloody hell," Pat said as he followed the towering cliffs down to the sea. He lowered the binoculars into this lap, let out a deep sigh and prepared himself for a long wait.

***

Aden was surprised at how long the boat was taking to cross over, as its little engine battled against the waves. The man hadn't said a word since they'd set off. He held the wheel tightly with a worried expression on his face, as though driving the boat against its will.

The craft seemed ancient, with patches of rust every-where and every type of accessory a fisherman would ever need. As Aden watched the driver and looked around the deck, he noticed the distinctive shape of the handle of a flare pistol in a holster hanging up beside him. *Understandable*, he thought to himself.

"So," Aden shouted over the sound of the engine, wind and waves, "have you been a fisherman long?"

The man turned as though he thought it impertinent to ask a question whilst he was driving. "Yes," he said and turned his attention back to the sea.

Aden shrugged his shoulders. He gazed back to the mainland and wondered what Pat was doing, given his intolerable lack of patience. His thoughts turned to Caren. She popped into his mind now and again but he avoided thinking of her too much. He had tried not to worry about her. He knew William would make sure she was safe …

Suddenly, something didn't feel right. Aden looked round. He realised they had significantly changed their heading and were going in a different direction – away from the island.

"What are you doing?"

The man turned. "We go there," he said, pointing to the open sea.

"We had a deal. You take me to the island," Aden said.

"We go there," the man insisted, pointing.

Aden looked around the boat. He looked at the pistol again and realised it wasn't a flare pistol after all; it was an old Chinese service revolver, still in its holster, which probably dated back to the Second World War. Aden checked out the other items on the boat. There were weights and lots of rope – enough to tie him up, weigh him down and drag him to the bottom of the sea.

The man was driving the boat intensely, his eyes fixed rigidly forward. It was now or never. Aden had to do something to take control of the situation.

To his right, just out of reach, was a toolbox. He could see the handle of a hammer sticking out from under the lid.

If he grabbed the hammer, he could knock the boatman out, take control of the boat and drive himself the rest of the way to the island. It was a good plan. It was his only plan.

Aden began to shuffle slowly to his right. He had to make sure the boatman didn't notice. A little further. The toolbox was almost in reach – just a little further.

Before Aden had a chance to reach for the hammer, the boatman turned. He locked his eyes firmly on Aden as though he had read his mind. "Currents strong here. We make turning and they take us to island," he said and swung back, focusing once again on the sea ahead.

Aden let out a sigh of relief.

***

Pat sat in the car, singing to himself.
"Tim Finnegan lived in Walkin Street,
A gentle Irishman mighty odd.
He had a brogue both rich and sweet,
An' to rise in the world he carried a hod.
You see he'd a sort of a tipplin' way,
With a love for the liquor he was born.
And to help him on his way each day,
He'd a drop of the craythur ev'ry morn ..."

"Feck me, I'm almost comatose with boredom." Pat picked up the binoculars from the dashboard. He could see the boat bobbing up and down on its way to the island. He put the binoculars down and sighed.

He ran his fingers around the outline of the steering wheel and pondered for a moment. "Clover, that's what I am going to call you," he said, after some deliberation. "I wonder how old you are? When were you born?"

He imagined a production line with other little Clovers rolling off it, some ending up as hire cars just like this one.

He folded his arms and felt the immediate sensation that something was missing. He tapped his jacket pocket. "Oh no," he said, as he reached inside. Nothing. He desperately tried the other side. Both pockets were empty – his passport and wallet weren't there.

He checked on the passenger seat, in the footwell and on the back seat. He opened his bag and rummaged inside, in the main section, in the rear pocket, in the side pocket, every pocket. He shook his head.

He was suddenly filled with hope as he remembered that when they had come out of the climbing shop, they had tossed everything into the boot. He had paid – so his wallet and passport must be in there too. He got out, rushed around the back of the car and opened the boot. He brushed aside the labels, tags and plastic packaging, but he couldn't see either passport or wallet. He searched and searched but they weren't there. The hope rapidly turned to disappointment.

A dozen thoughts ran through his head: *it was his money and his identity; he couldn't get out of the country without his passport; Aden was almost on the island, what if he needed him? Did he forget them or were they taken and, if they were taken, who would have taken them and when?* His mind replayed the events since he last remembered having them.

"You dopey bleedin' eejit! You left your bleedin' wallet and passport in the bleedin' shop! Bollocks!" he said as he rushed back into the car.

He knew exactly where he had left them – on the counter, next to the cash register. It was when Aden had asked him to help pack the bag.

"Arse!" He hammered the steering wheel. Something went crack and the wheel wobbled under the impact. "Oh, Jesus, what have I done? Sorry, Clover," Pat said, feeling guilty as if the car had actually felt the force of the blow.

Pat had to go back to the shop; he couldn't leave his wallet and he definitely couldn't leave his passport. He didn't want to leave his partner either in case he needed him, but he had no choice.

"I know, I'll text him," he said aloud. He typed a quick message.

`I'm an eejit, left my wallet and passport in the shop. If I drive back now I should be back in just under an hour. All the best. P.`

Pat stabbed the send button. "There we go," he said, starting the engine. There was an odd sound. "That's weird."

He left the engine running.

"What was that, Clover?" Pat asked the car.

What he had just heard sounded like a text message arriving but it definitely wasn't his ringtone. It sounded like Aden's phone.

He looked at the phone on the seat – it was blinking.

"But I thought this was your personal phone. Why would you leave it behind?" Pat said to himself as he picked it up. He struggled to remember Aden's instructions – *check this ... check that ... I've got my phone.*

Then it clicked – *check that I've got my phone!*

"Eejit, eejit, eejit!" he despaired. Then, "Aden's a big boy, he'll adapt to the situation. If he needs me, I'm sure he'll send me a signal somehow. Right, Clover, if we're going to do this, we'd better get going."

Pat crunched the car into gear and reversed out of the parking space. "Okay, Clover - back to town."

***

"I go slow here. Rocks under surface," the boatman said, bringing the boat up near the base of the cliff.

Aden put the backpack on and the rope around his shoulders. He struggled to stand upright in the bobbing boat.

"You have to jump, no closer."

Aden stepped forward and steadied himself. He looked over the forward bow at the waves splashing and the rocks below.

"You jump. You jump," the man gesticulated.

Aden nodded and swallowed hard. He knew full well that one slip and he'd be crushed between rock and boat.

"Thank you," Aden said, handing the man a wad of notes.

The man took the money and nodded. "You jump. Quick. Tide turn."

Aden returned the nod and staggered towards the front of the wobbling boat. He held on tightly. He noticed a gap in the rails. He stepped between and got into the rhythm of the boat – up and down, up and down. He planted one foot firmly on the side – up and down, up and down. He readied himself, aiming squarely for a large rock in front of him – up and down, up and down.

He jumped.

Aden landed solidly on the rock with both feet, but he hadn't accounted for the weight of the backpack and the rope. He started to topple. He glanced behind frantically. The boat rocked. He rocked, the dark water sinking into murky depths that his eyes couldn't penetrate. He swiftly adjusted his weight, shifted his balance and thankfully managed to remain upright.

He sighed heavily. The boatman waved. Aden forced a smile and waved back. The boat pulled slowly away.

Aden stepped from one rock onto another and another, before climbing the short distance up onto a ledge at the base of the cliffs. He removed the rope from his shoulder, took off the backpack and put them down on the ledge.

He arched his back and watched the boat as it veered around and sailed off. Then he turned his attention back to the towering rock face above him. *They always seem so much higher when you're standing right in front of them.*

He reached out and placed his hand against the cliff. He smiled. It was beautiful to the touch. He looked upwards. This was perfect climbing rock. It felt rough, which would give him traction and there were plenty of holds.

"6A," Aden said aloud, "on average."

He would be lying if he'd said he hadn't been looking forward to this. Even so, it had seemed the best plan. There was no road, so they couldn't drive over, and they couldn't charter a helicopter (which was presumably the usual way on and off the island), at least not without alerting the inhabitants to their presence. This would certainly give him the opportunity of approaching unannounced with the element of surprise he needed.

I'll just give Pat a call to let him know I'm here, Aden thought to himself.

He opened the backpack and delved inside. "That's weird." His rummaging intensified. He couldn't find his phone. He checked again and again. He distinctly remembered asking Pat to check he'd got his phone. He must have been so engrossed in sorting out the climbing equipment that he'd forgotten to put the phone in his bag.

"You dopey eejit!" Aden shouted, doing his best Pat impression. He sighed. "Oh, well, I'll just have to work with what I have."

He took the rope out of its bag, which folded outwards as a little mat to protect it from the ground. He unfastened the helmet from the bag and secured it firmly to his head. He heaved the backpack onto his shoulders and made sure the straps were firmly tightened around him.

He looked upwards at the rock, tracing his route with his eyes, in his mind planning and memorising the path up the mountain.

Aden dug a foot into the first hold, steadied himself and looked up again. Focusing on a handhold just above his head, he took a deep breath and pushed himself upwards. This was the start of a very long climb.

Chapter 62

The Forgetful Eejit

"Eejit, eejit, eejit," Pat kept repeating to himself as he revved the little car back towards the town. Driving through what was now familiar scenery, he recognised the route.

He pulled up outside the shop and rushed in.

The shopkeeper recognised him straight away and started to bounce up and down excitedly.

"Sir, sir, you forgot things."

"Yes, yes, thank you, that's why I came back."

"Passport and wallet – left on here," the man said, motioning towards the counter.

"Yes, thank you," Pat said.

"You forget," the man said, handing Pat his belongings.

"Yes – me eejit!" Pat said, taking them from him.

The shopkeeper looked confused for a moment before replying, "Yes, yes, you eejit," and smiled.

"Tell me about it! See ya. Bye," Pat said, placing the wallet and passport very securely in his jacket pocket as he left the shop.

Chapter 63

A Stranger in a Strange Land

Caren walked through Arrivals at Shanghai Airport feeling like a complete stranger in a very strange land. Everything was glossy and white, the floor, the walls and even the ceilings. Many of the notices and shop signs were in English, but people chattered around her in a language that was completely alien to her. She had never been anywhere where she couldn't even recognise the alphabet. Suddenly she felt very alone.

She opened her bag and pulled out her phone. She had been waiting so long for this moment when she could surprise Aden and hear his voice at the other end. She wondered how he would react and what he would say. Would he be as excited to see her as she was to see him?

One of the great things about Aden's name, she thought to herself, was that it appeared first in her phonelist. She went into contacts and there he was. She pressed dial.

Beep, Beep, BEEP – This number is out of service.

Beep, Beep, BEEP – This number is out of service.

Caren felt a massive wave of disappointment as it dawned on her that Aden had had to get a new phone – and of course she hadn't got his new number.

She hung up and stumbled over to a nearby seat.

She sat down with a thump, feeling completely isolated.

As she sat forward and stared at her phone, suddenly there was a glimmer of hope. She braced herself and dialled a number.

Chapter 64

The Surprise

Pat turned the key. The engine revved, but there was something else – there was that sound again. This time it wasn't just one sound, it was a whole sequence of them.

He tried to work out where the sound was coming from and then opened the glove compartment. It was Aden's other phone, his personal phone, and this time it was ringing.

"Hello?" Pat answered.

"SURPRISE!" shouted the voice from the other end of the line.

Pat was thrown for a moment. He recognised the voice and the name that came up on the phone confirmed it.

"Caren?"

"Pat?"

"Yes. Is everything all right?" Pat asked.

"Where's Aden? Why are you answering his phone?"

"Er, he's a bit tied up at the moment. Where are you?"

"I'm in Shanghai."

"You're here? In Shanghai?"

"Yes. It was meant to be a surprise."

"It certainly bloody is."

"So where is Aden?"

"Well, he's, er, climbing a sheer cliff on an island at the moment."

"He's what?"

"He's ... Tell you what, why don't I just pick you up?"

"Yes, okay."

"Where are you?"

"I've just arrived at the airport," Caren said.

Pat did some mental reckoning. "Okay, that's about an hour away, plus I'm half an hour from the harbour. It'll take too long," Pat said, realising he couldn't fetch Caren and still have time to get back for Aden if he got into trouble.

"What do you mean it will take too long?"

"The distance – it'll take too long. Aden doesn't have his phones and he might need me."

Caren looked around the airport terminal and swallowed. "But, what will I do?"

"I know." Pat had an idea. "Get a taxi and I'll meet you halfway."

"But I can't speak the language," Caren said, feeling anxious.

"Doesn't matter, the taxi drivers speak English."

"And anyway, how will I know where halfway is? How will I find you?"

Pat thought for a moment. He remembered the main routes they had driven from the airport but he had no clue where halfway was. He needed a plan.

"Pat?" Caren said.

"One sec, Caren, I'm just working out where halfway is," Pat said, struggling to think of something.

He looked around, craning his neck to see out of every window, then spotted something that gave him a rather clever idea.

"Okay, Caren?"

"Yes, Pat."

"I'm going to forward you a text that the Chief Inspector sent to Aden. It'll show you the location of the monastery he's headed for, with map, everything."

"Okay," Caren said.

"Tell the driver to go there."

"Right, but Pat?"

"Yes?"

"How will I know where halfway is?"

"I've thought about that," Pat said. "The driver will go along the main roads on the map. I'm going to drive towards you as you drive towards me. Start to look out for me after about twenty minutes."

"What do you mean, look out for you?"

"Don't worry, you'll know it's me!" Pat insisted. "Any problems, you've got my number – or Aden's number. Ahh, you know what I mean."

"Okay," Caren said, not convinced. "See you soon."

"Aye." Pat hung up.

He opened the door and got out of the car. "Now this'll be interesting."

Chapter 65

Don't Look Down

Aden was in a good position with good holds.

"An ideal spot for a rest, I think," he muttered.

He hammered a piton firmly into place and another a few inches to the right. He fed a carabiner through each one and a sling through each carabiner, and tightened the locking nuts. He attached the other end of the sling to the carabiner on his harness. He checked and double-checked and, when he was securely anchored to the cliff face, exhaled and relaxed.

He leant backwards and shook his arms out to the sides to help the blood flow back into them.

He looked down.

As he did, he distinctly heard the voice of an old climbing instructor saying, "Never look down", although he'd never understood why. *How do you know how far you've come if you don't look down, and how else can you appreciate the view?* Aden had never found it a problem. He had always been very comfortable with heights.

So far it had been quite a challenging climb, more so than he had expected. It started off relatively simple with holds at easy to reach intervals, but things had become more and more demanding as he progressed. He had been enjoying it so much, he had almost forgotten why he was there – almost.

One of the many things he loved about climbing was how relaxing it was. As well as being a perfect exercise for the whole body, it helped to calm the mind. You didn't have the opportunity to think of much else other than the 'here and the now' and the rock in front.

He wondered how Caren was. She had popped into his head earlier. He'd felt a shiver run through his bones and had sensed something odd, as though Caren was somehow there with him, in Shanghai. He tossed the idea away. He must be missing her.

He shook his head and prepared to remove the anchor. He looked up. He still had a way to go.

Chapter 66

A Close Shave

Pat drummed his fingers on the steering wheel, glanced at the clock and slowly edged forward. He was still a mile from the motorway and he desperately didn't want to let anyone down.

He thought about Aden climbing the rock and he wondered about Caren in the taxi heading towards him. He was making very little progress.

There were two cars ahead of him and, in front of them, a large cart being pulled by two elderly donkeys.

"Only in China!" Pat said aloud.

He could hear the honking of horns from the cars behind and looked in his rear-view mirror. He did a double-take and looked again. Edging out of the traffic was a black Citroen.

"Sweet Jesus!" Pat exclaimed, craning his neck to get a better look at the car.

He couldn't see the registration number, but it was definitely the same make, model and colour of the car that had been tailing them in France. Had the car been following them all along without them noticing?

He kept looking behind. The car edged out a little further. It was then he saw the Chinese number plate and the Chinese driver.

"Phew," Pat said. "Gave me a fright there it did, Clover. But it looks like we're okay."

On reflection, he thought, *how would they drive all this way from France to China? Eejit.* He chuckled to himself.

Pat hammered his hand on the steering wheel as he looked out at the commotion in front of him. "Come on ... come on!"

He decided – he couldn't hang around anymore.

There had been a steady stream of traffic from the other direction and he had been waiting his turn patiently, but now the waiting was over. He looked ahead, craning his neck to see around the cart. There was a gap in the traffic. The two cars in front didn't seem to be making any effort to overtake, so he would have to make the move. He checked the mirror, slammed the car into gear and rammed his foot hard down on the accelerator. The car stumbled forward, reminding him he was driving a clapped-out hire car in China.

"Damn! Come on, Clover," he said, with loving encouragement and a small helping of desperation.

He was in the oncoming lane and, with alarming clarity, he could see cars heading straight for him. They flashed their lights and beeped their horns but he remained committed.

He kept the accelerator hard on the floor. The car chugged and choked and coughed forward, gathering more and more momentum.

Pat turned and smiled. "Hello donkeys!"

Up ahead the cars were approaching fast. Pat's nerves went into overdrive as the advancing vehicles didn't appear to be slowing down at all; they were still heading towards him at speed.

He rubbed a palm across his sweaty brow, willing the car to go faster. The looming cars beeped and flashed. Pat was nearly clear – just a little further. He snatched the wheel and pulled in at the last minute to the sound of a very angry horn.

"Well, bugger me, Clover – that was close. You nearly gave your Uncle Pat a heart attack, so you did."

Pat regained his composure. He kept his foot on the accelerator, looked behind and watched the donkeys disappear into the distance. He needed to get on his way quickly. He had some ground to cover.

Chapter 67

Pat's Clever Idea

Caren sat in the back of the taxi and fiddled with the phone on her lap.

She brought up the information on the monastery again and zoomed in on the picture. She imagined Aden climbing the precarious cliff walls and hoped he was safe. She wished she was there with him. Aden had taken her climbing a few times and she had quite enjoyed it, but not as much as he did. It was fun but it clearly meant much more than that to Aden.

She suddenly realised the time. "Look out for me after twenty minutes," Pat had said. She pressed a button on the phone and turned the screen off. She leant her elbow on the side of the door, rested her chin on her palm and studied the opposite lane of traffic.

The taxi sped along in the middle lane of what she considered to be the Chinese equivalent of a motorway. There was a central crash barrier and signs overhead, most of which were in English as well as Chinese, which she found comforting.

Exactly how would Pat identify himself to her? What would he be driving – a tank? And, Caren wondered, how would he catch up with her with a central reservation in the way?

She gazed at the road ahead, mesmerised by the passing cars and the unremarkable scenery. She noticed an exit.

The region was very flat with a mixture of houses, farm outbuildings and small fields occupying every little patch of land available. She noticed there was a lot of water around; in fact, there were waterways everywhere – off to the left, off to the right, intersecting the fields. It struck her this must be very fertile land.

Suddenly, something in the distance caught her eye.

"Is that a ...?" Caren stared until she could see more clearly. "Is that a dragon?"

Yes, it was! Hovering above a little car driving with all its might in the middle lane of the opposing carriageway was a large red and gold dragon, bobbing about in the wind.

Caren sat bolt upright and gripped the seat in front.

"That's my friend; I need to get to my friend," she blurted out, pointing to the car with the dragon attached.

The driver glanced to the left and shook his head. "Cannot."

"But you don't understand, I need to catch up with that car."

"Motorway," the man said, pointing forward.

Caren waved her arms frantically but it was no use. The car with the dragon floating above it whizzed past.

She felt deflated.

She remembered – the phone. She hastily re-dialled and Pat answered.

"Caren," Pat said, "where are you?"

"Is that you with the dragon?"

"Heh, yeah – didn't I say you'd see me?"

"You've just passed me."

"Oh, what?"

"You obviously didn't see me waving at you."

"No, I didn't," Pat said. "I need to get to you. The exits are few and far between on this road."

"There is an exit – we just passed it so you must almost be on it by now."

"Yes, yes, I see it," Pat said. "Just ahead. I'll call you back."

The line went dead.

***

Pat indicated, pulled into the slow lane and came off at the exit. As he approached the end of the slip road he wondered how fast he could take the corner. He looked ahead, read the road and timed it so he'd go round in the gap between the cars. He slowed a little, still trying to keep as much speed as he could. He got to the corner, held onto the wheel, which seemed to be wobbling more than ever, and cambered around the corner. He held on tightly. The wheels screeched. He could feel the car tip slightly but he made it.

"Good girl, Clover. You can do it."

He sped along the intersection of road back towards the motorway, round the other corner, along the slip road and onto the opposing carriageway.

"Right, Caren, let's see if we can catch you up."

He put his foot to the floor, veered amongst the traffic and fumbled with the phone. "I'm going as fast as I can but this little car doesn't have much in it."

"Oh, okay. One sec," Caren said and lowered the phone away from her mouth.

"Excuse me, driver?"

"Yes?" the driver said, turning his head.

"Can you slow down a bit, please?"

"No slow, motorway," the driver replied and pointed.

"My friend is trying to reach us."

"Motorway," the man pointed.

"Driver won't slow down. It's a motorway apparently," Caren said as she raised the phone back to her mouth.

"No shit," Pat said. "I'll just have to try and get more out of the dragon-mobile. Stay on the line."

"Okay," Caren said. Just at that moment something caught her eye. "Big white building, blue roof," she blurted.

"What?" Pat said.

"We've just passed a big white building with a blue roof."

"Okay. I have literally got the pedal on the metal so let's see how quickly I can get to it," Pat said. He made a mental note of the mileage and looked ahead for a white building with a blue roof.

"How do you think Aden is?" Caren said.

"I am sure ya man is fine. He seems to know what he's doing." Pat saw something come into view. "I've got it – big white building with a blue roof."

"Yes, that's it, that's the one."

"What speed you doing?"

"Erm, not sure, hold on," Caren said, glancing at the speedometer. "About ninety kilometres per hour by the looks of it."

"Okay, well, I'm doing one hundred and forty. So, if I'm

doing an extra 50kph and there is approximately 1.5km between us, then I'll get to you in ..." – Pat thought, trying to work it out – "... in ... no bleeding idea. Never been good at maths."

"You're approaching me at 50kph and there's 1.5km between us," Caren said, "so you'll catch up in about two minutes."

"That's not too bad," Pat replied. "Let's count down," and he kept his eye on the speedometer.

Caren listened. She found it very reassuring to know he was almost there. A thought popped into her head. She laughed to herself. Pat heard.

"What is it?" he said, trying to keep count at the same time.

"I was just imagining you whizzing along with a big dragon bouncing around above you."

"Hah, yeah – it's along for the ride now." Pat looked at the clock. "Okay, that's about halfway. It's quite busy here. Hang on."

Caren turned and looked back. There was a lot of traffic in the road behind but not as much as in front.

If Pat was going to catch up, he needed to get through this section of traffic without delay. He looked behind. He could just about squeeze in if he were quick. He changed lanes. The car behind beeped its horn. Pat waved and kept his foot down. He weaved in between a few other cars and came out the other side.

"I can see you!" Caren said as she saw the dragon bobbing above the approaching car.

"Brilliant. What car are you in?"

"I don't know what car it is," Caren said.

What is it with girls and cars? Pat thought to himself. "Okay, what colour is it?"

"It's sky blue on the top and silver at the bottom."

"Aha. Does it by any chance have a little red taxi sign on the top?"

"Yes, that's the one."

"Gotcha!" Pat said. "Can you get your driver to pull over?"

"Excuse me, can you pull over onto the hard shoulder, please? I need to get out here."

"No stop, motorway," the driver pointed forward.

"But it's really important. My friend is in the car behind."

"Motorway," the driver said.

"He won't stop," Caren said. "I don't think he really understands what I am saying."

"I'm sure you can think of something," Pat said.

"Actually, I just have. I am going to hang up – watch this."

"Okay," Pat said. The line went dead.

Caren put the phone in her bag. "Driver, can you pull over now?"

"No stop, motorway."

"But ..." Caren lunged forward and grasped the back of the seat. "But I am going to be SICK!" she said as she made a vomit-inducing wretching sound.

"No ill in my car!" the driver shouted and turned round to see Caren with her hand over her mouth and eyes wide, pleading with him to pull over.

"No ill in my car! We stop, we stop!" The driver rapidly indicated, veered into the slow lane and onto the hard shoulder. He slammed hard on the brakes and pulled the car to a stop. "You go, you go!"

Caren opened the door with one hand whilst keeping the other firmly across her mouth. She grabbed her bag, jumped out and slammed the door closed. The driver sped off back onto the motorway.

Hovering above the traffic was a large red and gold dragon. It was approaching fast.

Pat stopped the car on the hard shoulder a little way ahead. Caren ran up to it and opened the door.

"Hello, ma'am," Pat said.

"Thanks, Pat," Caren shouted over the noisy traffic.

"No problem."

Caren was about to get in when the dragon caught her eye, dancing above the car.

"What do you want to do with the dragon?" she said.

"I suppose you'd better let it go."

"Okay, do you have a knife?"

"No need. See the long dangly end of the string? Just pull it and it'll come apart."

"Okay."

Caren reached over to the centre of the roof where the dragon was attached to the aerial, and pulled the end of the string. The knot simply came apart in her hands. She held it for a moment, looked up at the red and gold dragon waving about in the breeze, and let go. It flew upwards as if happy to be free.

"Bye bye, dragon," Pat said as he looked out of the window and watched it drift lazily towards the fields.

Caren sat in the car and pulled the door closed.

"Ready?" Pat asked.

"Yes," Caren said as she buckled her seatbelt.

"I wasn't talking to you, I was talking to Clover."

"Who's Clover?" Caren asked.

"Who's Clover?!" Pat said as he rolled his eyes, and patted the dashboard. He checked the mirror and pulled out into the traffic. "So what are you doing here?"

"Not pleased to see me?"

"It's not that, ma'am, obviously, it's just we didn't know you were coming."

Caren smiled. "It was meant to be a surprise – for Aden."

Pat glanced across at her. "Okay, let me rephrase that. Why are you here and what happened back at home?"

"Two men tried to kidnap me."

"Aden said you'd been attacked and you went to hospital."

"Yes, that's right. But they tried again – when we left the hospital."

"They tried again?" Pat glanced, shocked. "So what happened the first time?"

"I was on the way to the bank, a white van pulled up, two men got out and tried to grab me," Caren said, clearly a little emotional as she relived the event.

"Thankfully Sam ..." She paused, realising Pat might not know who he is. "Sam's one of ours. He was walking down the street and heard me scream – came to my rescue and they took off."

"That was lucky timing," Pat said as he changed lanes. "And the second time?"

"Well, Sam took me to hospital because of this cut on my head. I was there a while and he waited for me. But they tried again when we were on our way back."

"What happened?"

"We'd just left the hospital and as soon as we'd pulled out of the car park the same white van rammed us from behind," Caren explained.

"Ouch!" Pat said.

"We were jammed in and they were smashing our windows. One of them even attacked a taxi driver who came over to help."

"So how did you get out if you were jammed in?"

"Sam. He just kept going forwards and backwards until he managed to make enough space."

"Wow," Pat said with another glance across.

"We were so lucky," Caren sighed.

"Yes, you were!" Pat said, picturing the scenario in his mind. "But, that still doesn't explain why you're here?"

"Oh right, yes!" Caren said, dragging her thoughts back to the main point. "We – well, William – thinks it's an inside job and I have to agree with him."

"Inside? But who?"

"Yes. William thinks it's the Deputy Prime Minister."

"Away on with ye!" Pat snapped his head round to look at her. "Slimy Greg Willis is behind all this?"

"Yes," Caren said.

"Yer arse is parsley!"

"What?" Caren said, mystified.

"I don't believe it," Pat said.

"We went through it several times. It all adds up. Apparently Home Office have been updating him on the case – what we were working on, where we were," Caren said. "That's why they seemed to know what we were doing all the time."

"Well, bend me backwards and poke me sideways with a stick!" Pat said as he struggled to get his head around the situation. "In fact…" A glimmer of a thought appeared in the back of his mind.

"What is it?"

"Just something you said," Pat reflected. "You said the Home Office were updating him."

"Yes."

It suddenly came to him. "That's what must have happened in Paris."

"What?"

"We were being followed in Paris by this bloody black Citroen. It was following us on the way to the airport but it suddenly it broke off."

"And?" Caren prompted.

"Well, Aden had already reported our destination so, if Greg had been informed, he could have passed it on to whoever was following us, allowing them to back off – because they knew where we were going."

"Yes, that's it," Caren said. "As I say, they've known what we were doing all the time." She had a troubling thought. "And that means they know we're here?"

"Er, yes, most likely," Pat said.

"That means they might know where Aden is?"

"Possibly."

"He might be in trouble."

Pat knew where Caren was going with this. "No, I'm sure he is fine."

"You don't know that."

"I'm sure he's fine," Pat insisted, attempting to calm her down.

"Won't this thing go any faster?"

"It has a name," Pat insisted.

Caren sighed. "Won't Clover go any faster?"

"Er, not really, no," Pat said, looking at the road and reading the signs. He noticed a familiar one. "Ooh this is our exit."

He changed lanes and pulled off.

***

"How long?" Caren asked.

"About five minutes. It's just at the bottom of this road."

Caren nodded as she looked out of the window, watching the world go by, thinking of Aden and thinking of home when, abruptly, she was tossed from side to side.

Pat wrenched the wheel, narrowly avoiding the dog that had just run into the road.

"Bugger me, that was close – stupid mutt."

"Is it okay?" Caren said, trying to look out of the back window.

"Yes, it's fine," Pat said, watching it running off behind them, "They obviously don't teach their animals the Green Cross Code out here."

Caren smiled.

Pat jiggled the wheel slightly from left to right and back again.

"What are you doing?" Caren asked, concerned.

"It's the steering wheel. It was wobbly when we picked it up, but now there just seems to be so much play in it – look," Pat said, turning it from side to side without affecting their direction. "It's really weird!" he added, still fiddling with it.

"It's almost as if it's going to ..." – Caren spoke as if she'd had a premonition – "... come off in your hand!"

"Bugger me! That's not good," Pat said, turning to Caren with the detached steering wheel in his hands. "It's banjaxed!"

She looked at the steering column; looked at Pat holding the wheel. She looked out of the window ahead of them.

"Oh, my God!" Caren screamed. "Look out for the ..."

Chapter 68

Tricky Ascent

Aden was stuck.

"Damn!" he said as he held on tightly and checked his surroundings.

He had climbed himself into a position where he couldn't continue. The rock was smooth with no holds, no cracks, no crevices – nothing.

"I don't believe this."

He had already been having doubts about himself as a climber, but this was the final straw. How could he have allowed this to happen? How could he have got himself into this spot? He had nowhere to go.

Pull yourself together!

It was an easy mistake to make. Any other climber could have done the same. There had been a slight overhang and this had meant he couldn't see much further ahead. He had climbed over an obstacle, kept on going and now he was here. But this is what climbing was all about: the unknown, the challenge.

He knew it was a waste of time trying to hammer a piton into place as they needed some kind of crack or fissure to be hammered into. He had tried earlier on a smooth face, but had just ended up chipping the rock and not doing much else.

He had to do something and he didn't fancy down-climbing back past the overhang. There must be a way. He was determined to continue.

Even with the security of the rope attaching him to the rock, it was still a little nerve-racking. Aden adjusted the rope. It felt light at one end. He realised there was hardly any left.

"Great! Just what I need!"

The first length of rope had been looped through the anchors throughout the climb, but at some point he should have tied off one end and started with the next length of rope. However, in an attempt to get the maximum length out of the rope, he'd misjudged it. He looked down. There was only about four to five feet of rope left.

He had to think.

He steadied himself and leant back as far as he could. He noticed there was a crack in the rock about two feet above him and to the right. It looked about three inches wide.

He raised himself up on tiptoes and tried to reach it but it was just too far. Even launching himself would be difficult and he wouldn't be able to rely on the security of the rope as it was.

He thought for a moment and decided to tie off the end of the rope to himself. He knew it was a risky strategy as he needed to allow enough length to move forward, whilst keeping it short enough so that if he did fall he wouldn't fall too far, otherwise the jolt from the rope might be too much for his body to cope with.

He held on with his right hand and fingered the rope through his left. As he got near the end, he fed it through the carabiner and back through itself and in an instant he had a perfect bowline knot.

He let out a small sigh of relief, knowing he was secure once again.

Holding on with his left hand he let his right arm drop and shook the blood back into it. He had one more problem to deal with: where to go next. The crack to his top right was the best bet.

Grasping on tightly, he leant back to try and get the best possible look at the crack. Again he estimated it was about three inches wide and narrowing at the bottom. He had an idea.

He held on with his left hand, looked down and chose an appropriately sized nut. He carefully removed it from his harness and gripped the wire between his teeth. He removed a sling and attached it to the nut.

He threaded his hand through the end of the sling and flung the nut upwards towards the crack. It hit the rock to one side and flopped back down. He steadied himself and flung it again. It missed. He tried again – missed. He tried and missed yet again.

"Oh, come on," he said getting irritated.

He knew that losing his patience wouldn't help. He took a moment, held the nut and aimed as precisely as he could. He threw it towards the crack and this time it went in.

"Yes!" he shouted.

Before he put any weight on it, he checked it methodically. He tugged and pulled; it was firm. He yanked it one more time and it held.

He put all of his weight on it. It gave slightly but was

firmly in place. "Okay, it's now or never."

He gripped the sling with both hands and spread the soles of his shoes flat against the rock. Using the grip of his shoes he began to walk up the smooth face and, hand over hand, he eventually reached the crack.

Aden formed a fist and put his hand into the cavity, providing a more secure hold. Thankfully from this point he could see more and more holds. He reached out with his left hand and grasped one. He took his right hand out of the sling and let it drop. As he put his foot in the loop and his hand back in the crack, he breathed a sigh of relief. There were holds and cracks as far as the eye could see.

Now that he was safely in place, he needed to work out what to do with the rope.

Chapter 69

Distant Observation

"Pat – do something!" Caren pleaded as the car started to veer off the road.

She gripped the edge of the seat tightly with both hands and looked around. She could see people going about their business in the paddy fields alongside.

"Erm, I'm trying, hold on," Pat said as he fumbled about, trying to align the steering wheel with the shaft on the end of the steering column.

He looked up. The car had slowly drifted and they were about to graze the side of the road. He felt the wheel click into place. He turned it and, to his great relief, the car straightened. They both breathed an enormous sigh.

"Holy Mother of God, wasn't that exciting?" Pat said, turning his head and grinning.

Caren just stared.

"Now, I've just got to try and keep it on 'til we get there."

"How long now?"

"Not long at all, it's just at the bottom of this road."

"Is that the sea?" Caren asked, pointing towards the grey shimmer in the distance.

"It is indeed," Pat said, heading straight for it.

***

"But – it's huge," Caren said. She was seeing the island and the scale of the cliffs for the first time in real life.

"Yep, rather him than me," Pat said. He turned off the engine and picked up the binoculars from the back seat.

"Can you see him? Is he okay?" Caren asked impatiently.

"Give us a chance," Pat said, moving the binoculars around to try and get Aden in his sights. "Got him – he's fine. I can't believe he's been climbing all this time."

"Can I see?" Caren asked.

Pat handed her the binoculars. She held them to her eyes and looked.

"How do you focus?"

"This knob, here," Pat said, showing her how to adjust them.

"Where is he?"

"Left-hand side – yellow helmet."

"I can't find him."

"Find the top of the island, move to the left and find the edge. You'll see a sticky out piece of rock that looks like a nose – just follow it down the side of the cliff a bit."

Caren steadied the binoculars. She followed the edge of the cliff and found him. "Wow, he looks so small," she said, peering through the lenses.

"Aye."

"It's weird," Caren said, taking her eyes away to look at Pat. "There's Aden, all the way over there, climbing up a steep cliff and we're here watching him." She put the binoculars back to her eyes.

"Aye, that's the wonder of these specialised optical devices."

Aden had removed the other length of rope from his shoulder and anchored it with a piton to the cliff face. He reached upwards and felt the width of a gap in the rock, inserted a cam and let it expand into place. He ran the rope through a carabiner, giving him two strong anchor points.

He slowly and deliberately fed the new rope through the harness and untied the bowline knot in the other. He let the first rope fall free. He reached up to a nice firm hold and pushed with his leg. This section of rock was much easier to climb than the previous one. The holds were so well spaced it was almost like ascending a ladder. He kept going and going until he realised he hadn't anchored on for a while. Irrespective of how easy it was, he knew one wrong move could cause him to fall and, with no anchor point, that could mean trouble.

There was a small fissure in front of him. He pulled out a cam, inserted it and expanded it into place. He ran the rope through a carabiner and continued to climb. At this pace he would reach the top in no time at all.

***

"He's going so fast," Caren said, continuing to watch Aden through the binoculars.

"Where is he now?" Pat asked.

"He's not far from the top. It starts to slope off so I presume that'll make it easier."

"I guess so," Pat said.

***

Aden looked up. Not far now.

But still, he thought to himself, *better to be safe than sorry.*

In front of him was a wide cavity. He chose a larger cam, shoved it in and ran the rope through a carabiner. After two more holds he hammered a piton into place, attached a quickdraw and fed the rope through. He climbed further, hammered in another piton, and repeated the process for another few holds.

Chapter 70

Intruder Alert

Pearl walked along the beach back towards the stables, the reigns of the horse held firmly in her hand.

She stopped and listened to the waves lapping against the beach. She turned to Emerald Princess and stroked her nose.

"Not long now, my beauty. Mr Liang will be arriving at any moment to take you, Onyx and Peppermint to your new home. I'll join you very soon."

The horse whinnied. She smiled and began to hum the first few notes of her melody.

Without warning, the horse snapped her head sharply. Pearl turned.

"Morgan, I do wish you'd stop sneaking up on me!"

"Sorry, Pearl," Morgan stuttered. "I ... I need to talk to you."

Pearl just didn't know what had got into Morgan. He was behaving more strangely by the day. He stood in front of her, almost pathetic, with one arm behind his back and his head hung low.

"Is everything okay? Is there something wrong with the data upload?"

"The data upload is fine. It's not that."

"Then what is it?" Pearl asked.

"I just wanted to say … I'm …" Morgan found it difficult to speak the words he had been going over in his mind. He had practised so well in the mirror. "I am …"

Pearl looked at him and held the reigns of the horse tightly. The horse whinnied nervously.

Morgan opened his mouth. "I …"

The radio crackled: "Threat detected – repeat: threat detected. Security alert. Please report to the operations room. Repeat: please report to the operations room!"

"Morgan, whatever this is, it'll have to wait," Pearl said as she led the horse back to the stables.

Morgan bit his lip and watched Pearl hurry off.

"I'm sorry, I'm sorry …" he said, breaking down. He pulled his hand from behind his back, frantically trying to wipe off the blood.

***

Pearl stormed into the operations room. "Right, what's going on?"

Pierre stood up. "Our movement detectors have sensed someone climbing the cliff."

"Climbing? But it's sheer!"

"Yes, Pearl. I thought it was birds at first but it's too large, too consistent in the way it's moving."

"Have we got it on camera?"

"No, not yet, the cameras can't see over the edge of the slope. We'll get a glimpse soon though."

"We don't need this distraction. And you're sure it's someone climbing?"

Pierre nodded. "One person, definitely."

Pearl thought for a moment. "Okay, release the stones."

Pierre nodded, tapped a few keys on the keyboard and said, "Releasing in three, two, one."

He stabbed a key, "Done."

***

Aden hammered in another piton, attached a quick-draw and threaded the rope through. He attached a sling to the piton and to his harness. He leant back on the rope and shook his arms to his sides to get the blood flowing into them again.

He looked up and smiled. *Not long now* he thought, proud of his accomplishment.

He took a moment to look around and noticed something hanging against the edge of the rock. He squinted and stared. They were devices of some kind. And then he realised – they were sensors which had been lowered down from the top of the mountain to detect intruders.

Damn, they must know I'm here.

Aden could hear a noise above – a rattling sound which rapidly grew louder and louder. From over the edge, stones and rocks started tumbling towards his head.

"Oh, no!"

He hugged the rock and pulled himself in tight against it. The first few smaller stones bounced off his plastic helmet, but it was the larger rocks he was worried about.

To his right he remembered seeing a hollow in the rock. It was large enough to shelter him. If he held himself inside it, the rocks would hopefully pass him by. He knew he had no time to waste. The manoeuvre would involve swinging on the piton he'd just hammered in to place. He knew it should take his weight, but they were meant to be for emergencies only. *But this is an emergency,* he reasoned, as another piece of rock struck his helmet. The clattering grew louder as more and more rocks began to fall.

Aden rocked on his left foot, leapt to his right-hand side and swung on the rope. His feet landed firmly on a small ledge and he reached out and grabbed a hold. He noticed a large crack to his right. He formed a fist and wedged his hand into it. Tons of rock came crashing down the cliff face. Smaller bits clattered against the edge of his helmet and suddenly he was jolted backward by a large rock striking his backpack. His left hand came loose as he struggled to maintain his balance. He looked up and, as he did so, he saw a massive rock plummeting straight towards him.

***

"Anything on the sensors?" Pearl asked.

"No, nothing, I think that must've worked," Pierre said.

"And the cameras?"

Pierre pressed a couple of keys. "No, cameras clear too."

Pearl nodded, "Good." She sat down in her seat. "In that case we'll just wait for the upload to finish."

She felt a jolt of guilt rush through her. She hadn't wanted to hurt anyone but she was too close now and nothing could jeopardise the project at such a crucial stage.

Chapter 71

The Pinnacle

Aden held on tightly with his face against the cold stone. He waited until the sound of the rockfall subsided. He still couldn't believe he'd managed to regain his balance and pull himself into the recess at the last minute. He could have been pulverised.

He glanced around. He could see the last piton he'd put in place had been smashed out. It was dangling in the air with the rope flapping beneath him.

He took stock of his surroundings. Both feet were resting on a small ledge, while one hand gripped a round hold and the other was still clenched into a fist in a crack. He was stuck in a hollow. Above him was an overhang that was so smooth there was nothing to grip onto. He couldn't go to his right and the holds to the left were too far away, especially now there was no piton to take his weight. He was completely stuck.

"Bloody brilliant!" Aden said to himself.

He knew the only option was to let go and let his body swing with the rope. Hopefully the previous piton would hold. He had nailed them in well but there was a chance the jolt of his fall could yank it out. He looked around again, checking one last time. There was definitely nowhere else to go.

He took a deep breath. "Here goes!"

He let go.

For a second he was weightless but then the air rushed past him and he felt himself being jerked violently to his left as the rope swung underneath the existing piton. He could feel something strike his head. It was the piton and the quickdraw that had been dislodged from the rock. The harness dug into his waist and pinched his crotch; he swayed from side to side.

Aden exhaled. The fall had jarred his body but he seemed okay.

He let himself swing for a moment and caught his breath. It was then he felt another unexpected jolt on the line.

***

"Can you see him? Where is he now?" Caren asked.

"Hold on, just trying to find him again," Pat said. He had no idea what was happening but he had just seen Aden fall. He certainly didn't want to say anything in case Caren started to panic.

"Well?" Caren insisted.

Pat watched Aden dangling from the rock. He swallowed hard. "Yep, I got him, he's fine."

"Let me look," Caren said, holding out her hand.

"Er ... hold on a moment. I just need to check the top of the cliff and the monastery and then you can have them," Pat said, stalling for time. *Come on, partner, what the hell are you doing?*

***

Aden felt the rope give a little. He was hanging three feet from the face of the cliff. He looked up. He could see another piton working itself loose.

He looked at the route. He remembered the holds.

Very carefully he reached forward but couldn't quite make contact with the rock. He needed to push himself away with his legs and grab the holds as he swung back. In his mind it sounded so easy, but he knew one tug could dislodge the piton and, if he fell any further, the remaining pitons could work loose.

He didn't want to think about it, he had little choice – it was something he had to do.

With his feet against the surface and his legs slightly bent, he pushed himself away from the rock. He looked up and he saw the piton move. He swung outwards and back towards the face of the cliff. He felt the rope above him slacken and heard the piton break free.

His body began to tumble but he lunged and managed to grasp the holds. He smashed into the rock. He turned his head as it struck the side. He could feel his whole body-weight on his arms. He shook his head. His senses returned. He pulled himself up on his arms as his feet frantically searched for a foothold. They found one. He held himself against the cliff face, gasping for air. It took a moment to recover.

Damn that was close. He might not be dead but he still had some work to do to get out of this situation alive.

There was now a large loop of rope beneath him, with two pitons and quickdraws dangling from it. He needed both hands free in order to hammer in a piton and he just didn't have the footholds to help keep him in place. He looked up and about two feet above his head he could see a crack in the rock. Holding on tightly with his left hand, his right hand reached towards the back of his harness. He felt the equipment on the belt and located a camming device. He gingerly took it off the harness and held it between his teeth. He gripped back onto the rock with his right hand.

He looked up at the crack. It would be quite a stretch but he should be able to do it. He adjusted the cam between his fingers so it would fit into the rock. Holding on tightly he raised his hand and tried to wedge the cam in place. It was so close – almost there – he just needed another inch. His left hand tightened even more as he gradually raised himself onto the tip of his toes. With one last push, he jammed it in the crack and let go. He tugged on it; it was firm and it held.

Aden carefully fed the rope through his fingers. As the loop got smaller and smaller he finally managed to catch the quickdraw that was still attached to the piton. He pressed the clasp and fixed it to the cam.

With his anchor back in, he climbed another four feet and put a cam in the rock. He anchored the other quickdraw with the piton hanging off it, tugged and looped the rope through it.

He was back to where he had been earlier. He looked up to his right. The sensor that had given him away had been damaged by the rock fall. This gave him back the advantage.

Every so often, as he continued to climb, he hammered a piton in place, attached a quickdraw and fed the rope through, followed by another and another. The pitons were now much closer together; he wasn't going to make the same mistake twice.

Hand over hand, hold after hold he progressed.

***

"Can I see now, please?" Caren snapped.

Phew, Pat thought as he watched Aden sort himself out. "Here you go," he said and handed the binoculars to her.

Find the top, move to the left, find the edge, piece of rock that looks like a nose and follow it down, she thought to herself. *There he is.*

"He doesn't have far to go now," Caren said as she watched. "When do we go in?"

"We don't," Pat said.

Caren lowered the binoculars to her lap. "What do you mean, we don't?"

"Aden said he was going to check things out and would only signal if he needed help."

"But he might need us."

"Then he'll signal."

"But it may be too late by then."

"I am sure there's no need to worry, Caren," Pat said, trying to reassure her. "He's met Pearl already and he's only there to find out more about what's going on."

"But what if Pearl really is a killer?"

"Aden seems certain she's not. He thinks we've got the wrong end of the stick."

Caren raised the binoculars to her eyes and kept watching.

"He knows what he's doing, Caren," Pat said.

She lowered the binoculars again. "I know. I can't help it. I suppose I care too much," she sighed.

Uh-oh, she's gonna get soppy, Pat thought to himself.

He hadn't known many women in his line of work and he always found it a little uncomfortable when it came to emotions. He tried his best to pay no attention and wondered how his partner was getting on as he neared the top of the cliffs.

"My friends did warn me that relationships and the job don't mix, but you don't listen when you're in love," Caren continued.

Pat didn't answer and just stared out of the window.

"Aden felt the same way at first. He said his motto was: don't get involved with women at work." Caren turned to him. "Do you believe that, Pat?"

Pat wasn't really paying attention. *I'll play dumb*, he thought. "I wouldn't know about that."

Caren looked at him and thought for a second; then it clicked. "Oh, I see. Sorry, I didn't realise."

"Realise what?" Pat was confused.

"You're gay."

"Get away with ya – I'm no effin' arse bandit!" Pat snapped.

"But you just said ..."

Pat jumped in. "I've always worked with men that's all, never women, so I've never had a chance to get involved with women on the job."

"Oh, God, I'm sorry." Caren blushed with embarrassment.

"Bleeding gay!" Pat shook his head.

Caren glanced at his face. He looked so indignant. She giggled and as Pat looked at her, she began to laugh uncontrollably. He smiled. He could see the funny side and in the end he had to laugh with her.

"Keep an eye on ya man," Pat said and nudged her arm.

Caren raised the binoculars and followed the routine again. *Find the top, move to the left, find the edge, piece of rock that looks like a nose.*

***

Aden looked above him. There was an overhang. He had known it was coming and now it was here. It only jutted out about a foot but any overhang was a challenge.

Aden reached round the back of his harness to grab another cam. He couldn't find one. He checked with his other hand, reaching around his backpack, but he'd run out.

"Damn," he said aloud. He was down to two pitons and one choc.

Just to his left was a crack. He unclipped the choc and jammed it into the hole. A cam would have given him so much more security but a choc was better than nothing – as long as it didn't pop out.

As Aden contemplated the best way over the overhang, he checked the remaining rope. It seemed the overhang and the choc were the least of his worries – he didn't have much rope left either.

"One thing at a time, "Aden said calmly.

There was a gap underneath the overhang. Aden reached

up, formed a fist and wedged it into the gap. He raised his left leg, found a great hold, braced himself and launched himself upwards.

It was yet another leap of faith as he couldn't see over the overhang and had no idea if there would be any holds up there or not. His left hand slapped down on the rock. It was smooth. His hand began to slide and, just as it was about to slip over the edge, he managed to get a finger hold. It wasn't much, but it was enough. He raised his right leg, found another good hold and pushed himself upwards again.

He relaxed the fist of his right hand, removed it from the gap and threw his arm over the top of the overhang. Almost immediately he found a hold. *Thank goodness*, he thought, and heaved his body upwards and over the edge.

The overhang made a nice little platform for him to rest on as he gathered himself together. He glanced around but noticed a security camera pointing in his direction. He swiftly took stock. His rope was running out, he only had a short distance to go and he was out of cams and almost out of pitons as well.

The remaining distance up to the top was more of a steep slope than a climb. Aden rubbed his foot on the rock. The climbing shoes gave more than enough grip, or so he hoped. It was risky, but it might just pay off.

"Go!" he said to himself.

***

"Oh, my God, he's dropped his stuff!" Caren cried out.
Pat jolted in his seat. "Damn, you made me jump!"

"But he's dropped his stuff," Caren said with panic.

"Let me look," Pat said and snatched the binoculars from her.

He could see Aden clambering up a slope towards the top of the island. He followed the slope backwards and could see the bit that looked like a nose with Aden's bag and harness dangling underneath.

"It's okay. He let it go on purpose. He's on the last bit, see, he's clambering up the slope. He handed the binoculars back to Caren.

"Oh, I see. Wow, he's going so fast. He'll be there in a moment."

***

Pierre pressed a few buttons on his keyboard and brought up the sensor display again. No readings, nothing there.

He pressed another few buttons and brought up the live feed from the camera. Just as the picture appeared he turned his head. Someone was calling his name. It was Pearl, beckoning him over to her desk. He nodded and raised his hand to tell her he'd be with her in one moment.

He looked back at the camera. *That's weird*, he thought to himself – he was sure he saw something disappear from the edge of the picture. He studied the image carefully but he couldn't see anything. *Probably just a bird*. The rockfall must have had the desired effect.

I wonder who it was? he thought to himself, *and what were they doing here?* Maybe it was just a climber, but it would be strange to be climbing here, of all the places in

China. He had done a bit of climbing himself in Fontaine-bleu, south of Paris, and he knew it would be unusual for someone to climb on their own. *Maybe he wasn't alone?*

He got up and walked over to Pearl's desk.

"All clear?" Pearl asked.

"Yes, Pearl, all clear. Nothing on the sensors and nothing on the cameras."

"Good. Thank you."

"I just wondered something, though."

"Yes, Pierre?"

"Climbers don't often climb alone. There might be some-one else out there."

"But there was no one else on the cameras?" Pearl said.

"No, no one," Pierre replied.

"And nothing else on the sensors?"

"No, nothing at all," he confirmed.

"I'm sure there is nothing to worry about. It was just one person out climbing where they shouldn't be," Pearl snapped, still haunted by the guilt – *the project must complete.*

"Yes, Pearl," Pierre said.

Pearl stood up. "I'll be back in ten minutes."

Pierre nodded and returned to his desk.

***

Aden clung to an outcrop of rock at the top. The monas-tery was now clearly in view.

He watched and waited.

There was no sign of activity.

The monastery appeared to have two levels. The first level had a wide roof which curled up at the edges and there was a second level above that. Aden realised that, from where he was, he could jump onto the first level. He calculated he could walk along the roof and get in through a partially open window. That's what he would do. He just needed to get over this outcrop first.

He strained, lifted himself upwards and over – and he had done it; he had reached the top.

**

"He's done it. He's done it!" Caren said.

"It's about bloody time – the ol' slowcoach."

Caren looked at Pat. She still hadn't quite got used to his humour.

"What now?" Caren asked.

"We wait," Pat said.

**

It was an amazing view from the top of the island, looking over the monastery out to sea and, in the other direction, over to Shanghai. Unfortunately, Aden didn't have time to take it all in. Instead, he rushed to the edge of the rock and assessed the situation.

The gap between the rock and the roof was actually larger than he had thought – probably four foot. Jumpable, but nasty if he slipped.

He took a few steps back and readied himself. *Here we go.*

He ran forward and jumped. He landed heavily on the roof and fought to steady himself. He just hoped no one was in the room below after his rather noisy landing.

He stood for a moment. The rock-climbing shoes seemed to grip the roof well and, after testing it with a few tentative footsteps, he was satisfied the roof tiles were perfectly strong enough to take his weight. He tiptoed up the slope.

The window opened vertically and was loose on its hinges. Aden lifted it upwards. The sun reflected off the glass as he opened it. He let it go and it fell back into place. He lifted it again and looked inside – all clear. Holding the window open, he inched his way to the edge. The frame rubbed against his back as he lowered himself through the opening. He jumped down into the room.

The window swung back into place.

***

"Wow, did you see that?" Pat said as he shielded his eyes against a beam of bright sunlight.

Caren turned her head. "Do you think that was Aden's signal?"

"It might just have been someone opening a window. We'll wait and see if it happens again."

There was another blinding flash.

"It must be Aden."

"Hang on," Pat said.

Another flash.

"That must be the signal."

"Yes, I'm inclined to agree with you," Pat said with a melancholic voice.

"What's the matter?"

"It means I have to go on the water."

"So?"

"I hate the water and I can't swim."

"It'll be fine. Come on."

Caren jumped out of the car.

Pat reluctantly got out too and they both ran down to the quayside.

"Which boat did Aden go on?" Caren said.

"Dunno, they all look the same."

"You must have some idea."

"I don't think it's here," Pat said.

They walked along the harbour wall. There were lots of boats but most of them were empty.

"How long did it take him to get across?"

"About half an hour, I suppose."

"We need to get there sooner than that. He might need our help …There!" Caren said, pointing.

Up ahead was a young man who appeared to be getting ready to go home as he was busy making the final checks to his boat.

"Come on, Pat, quickly," Caren said, rushing over to him.

The boat was very sporty with a low slung hull and tapered nose. It had a gold trim and a red 'go faster' stripe down the side.

"Excuse me," Caren said.

The man looked round and nodded his head.

"Do you speak English?"

The man shook his head.

"I need to get to that island," Caren said, pointing to herself and then to the island.

The man looked at her, looked at the island and back at her. He shrugged his shoulders.

"I – need – to go to the island – on this boat," she said, again pointing as she spoke.

The man pointed to himself, his boat and towards the island.

Caren nodded and smiled. She turned as Pat appeared beside her, and pointed to Pat, herself, the boat and then the island.

The man seemed to indicate he was planning to leave. He lifted his bag and walked towards the back of the boat.

"Pat, quick – money. Give me money!" Caren said as she held out her hand.

The binoculars, the climbing stuff and now this – what am I, an effin' bank? Pat thought to himself.

He reached for his wallet. "Do you take credit cards?"

The man looked blankly at him.

"Pat – cash!" Caren snapped.

Pat pulled some cash from his wallet and handed it to Caren.

Caren seized the cash and stepped forward. "Please help us. We need to get that island." She held out the cash. "My husband needs our help and we've got to get there as soon as possible. Please help us. We can pay to cover your time and your fuel."

The man looked at the desperation in Caren's face and the cash in her hand and nodded.

He said something in Chinese and placed his bag down again. He held out his hand to help Caren aboard.

***

It was obviously someone's private quarters. Aden had climbed through into some kind of dressing room area. To his left was the main door and to his right a small corridor leading into a bedroom. He could just about see the corner of the bed and a wardrobe.

He turned to the door and pushed his ear against it. He gingerly gripped the handle and opened it without making a sound, but as he did so, he could hear footsteps in the hallway. He promptly closed the door.

He listened. They were getting closer.

I need to hide, he thought and looked around – *the bedroom.*

He had only been able to see the corner of the bed from where he'd been standing before but, as he walked towards it, he did a double-take. His heart skipped a beat. The sheet was stained with blood and he could see the outline of someone underneath.

He walked round the side of the bed and lifted the corner of the sheet.

Underneath lay the body of a young woman with a lithe figure. Her throat had been cut.

The door opened.

Aden looked around – there was nowhere to hide.

Pearl walked in.

"Sinead? Are you here, my darling?"

"Sinead?"

The moment was frozen in time as Pearl stood, mouth agape, staring at the bed with the sheet resting upon Sinead's bloodied corpse.

Aden felt helpless.

Pearl was in shock. Her stomach tied itself into knots of rage. Tears welled up in her eyes. She felt anger bubbling up from within. She looked down at the floor. There was a knife, its blade covered in blood – Sinead's blood. She reached down, seized it and rushed at Aden, thrusting it towards his chest.

"Pearl – wait!" Aden begged, taking a step backwards to avoid the blow.

Pearl hesitated.

"It seems you have an enemy in your camp and I am not your enemy," Aden said.

Through teary eyes, Pearl looked at the bed and back at Aden.

"You did this. You killed her!" she screamed.

"No, I didn't. I would have no reason to kill her and, look, there's no blood on my hands," Aden insisted.

"That was you, climbing the cliff."

"Yes, it was."

"Why are you here?"

"Let's just say we're interested in knowing what you're up to."

Pearl looked into his eyes. There it was again, the feeling she could trust him. She looked at the knife in her hand covered with Sinead's blood. She let out a tortured scream filled with anger and pain and threw it to the floor.

"Why?!"

"I'm sorry," Aden said, placing a comforting hand on her shoulder.

A thought entered her mind. "Morgan!"

"What?"

"Morgan did this!" Pearl screamed.

"Who is Morgan?"

"He is my ... my second-in-command. He's been behaving oddly for a while now. He came to me earlier acting strangely and was trying to say something. I could tell something wasn't right," Pearl said, dragging the back of her hand across a wet cheek. "He did this – he did this!"

Pearl tried to storm out of the room, but Aden held her back.

"Wait. Tell me what's going on."

"Let go of me. I must find Morgan." Pearl pulled away.

"Wait a moment. Tell me what's happening."

"I must find Morgan."

"Hold on. Please," he implored, looking deeply into her eyes. "You said he's been behaving oddly for a while and he's killed your friend, obviously someone you cared very deeply about. If he's up to something, you could be next. I'm here to help. I want to help. Just tell me what's going on," Aden said.

"Okay." Pearl wiped the tears away from her face, looked back at the bed and stared.

"Let's go somewhere else."

Pearl nodded, but she couldn't move. She stood transfixed. So much blood – so much of Sinead's blood. "She was such a lovely girl, so beautiful ..." She sniffled. "Bastard!"

Aden put his arm around her and guided her out of the room.

**

Morgan closed his door and tried to steady himself. His heart was beating at a pace he had not experienced before; he felt exhilarated – alive.

He rushed into the bathroom and turned on the tap. He thrust his hands under the flow of water and watched the streams of bloody liquid spiral down the plug hole. "I have a mission," he announced proudly.

The events replayed in his mind.

He had been trying to find Pearl but she wasn't in the control room or in her room either. He'd checked the cameras to confirm she wasn't on the beach, so the only other place she would be was with that bitch, Sinead. But when he'd got to her room, Pearl wasn't there, only Sinead.

Sinead was suspicious. She kept asking questions, and then the insinuations started. Morgan had to do something straight away, he had to do something to shut her up. So he cut her neck.

He remembered what it was like, holding her down while she thrashed against him, trying to defend herself; the first stab of the knife to her throat; the way she tried to claw at her neck. The first little scream and how that scream turned into choking and eventually coughing up her own blood. The horror in her eyes – those eyes ...

He shivered. It was an unexpected reaction. He felt a jolt of guilt. His conscience was interfering with his mission.

"No!" he shouted as he looked at himself in the mirror.

What was happening to him? What was he doing? He stared into his eyes, but for a moment he saw someone else's eyes – those eyes!

"Arrgh!" Morgan screamed, thrusting his fist into the mirror. It shattered, scattering shards of broken glass into the sink.

He turned off the tap and lowered his head. He could see his reflection a dozen times in the pieces of broken mirror. A dozen eyes – those eyes ...

He turned, rushed into the bedroom and over to a chest of drawers. He bent down, opened the bottom drawer and rummaged beneath some clothes. His fingers made contact with cold metal. He pulled out a submachine gun and held it close to his chest. *He had a job to do.*

***

"Is this your room?"

"Yes," Pearl said as she opened the door and led Aden inside.

Behind her, Pearl heard the click of the lock and stopped in her tracks.

"Don't worry," Aden said. "If this Morgan fella is on some kind of murderous rampage, I just want to make sure we've got something between him and us."

Pearl nodded and lowered her head. "Want a drink?"

"Yes, please."

Pearl beckoned him to sit at her desk and walked over to a table in the corner. She picked up two glasses and poured them both a drink.

"What's this?" Aden asked, inspecting the contents of the glass.

"It's called Baijiu – it's essentially Chinese vodka."

He took a sip. It was strong.

He placed the glass down on the desk and looked at the blank computer screen in front of him.

"Press a key," Pearl said.

Aden reached forward, pressed a key on the keyboard and studied the display on the monitor.

"Numbers – lots of numbers. It's a data transfer of some kind," Aden said.

Pearl nodded. "I'm one of the key people involved in the IPV6 strategy, which is basically the next era of the internet. Through my company, Pearl Technologies, we have developed IPV6 routers, bridges and other equipment – the equipment that forms the backbone to the internet. We've installed them in all the major ISPs, hosting companies and even government departments and secret military buildings," Pearl explained, sipping her drink.

"Impressive."

Pearl continued, "Flash memory is built into each device and, by using a clever compression algorithm, which I developed myself, we can store massive amounts of information that is being passed through it – documents, emails, images, web pages, whatever it may be. We've now triggered the download from all those devices.

"Hang on …" Aden said. "You're stealing data?"

"No!" Pearl snapped, slamming her glass down on the desk. "I'm looking for the truth. My parents' life was ruined because of something the French Navy did to the marine life in Tikehau. They killed my parents and destroyed my home. I'm looking for the truth."

"You're collecting everything that gets sent through the equipment?" Aden said as the enormity of the operation began to sink in.

"Well, no, not quite. It's fairly specific information we're looking for, based on very detailed algorithms with keywords and phrasing."

Aden interrupted. "Okay, fine, it's clever stuff, but at the end of the day, you're still stealing information. It's illegal. What would the French Government do if they found out?"

Pearl sighed and shook her head.

"You met with a French minister recently. Does he know?" Aden asked.

"Oh, God, no! He's part of the French Government that commissioned the equipment. There's no way I could tell him what I was doing."

"Then why did you meet with him?"

"We'd just finished an upgrade in the last of several government data centres. It was the final step before we could begin."

"Begin?" Aden said. "With the data transfer?"

"Yes," Pearl said.

"Did you have anything to do with his disappearance?" Aden said directly.

"Disappearance? What disappearance?"

"The French minister. Shortly after meeting with you he went missing and hasn't been seen since."

"François? Oh no ..." Pearl was obviously taken aback. "He has a family, what about them?"

"They're all okay as far as I know. It's just the minister who's gone missing." Aden sat back and exhaled deeply. "I just can't believe you're collecting – stealing – all of this information from France." He took another sip from his glass.

"France? Not just France – the world!"

Aden sat bolt upright, almost choking on his drink. "The world? You're stealing data from the world?"

"Yes, of course, it's the only way to guarantee I find the information I'm looking for."

Aden was gobsmacked. "The world's data – that's wrong. No one person should have access to all that information."

"I don't care about the other stuff on there. I've no intention of using it for anything other than to find the information I need – what happened to my parents and my home. The truth!"

"I'm staggered. How have you been able to achieve this?" Aden said.

"Hard work, commitment and dedication, just like building any business," Pearl said matter-of-factly.

"But who knows about it?"

"Only my team."

Aden couldn't believe she had been able to keep it a secret for so long.

"Where is the equipment made?"

"At a fabrication plant, here in China."

"And no one there knows?"

"No. They just connect up all the components and box them up."

"So they don't question why they are putting so much flash memory in there?"

"It's a sealed memory unit. They don't know its capacity

and they wouldn't care. They just build the equipment; they didn't design it."

"What about the head office – in Paris?"

"It's just admin. Someone wants a particular piece of equipment, they put the order on to the computer and it gets despatched from here in China."

Aden shook his head in disbelief. He thought for a moment. "Okay, but surely government departments must have their own engineers to inspect the equipment and confirm it's okay – and also to check you're not trying to do the very thing you're doing?"

Pearl smirked. "Actually, you'd be surprised. Most companies, and even some governments, just take the equipment on face value."

"But what if they did try taking it apart?"

"That's fine. They'd just see the inside of the machine. All of the clever stuff is done with its programming and that's embedded within its BIOS and its memory."

"Okay, so what if they took the sealed memory apart and realised exactly how much memory was included?"

"The manual explains it's used for the operational programming of the machine, the BIOS and the buffering technology, so that, in the event of an outage, data isn't lost."

"But what if someone was suspicious of such a large amount of memory?" Aden asked.

"We would just explain we wanted to make sure the buffer was large enough. But they can't really find out as it's sealed and off limits to them. There's no way they could access it."

"But what if they did?"

"They can't."

"But what if they tried?"

"It's all encrypted using an algorithm; it's impregnable."

"Nothing is ever completely impregnable."

"This is." Pearl became animated. "I designed it myself. It's the strongest encryption ever and only I have the key."

"But what if they break the key?"

"There's no way they can, but if – if – they did, there is another failsafe."

"Which is?"

"The equipment is programmed to re-flash itself."

"Re-flash?"

"Yes, basically to re-programme itself from a clean operating memory so the data collection algorithms and transfer code are all erased. That way it can never fall into the wrong hands and never be traced." Pearl crossed her arms. "I've thought of everything."

"Well, not quite."

"What do you mean?"

"You've obviously got a brilliant mind and I have to agree, you've thought of everything from a technical point of view, but there is one thing you've failed to take into consideration."

"What?"

"The human element."

Suddenly Pearl's memory returned to Sinead.

"Morgan!"

"Exactly. He took your friend's life – he's up to something." Aden sat forward. "Do you realise the value someone would put on this? The world's secrets handed to them on a plate."

"But I've been so cautious. I'd never considered that could possibly happen," Pearl said.

"Well, I guess up to this point you didn't need to."

Aden heard something.

"What was that?"

"Oh, it's my radio. It's how we keep in contact with each other."

"Pearl, Pearl, are you there?" Pierre's voice crackled over the air.

Pearl picked up the radio. "Yes, Pierre?"

"Something's up – we need you in the control room immediately."

"Okay. I'll be right there." Pearl made a dash for the door.

"Wait." Aden placed his hand on her arm. "How did he sound?"

"What?"

"Pierre, how do you think he sounded?"

"Now you mention it, a bit agitated."

"Exactly. It could be a trick."

"A trick?"

"Morgan could be in there. It could be a ploy to get you up there."

"Oh, I see. What do you think he wants?"

"Well, my guess is to kill you all and sell the information to the people he's involved with, who could then potentially hold the entire world to ransom. What do you think?"

Pearl's face dropped into her hands. "Oh, God, what have I done?"

"Where's the control room?"

"At the end of the building, along the corridor."

"Are there any other ways in?"

"No, just the main door. It's the most secure room."

"Okay, I'll come with you."

Pearl stopped in her tracks. "If you come, he might try and kill you too."

"Don't worry, I will get him before he gets us." Aden unlocked the door.

"Are you sure?"

"Of course – trust me, I'm a professional," Aden smiled.

***

Caren held Pat's hand as they sat huddled in the back of the boat. He was gripping so hard she was in desperate pain, but she hadn't the heart to tell him to let go. She looked at him. His teeth were clenched and his face fixed with intense concentration.

"See, it's fine," Caren shouted over the noise of the engine as the boat skipped over the waves.

Pat shook his head and stared straight ahead.

"We'll be there in a moment," Caren tried to reassure him. She couldn't believe how fast the boat was. The island was already looming large.

The driver turned round. He pointed ahead to a beach on its far side.

Caren squinted through the wind and spray. She nodded and raised a thumb with her free hand.

"We're almost there, Pat," Caren shouted. "We're just going to land on that beach."

Through gritted teeth, Pat managed a nod.

***

Pearl grasped the handle of the control room door and paused.

"It's okay, I'll be right behind you," Aden said and smiled.

Pearl nodded, turned the handle and walked in.

Once inside, she felt sick. Standing in the centre of the room was Morgan. He had a silenced submachine gun in his hand and his clothes were covered in splatters of blood – lots of blood. There was no sign of her team.

"Finally! Come on, come on in. Join the party," Morgan said. He held the gun aloft and strutted around the room like a madman.

"What have you done with my team?"

"Dead – all dead!"

Pearl held her hands to her face. "Why, why?" she sobbed.

Aden followed her in.

Morgan swiftly raised his gun.

"Who's this?" he said, thrusting the gun forward. "Who is this?"

"This is Aden. He's an old friend. He came to visit."

"You've never mentioned him before. You've never mentioned another man."

"Another man? What do you mean?"

"I am the only man in your life."

Pearl looked confused.

"We work together, Morgan."

"Yes, but we talk and you invite me to your room."

"Yes, but it's all been work-related … So this is why

you've been acting so oddly over the last few months."

"You don't know anything," Morgan said, waving the gun about menacingly.

"What do you mean?"

"I am on a mission."

"Mission? What mission?" Pearl said.

"I am going to be rewarded."

"Morgan." Aden stepped forward.

Morgan pointed the gun at him, his hands shaking nervously.

"You say you're on a mission and that you're going to be rewarded?"

"Yes."

"Rewarded with money?"

"Yes."

"How well do you know these people?"

"What do you mean?"

"I mean, how well do you actually know these people who are going to reward you?"

"A friend of a friend introduced us."

"Explain."

"I got in touch with an old friend and told him what I was doing."

Pearl snapped, "You told someone what we were doing here?"

Aden interrupted and raised his hand. "Sorry, Morgan, please continue."

"I told the friend what I was doing, and the next day I got a phone call from a man who said he worked for someone very important who would give me a lot of money for any information we found. Not only that, but the information I delivered could help change the world!"

"What was the man's name?"

"I don't know. He said it was best I didn't know his name for security reasons."

"How many times have you spoken to him?"

"About five times, but I spoke to the important man for the first time last night."

"Last night? What did you say?"

"I gave him an update and said the upload would be finished by about four."

"And what was the plan?"

"That I would take the information and meet them ..." Morgan suddenly realised what was happening. "I don't have to explain anything to you. Who are you anyway? Are you the police?" He jabbed the gun towards Aden's face.

Aden raised his hands. "Sorry, I was only trying to help."

"Help? *Help*?" Morgan waved the gun from side to side again. "How can you help me?"

"It's just I've dealt with people like this before, you see."

"What do you mean, people like this?"

"Well, you realise they'll probably kill you rather than pay you?"

"No, they wouldn't. Why would they do that?"

"Because they'll want to save their money and you don't mean anything to them."

"No – he promised. He said I'd be the envy of everyone, with fast cars and a boat, and I could live anywhere I wanted." Morgan paused. "Monaco – I've always wanted to live in Monaco."

Morgan looked up and smiled, apparently deep in thought, contemplating what he would do with the money.

While he was distracted, Aden turned to Pearl.

"I need to set off a signal. Have you got anything that can do that?" Aden whispered.

"What?"

"A signal – something to attract someone's attention a mile away."

"Er, yes, we have some flares."

"Where?"

"On the roof – we can control them by computer."

"Set one off."

Morgan turned. "What are you doing?"

"I was just going to check on the status," Pearl said innocently.

"You know they want me to kill you. They wanted me to kill everybody. I don't want to have to kill you, I really don't, but they told me that I must. Monaco, the boat, the car – I've always wanted to live in Monaco."

Aden looked over at Pearl and nodded towards the terminal.

Pearl understood. "I just want to see the results, please. If you're going to kill me, then I would at least like to see how close we came to realising my dream," Pearl said as her fingers hovered over the keyboard.

Morgan paused. "Okay."

Pearl typed something and brought up the status screen.

"What was that?" Morgan stepped forward and looked around the room.

"What?"

"That noise, what did you do?"

"I just brought up the status screen."

"Before the status, you pressed too many keys." Morgan became agitated.

"Oh, I was just closing some other things down."

"You're lying. You did something else. You set off a flare – you signalled for help! Well, Pearl, there's no one that can help you now!"

Morgan raised the gun and pressed his finger on the trigger.

"No, WAIT!" Aden rushed forward. Morgan turned the gun on him.

"What?" Morgan demanded.

"Pearl, just tell the poor sod, will you?"

Pearl was confused. "Tell him what?"

Morgan frowned. His arm was trembling and the gun wobbled in his hand. "Tell me what?"

Aden paused and looked at them both. "Oh, I don't believe it. What is it with people who work so closely together? It was the same with me and my wife."

Pearl was completely bemused.

"What are you talking about?" Morgan snapped.

"Well – and it doesn't seem to be such an appropriate time to bring this up under the circumstances, but Pearl ... well, Pearl has a thing about you," Aden said, slowly stepping forward.

Morgan's eyes grew wide. He looked at Pearl, at Aden and back at Pearl.

"She told me. It's because she's such a professional she didn't want to let emotions get in the way of work." Aden swung his arms in an exaggerated gesture and took another step forward. "She said when this was all over she was going to tell you how she felt."

Aden stood between them, looking at them both as if they were childhood sweethearts too embarrassed to ask each other out. He waved his hands in mock exasperation.

Pearl still looked totally baffled. Aden turned his head towards her and winked – and her expression changed. She knew where this was going. She lowered her head and pretended to wipe a tear from her eye.

"Is this true?" Morgan asked.

Pearl looked up and smiled – a beautiful beaming smile that made her whole face light up. "You know what I'm like, Morgan. I'm a professional. I get so seriously focused on what I'm doing that I don't like anything to distract me – including affairs of the heart. I think that can often be the most distracting thing of all."

Aden looked at them both and swung his arms in disbelief again.

"I can't believe you didn't say anything. After all this time." Morgan's arm dropped to his side, the gun pointing at the floor.

"You guys – I can't believe it. I feel like Cilla Black on *Blind Date*." Aden swung his arms yet again and watched Morgan carefully. He was now close enough. One more swing of the arms to distract him and he would be able to disarm him and pin him to the ground.

Suddenly Morgan glared at Pearl and Aden.

"You're lying again," he said, aiming the gun at Aden. He

sneered. "I saw the look you gave her. No more tricks!"

He took a couple of steps backwards to create more distance between himself and Aden.

"Kneel." Morgan gestured with the gun. "Both of you – kneel!"

Aden dropped to his knees and Pearl knelt beside him.

Morgan pointed the gun. "Goodbye."

He placed his finger over the trigger; began to pull.

At that moment, the door opened. Simultaneously, their heads swung round.

They had no idea who was going to come through the door. As far as Morgan was concerned, everyone was dead apart from those in the room.

Pat walked in and froze on the spot. He held his hand out behind him to stop Caren following him in.

"Who are you?" Morgan said with surprise.

Aden was staggered that his partner could arrive so soon. But he had no time to think – he had to react.

"So, Morgan, I'm guessing this is who you've been speaking to on the phone – the man who promised you money for the information you've been collecting."

"But, I was meant to come and meet you," Morgan spluttered.

Pat stood and listened, catching on immediately. He held his rucksack in his hand and discreetly handed it to Caren who stood silently behind the door.

"As I said, Morgan," Aden continued, "you can trust me – I've dealt with people like this. They want to keep the upper hand. I bet, whilst he was on the phone, he kept trying to find out where you were, so he could come to you."

Morgan's face said it all. "Yes, you're right, he did." He looked over at Pat. "I was just going to ..."

"Morgan, well done," Pat said, walking over to him. "You've done a great job and you've certainly earned your reward."

Morgan didn't know whether he was coming or going. He had no idea who to trust anymore.

"Thank you, sir," he muttered warily. "But your voice – it sounds so different."

"This is my real voice. You don't think I'd speak on the phone without disguising it, do you?" Pat thought on his feet.

"Er, no, I guess not."

Pat stood beside him and folded his arms. He looked down at the man and woman on their knees.

"So, Morgan, what do we have here?"

"This is Pearl and this is ... her friend. He asks lots of questions," Morgan replied.

"Aye, I bet he does," Pat said, rubbing his chin. "And so, Morgan, do you have the information we're after?"

"Yes, I have it."

"Show me. I'll look after these two," Pat said as he reached for the gun.

Morgan pulled the gun close to his chest and eyed Pat up. "It's okay, I've got it," he said. He kept the gun pointed in Aden's direction and went over to his desk. He tapped a few keys on the keyboard and the screen lit up. "See, we have the data, we have everything. Do you have the money?"

"Oh, yes," Pat said. He raised his voice and called, "You can come in now."

Caren appeared from behind the open door with Pat's rucksack in her hand.

"Caren?" Aden said involuntarily.

Morgan stepped forward. He smelled a rat.

"You know her?" he said, noting the expression on Aden's face. "You know her!"

Pat could see in Morgan's eyes exactly what he was about to do. Acting on instinct, he rushed forward. Morgan turned the gun and fired. Pat dived.

Suddenly the air was filled with whizzing bullets and the muffled sound of suppressed gunfire. Computers exploded, chairs toppled over, and the walls were peppered with holes. The kick of the weapon on full-auto was unexpected and uncontrollable.

Morgan fought to keep the gun level, but Pat pounced from his crouched position and prised it out of his hands. He smashed its butt into Morgan's cheek. Morgan fell to the floor, out cold.

The room was silent.

Pearl lay on the floor and brushed the hair from her face. Pat looked over at Caren, who was lying motionless near the door.

Aden looked up at Pat, his expression spoke volumes. "NO!"

He rushed over and knelt next to Caren.

"Caren, can you hear me?"

Caren opened her eyes and looked up. Her face was white. A pool of blood was oozing from beneath her.

Tears welled up in Aden's eyes. He inspected her injuries. There were two bullet wounds, one a very clean shot near her navel and another, more jagged in shape, about six inches higher.

Aden lowered his head. "I'm sorry."

"It's okay. It's not your fault."

He placed his hand over the holes in her body, trying in vain to somehow seal them up.

Caren rested a hand on top of his. "We know the risks. It doesn't stop us doing the job. You still have a job to do. Get on with it."

Aden lowered his face to hers.

"That's an order," she said, her breath becoming shallow.

Aden's tears fell onto her cheeks. He kissed her. At that moment, he remembered: "I have something for you."

"You do?"

Aden pulled up his sleeve and unclasped the bracelet he'd brought from Tikehau . He'd worn it for safekeeping.

"It's beautiful." Caren struggled to speak.

"Like you," Aden said as he gently clasped the bracelet around her wrist. "I love you." His voice trembled.

"I love you too," she whispered.

Aden put his hand on her chest. He felt her final breath leave her body and, at that moment, part of him died with her.

Pat put his hand on Aden's shoulder. "I'm sorry, mate."

Aden looked over at Pearl. She was crouched by her desk, her face sad and drawn.

"This is all my fault," she said wearily.

"No, it's not, it's mine," Pat said, stepping away. "I shouldn't have wrestled the gun from him."

"No, it's not," Aden snapped, looking at Pat. "It's no one's fault." He looked at Pearl as he held on to Caren's hand – he couldn't seem to let go.

It was as if time stood still, leaving him in a vacuum of grief. He had no idea how long he stayed like that but, perhaps due to his training, reality finally filtered through and he remembered he did indeed have a job to finish. Other people's lives depended on his ability to accomplish it.

Forcing himself to return to the present, he focused on the situation in hand. Pat was standing a diplomatic distance from him.

"How did you get here so quickly?" Aden asked.

"We used the lift," Pat replied.

"What?"

"There's a lift from the beach," Pat said.

"Oh, right, I didn't know – but no, not that, how did you get to the island so quickly. We only fired the flares a few minutes ago. How did you get here so fast?"

"Flares? Don't know anything about any flares, but we got your signal earlier. The flashing light?"

"Light?"

"Yes, it was like you were signalling with a mirror."

"Mirror?" Aden repeated and then he realised. "Ahh, it must've been the window. Well, whatever it was, you saved my life – thank you."

"Aye, mate, you're all right," Pat said.

"You saved mine as well – thank you," said Pearl.

"Aye, you're alright too," Pat nodded.

Aden tilted his head upwards. "Can you hear that?"

Pat nodded. "Helicopters."

"Did you call them in?"

"No, not ours," Pat said.

Aden looked at Pearl. She shook her head and wiped a tear from her eye.

Aden looked back down at Caren. His heart was heavy and he felt sick. He wanted to stay with her as long as he could, holding her hand, but in his mind all he could hear was her voice – *You still have a job to do – get on with it – get on with it – get on with it.*

Suppressing his emotions, Aden stood and walked over to Morgan who was still out cold on the floor.

"Wake up," Aden said. "WAKE UP!" he shouted, kicking Morgan in his side.

Morgan groaned and partially opened his eyes.

"Are these your friends?" Aden asked.

Morgan clutched his stomach and curled into a ball. "My stomach hurts."

"That won't be the only thing hurting if you don't talk to me, you bastard. These helicopters, are these your friends?"

"I am meeting them in Bangkok," Morgan snivelled.

"What?"

"The plan was for me to meet them in Bangkok with the data."

"Then who the hell's in the helicopters?"

"I don't know," Morgan sobbed as his dreams of Monaco were slowly dashed.

Pat took off his jacket and covered Caren's body. He closed the door and rushed over to where Aden was standing over Morgan.

"I bet that was the tail," he said.

"What?" Aden asked.

"The tail – it all makes sense," Pat explained. "Ya man here tells them what's on offer. They make a deal they have no intention of keeping, and meanwhile they discover we're on to them. So they tail us hoping we'll lead them here."

"Clever bastards," Aden said.

"Yep, their plan worked brilliantly."

Pat was right. It had.

"Pearl?" Aden called over.

She looked up.

"Is there any way you can secure this room?"

"Yes. We have shutters for the main door, and the walls to this room are steel-lined."

"Okay, get the shutters closed."

Pearl got up from the floor and sat in the chair at her desk. Thankfully her computer had escaped damage. She swung the keyboard round and tapped in some commands. After a few seconds huge, metal shutters started to descend.

They were secure.

"We need to find a way out of here," Aden said to Pat.

Pearl stood up and walked over to them. She looked down at Morgan lying on the floor. She felt a knot in her stomach.

"There is a way," she said.

"There is?" Aden asked.

"Yes, the fireplace." Pearl pointed to the far end of the room.

Aden and Pat looked at each other. It was a huge stone fireplace – it didn't look like an escape route.

"You mean we're going up the chimney?" Pat asked.

"No, through the back. There is a hidden passageway behind the fireplace. It connects to a series of tunnels that lead down the mountain. It's always been there. I have just modernised it."

All of a sudden, they heard the metal shutters rattle followed by a loud banging sound.

"How long will they hold?" Aden asked.

"Depends what they try to do to them. They will hold, but not indefinitely," Pearl said.

Pat stood over Morgan and watched him like a hawk.

"If we're going to salvage anything from this situation, we'll have to act fast. How can we take your data away with us?" Aden asked.

"We can't take all of it, there's too much. We have a massive storage network and it's all stored on thousands of disks."

"Where?"

"Downstairs," Pearl said.

"Is it secure?"

"Yes, very, more than this room."

"So what do we do?" Aden asked.

"We have to interrogate the system and export the data we want."

"Like a search engine?" Aden confirmed.

"Yes, exactly, like a search engine."

"Well, this is your moment," Aden said as he gestured towards her desk.

Pearl nodded, ran over and sat down. Aden picked up a chair from the floor and sat down beside her.

Pearl opened a drawer next to the desk and grabbed one

of the memory sticks. She plugged it into the computer and began to type a search phrase: 'secret naval experiments tikehau'. She tapped the return key and results started to appear, with a preview of the information displayed. She tapped a few more keys to write the results to the memory stick. She typed another phrase, 'naval base tikehau'; another, 'marine experiments tikehau'; another, 'atoni kalua'; and another, 'elizabeth wilson'. Pearl watched the information appear in front of her, writing it to the memory stick as quickly as she could.

A news headline flashed up. 'Pearl farmer's wife found dead.' She couldn't hold back the emotion any longer and let out an uncontrollable sob.

Aden placed his hand gently on her arm. "It's okay. Keep going."

Pat walked over, keeping a watchful eye on Morgan.

Pearl continued to type: 'reef tikehau', and the results kept appearing. Pat leant over Aden's shoulder and watched in amazement. Results came thick and fast from top secret files of the US Navy, French Navy, US Government and more.

"This is incredible. Imagine if this ever got into the wrong hands – we'd be buggered!" Pat said.

"He's right. What can we do to make sure that doesn't happen?" Aden said.

"There is a self-destruct. We can arm it before we go," Pearl replied.

There was a sudden deafening boom from behind them. They instinctively cowered over the desk until the sound had subsided.

"Smells like C4," Pat said as he looked round at the door.

It had buckled slightly under the force of the blast. "If they keep going like that it won't be long before they're in here."

"Quickly." Aden gestured towards the terminal.

Pearl typed in a few more phrases which instantly brought up more results. She wrote them to the memory stick and waited until all the files had transferred.

"Okay, done," she said.

"That's it?" Aden asked.

"Yes," Pearl said.

"Years of research, planning and implementation – and that was it?"

"Yes. That's it," Pearl insisted.

"How much data have you got?"

"Er ..." Pearl checked her screen. "Just over thirty giga-bytes."

"Thirty gig of results, but it only took you a minute to search and not much longer to write."

Pearl seemed completely unfazed. "I told you, I designed it myself and I am using state of the art equipment." She pulled the memory stick from the computer and held it in front of her. "It's encrypted too!"

Aden had an idea. "Do you have another memory stick and do you mind if I use it?" Aden gestured towards the terminal.

Pearl pulled the drawer open and rifled through the se-lection of memory sticks. One of them had a label marked 'A'. She had almost forgotten about it. She took it and held it tightly in her hand. She took another and handed it to Aden. She stood up. "All yours."

Pat held on to the back of the chair and leaned over

Aden's shoulder as he watched him type in various search phrases.

Another huge boom reverberated from behind the door.

"Bloody hell," Aden said, his ears ringing.

Smoke began to billow into the room. Pat flapped his hand in front of his face and coughed. He looked over at the door. There was now a large dent in the shutters and they had buckled ominously at the bottom. "One more of those and they'll be in!"

"Yep, I know, just two more minutes." Aden swiftly dragged the set of results to the memory stick and performed another search. "Oh, my God!" he said as the results were previewed in front of him. There on the screen was a face he recognised.

"What is it?" Pat asked.

"I'll tell you later." Aden dragged the results and watched the little counter as it wrote gigabytes' worth of data to the memory stick.

Suddenly there was gunfire from underneath the door. Bullets ricocheted into the room.

"It's time to go, it's time to go!" Pat yelled.

"Just a few more seconds," Aden begged, lost in concentration.

A bullet came whizzing past. Pearl screamed.

"Are you okay?" Pat rushed over.

Pearl examined the sleeve of her blouse. The bullet had made a hole in it, narrowly missing her arm.

"Fuck this, we're out of here," Pat said grabbing Pearl's hand.

"Just a few more seconds!" Aden implored as the

progress bar on screen wrote even more astonishing data to the memory stick.

"Pearl, can you rig it to blow from this other terminal?" Pat said, kicking Morgan out of the way and reminding him who held the gun now.

"Yes, of course."

"How long will it take?" Pat asked.

"About ten seconds," Pearl replied, sitting down.

Pat looked back over to Aden, still sitting at the desk, and to the mangled metal shutters behind him.

At least they've stopped firing, but that probably means only one thing, Pat thought to himself.

"Aden! They're rigging more C4. They'll be in within seconds."

"Nearly there," Aden said. *This is game changing stuff,* he thought to himself as he frantically kept searching.

Pearl tapped some keys. "Okay, done."

Pat had anticipated flashing lights and a loud announcement over a speaker system or something. "Is that it?"

"Yes, of course, what did you expect?" Pearl replied.

"Erm – not sure – how long do we have?"

"Just under two minutes."

"Aden, we've got just two minutes before this whole place blows!"

"Yep, almost there!"

Pat looked down. Morgan had crawled under the desk and was huddled tightly into the corner. He held his legs to his chest and was cowering and trembling.

Pearl tapped a few more keys on the keyboard.

"What are you doing now?" Pat asked.

"You'll see." She pressed the return key and pushed the keyboard away from her.

The back of the fireplace began to move slowly upwards, revealing a passageway behind.

Pat looked at Aden and shook his head. This was taking too long.

"Aden, come on, that explosive could go off at any ..."

A massive blast wave knocked Pat off his feet. He shook his head and tried to focus. The ringing in his ears disorientated him. He couldn't see anything for the smoke in the room.

Shots rang out in all directions.

Damn, they're in, Pat thought to himself.

The smoke started to clear. He could see a figure approach. Pat raised the gun, his finger poised over the trigger. He couldn't make it out. He prepared to fire.

"Damn, that was close," Aden said, rushing forward towards them. "Come on, they're in!" He clutched the memory stick in his hand and crouched into the back of the fireplace.

The shooting stopped and they heard a voice shout: "There!"

Without delay, Pearl reached for a lever, pulled it and, in the blink of an eye, the back of the fireplace returned to its original position. They could hear muffled gun shots from the other side.

"Wait, what about Morgan?" Aden said.

"Let them have the bastard," Pearl seethed. "Now hurry, let's go, we've got just under a minute."

Pat followed Pearl down the tunnel. Aden kept closely behind, ducking slightly to protect his head.

The tunnel was about five feet high, three feet wide and sloped downhill, turning at angles as it traced the contours of the mountain. They had to stoop but at least they could be fast on their feet. Security lights were situated every fifteen feet or so, and they had to watch their footing on the rough stone floor.

"How far does this go?" Aden asked.

"About a quarter of a mile," Pearl replied.

"To the bottom?" Aden confirmed.

"Yes."

"Thirty seconds," Pat said, keeping a mental note of the countdown.

"How big will the blast be?" Aden asked.

"Pretty big," Pearl said.

"Twenty seconds!" Pat shouted.

They hurried as fast as they could, Pearl leading, Pat in the middle and Aden behind.

"Five – four – three – two – ONE!" Pat completed the countdown.

A few more seconds passed.

"Damn, what if it doesn't go off?" Pat said.

"It will. Come on," Pearl called out from in front.

"But, what if it doesn't, we'll be ..." Pat was interrupted.

At that moment, it was as if the whole mountain was shaking beneath their feet. A huge rumbling noise filled the air.

They froze in their tracks.

The boom echoed away into the distance and the shaking gradually stopped. The air was thick with clouds of dust ... and then there was a creaking noise.

"There could be a cave-in," Aden said.

No sooner had he spoken than there was an almighty crash from behind them.

"Run, quick!" Aden shouted, shoving Pat down the tunnel in front of him.

Another crash echoed.

"The shock wave must have loosened the rock."

The rumbling gradually stopped. But then something unexpected happened – the lights went off.

"Great!" Pat said.

They waited a moment. "Will they come back on?" Aden asked.

"No, the explosion will have taken out the generator and the battery room. We'll have to go the rest of the way in darkness," explained Pearl.

"I can't see a bleedin' thing!" Pat said.

"Hang on a minute," Aden said. "Pat – check the gun. It's tactical spec; it's got a torch on the front."

The tunnel was illuminated again.

"Well, getta load of that – well done, mucker! I didn't fancy going the rest of the way in the dark," Pat said.

"We've still got a fair way to go," said Pearl.

Pat took the lead, lighting up the tunnel. It snaked and wound down the mountain.

"Much further, Pearl?" Aden asked.

"We should almost be there. You'll notice it's levelling out."

They turned another corner and there, at last, was the end of the tunnel system.

Pat shone the torch at a large wooden door. "How do we get out?"

"We need to blow it," Pearl said.

"Great – more explosives!" Pat moaned.

"Point the torch here," Pearl said, edging past. There was a box on the wall. She opened it and pulled out a detonator. She started to unravel the cord attached to it. "We'll need to go back past that last corner."

Pat and Aden walked with her, Pat still shining the torch so that Pearl could see what she was doing. She finished un-ravelling the cord as they walked back to the last corner and crouched as low as they could.

"Cover your ears," Pearl said. She pulled the lever up-wards and then rammed it back down.

Nothing happened.

Pat uncovered his ears. "How long has this been here?"

"A few years now – what do you think has happened?"

"Could be the explosive has broken down. Maybe water got in, or it could be the contacts. Can I take a look?"

Pearl nodded and handed Pat the detonator.

"I think it's the contact terminals. They've rusted slight-ly. Do you have anything sharp?"

"Er, no – everything I had was in my bag, which I dropped off the cliff," Aden replied.

Pat looked at Pearl who shook her head.

"Never mind," Pat said, detaching the wires from the terminals. He scraped the ends against the rock face un-til he exposed bare metal. He rubbed the wires up and down against the contacts and then re-twisted them tightly around the terminals.

"Here you go, my dear, try again."

Pearl lifted the plunger. "Ears!" she shouted, and

rammed it down again.

A huge shockwave rushed past them and dust filled the air once more.

Pat uncovered his ears. "That did the trick."

Pearl coughed and spluttered and covered her mouth with her blouse. Aden exhaled after holding his breath and Pat still seemed to be holding on to his.

As the dust settled they could see light streaming in from the end of the tunnel.

They walked gratefully out into the bright sunshine. They were standing on a small rocky plateau at the base of the island with the sea lapping on the rocks just a few feet below.

Pat coughed. "God knows how much dust is in my lungs. I'm going to end up with asthma – or worse, consumption."

Aden coughed in sympathy.

Pearl stood quietly and looked up towards the top of the cliff. She watched the smoke billow upwards into the sky and imagined her monastery now in ruins.

"How does it feel?" Aden asked.

"A mixture of feelings really," she sighed. "Relief – sadness – grief. My poor team, they worked so hard for me. They helped me realise my dream, only to pay for it with their lives." She reached into her pocket and pulled out the memory sticks holding them tightly in her hand. "But there is also optimism. I am finally holding in my hand the truth about what happened."

"What's on the other one?" Aden asked.

Pearl thought about the question. "Oh, just some personal data," she replied and hurriedly put them back in her pocket.

Pat sat on a rock and watched the smoke rise from the top of the island.

"What will you do now?" Pat asked.

"I have a friend who works for a newspaper in Hong Kong. I'll go and see her. She always said she'd help me reveal the truth."

"Well, I wish you all the very best of luck," Pat said.

"Thank you," Pearl replied. She turned to Aden. "Thank you for helping me."

"That's okay." Aden reached into his pocket and pulled out his memory stick. "I believe you have also helped me and my country."

"You found important information?" Pearl asked.

"Yes, very, and I think it will explain exactly what's been going on."

Pearl lowered her head. "I'm sorry."

"What for?"

"You obviously cared very much for that woman."

Aden felt a jolt through his chest. It was as though a knife had been rammed through his heart. He hadn't forgotten he'd lost Caren, but with all the events which followed, he had deliberately cast his feelings to one side and put himself into 'automatic' mode for the assignment. It's what they had been taught to do – not to allow emotions to get in the way of the job. There would be time to grieve later.

"Yes. I did," Aden said, looking up. She was still there, lying on the floor, God knows in what state after the explosion. He tried not to think about it.

"Were you close?" Pearl asked.

"She was my wife," Aden said.

"I am so very sorry. She was a very lucky woman."

It took Aden a moment to realise what Pearl meant: "Thank you, that's very kind. And I'm sorry about Sinead," he said.

"Thank you," Pearl sighed. "I'll miss her."

Pearl put her arms around him. They held each other tightly for a few moments. It helped.

She kissed him on the cheek and whispered, "À cœur vaillant rien d'impossible."

"What does that mean?"

"To a valiant heart nothing is impossible."

Aden smiled. "Il faut casser le noyau pour avoir l'amande."

Pearl laughed. "You need to break the shell to have the almond."

"No pain, no gain," Aden said.

"C'est la vie!" Pearl said and smiled.

"Indeed," Aden replied.

Pat sat and watched. He considered himself lucky he hadn't lost anyone close to him on this mission, but then, he no longer allowed himself to get close to anyone. Bitter memories were still buried deep inside.

"Okay, Pat, you ready?"

"Yep, where to?"

"Back home. With what I have on this memory stick, we need to get there fast!" Aden turned to Pearl. "And how do we go about doing that?"

To their side was a large red box. Pearl gestured towards it. "Inflatable boat – stand back."

Pearl grasped a handle and pulled. There was a huge whoosh of air and in seconds an orange inflatable boat was taking shape in front of them.

"Is he okay?" Pearl asked as Pat's face turned a ghostly shade of pale.

"He doesn't like water – or boats," Aden explained.

"Oh, he's not going to like this then!"

Chapter 72

The Show Must Go On

The London traffic was heavy but at least it was moving.

"The Chief Inspector will have expected you to come in and debrief," Pat said.

"When he realises what's at stake, he'll understand," Aden answered, slowing down for a red light.

"You can drop me here if you like," Pat said.

"Okay, jump out at these lights," Aden said. "You got the memory stick?"

"Yes." Pat tapped his pocket.

"For God's sake, don't lose it!" Aden joked.

"Oh, shut yer beak!" Pat replied.

Aden brought the car to a stop.

"Right then, good luck. See ya later."

"Yep, see you later," Aden nodded.

Pat jumped out and slammed the door.

Aden adjusted the Glock 17 pistol in his shoulder holster.

The lights turned green.

***

He was approaching the Parliament building. Aden hadn't been here for some time, but he knew there was now a security wall between it and the road.

As he drew closer, he could see a point of access with three uniformed officers standing around.

Aden pulled in and got out of the car. He slid out his identity card and held it up so his photograph was visible.

The officers were alert. One of them stepped forward.

"Aden Fitch – SIA – on urgent business."

Inspecting the card, the officer nodded. "Okay, mate." He lowered his Heckler & Koch MP5.

Aden vaulted the crash barrier.

"Hang on – you can't leave your car there!" one of the officers shouted, but it was too late. Aden was sprinting towards the building and, in a moment, had disappeared inside.

"Where's the Prime Minister's office?" he barked at the receptionist.

"I'm sorry, sir, the Prime Minister is currently preparing for Questions at 12 noon"

Aden looked at her name badge. "Marjorie – that is not what I asked." Aden thrust his ID card in front of her face. "I'm SIA Officer Aden Fitch on urgent business. Where is the Prime Minister's office?"

The receptionist recoiled in her seat as if hypnotised to answer. "Second floor, fourth office on the right."

"Thank you."

Aden turned to run towards the stairs but as he looked round he could see the woman had picked up the phone and was about to dial.

"Who are you calling?" Aden called out.

"The Prime Minister," Marjorie replied.

"No!" Aden rushed over, grabbed the phone and slammed it down. "The Prime Minister is in grave danger. Whatever you do, don't call him. You could get him killed."

The woman was shocked.

"You wouldn't want that now, would you, Marjorie?"

She shook her head.

Aden rushed off towards the stairs. He raced up two steps at a time, heading for the second floor.

Marjorie watched him disappear from view, her hand hovering over the phone. She had been trained for these situations, although not one quite like this. She was torn. Surely she couldn't get the Prime Minister killed just by making a call. She picked up the phone.

Aden had reached the second floor. He ran forward past the first, second and third doors. He paused at the fourth. There, upon the dark oak surface, was a brass plate that read: 'Prime Minister'.

Without knocking, he turned the handle and rushed in.

The Prime Minister was sitting behind his desk on the phone. "Yes, it seems he has just arrived," he said, looking up and making eye contact with Aden.

Aden glanced to the Prime Minister's left. There, standing in the corner, was a man whose face he recognised from the data he'd downloaded.

The reason for Aden's presence immediately dawned on the PM's protection officer.

The protection officer was sharp. He reached for his gun and took aim – but not at Aden.

Aden rushed forward, drew his gun and fired. The protection officer ducked and fired back.

The Prime Minister cried out and then fell from his chair.

Aden side-stepped to his left and fired again. The officer fired back. The bullet whistled past and smashed into the wall, narrowly missing Aden's shoulder. Aden fired, and fired again in the direction of the officer. More shots were exchanged. Aden dived to the floor – and then there was silence.

Aden's ears rang as he got back on his feet. He could see the Prime Minister slumped behind his desk.

"Sir! SIR! Are you okay?"

The Prime Minister raised himself to his feet and rubbed his ears. "What on earth ...? That's my protection officer – you've just shot my protection officer!"

"Aden Fitch, SIA, sir," Aden said as he pulled out his ID card. "I've uncovered a plot to assassinate you, and your protection officer was going to carry it out – today, before Questions at 12 noon."

The Prime Minister looked over at the clock on the wall "Bloody Hell."

"I'm afraid there were a number of very powerful people who wanted you dead, sir," Aden said.

At that moment the door burst open and three armed police officers rushed into the office with their guns raised.

"Are you okay, sir?" one of the officers asked.

Two of them stood either side of Aden and the other inspected the body of the protection officer.

The Prime Minister got up from his chair. "Yes, I'm fine, lower your weapons."

"What happened?"

"Aden Fitch here just saved my life."

Aden held his ID card out for examination. "Aden Fitch, SIA Officer, SIA181."

One of the officers stepped forward and checked the ID carefully. "All, right mate. Good job."

"Thanks," Aden replied.

"Do you need any help?" the officer asked.

"No, got it covered thanks."

"Leave us for a moment, please," the Prime Minister said.

"Okay, sir," one of the officers responded. They looked at each other and left.

"Aden, you were saying?" The Prime Minister sat and made a sign for him to continue.

"A hitman, Mykola Liski, was sent to carry out the assassination – your assassination – but we got to him first."

"The one who fell in front of the train?" the Prime Minister said, the pieces of the puzzle beginning to fit into place.

"Yes, sir," Aden continued. "When that failed, they wanted to arrange for someone else to do it – someone closer to you. Someone who wouldn't fail this time."

The Prime Minister looked down at the body of his protection officer lying on the floor. "Draper."

"Yes, sir, Colin Draper," Aden said.

"And do you know who organised this?" the Prime Minister asked.

"Yes, sir. Greg Willis."

The Prime Minister hammered the desk with his fist. "That bastard! I knew he was up to something." He shook his head. "That's what he meant on that programme when he said, 'when I'm Prime Minister'."

"Yes, sir, exactly, sir."

"And how do you know all this?" the Prime Minister asked.

"We had some help uncovering the information, sir."

"And, more importantly, do you have evidence?"

"Oh, yes, sir, lots of it. It's all on a memory stick with my Chief Inspector."

"Okay, good work. Aden Fitch you said?"

"Yes, sir, SIA."

The Prime Minster stood up and walked around the desk. "Thank you, Fitch. I'll make sure you get recognition for this." The Prime Minister shook Aden's hand enthusiastically.

"That's very kind of you, sir, but I'm just doing my job."

The Prime Minister brushed himself off, straightened his suit and stood tall.

"Right, I must attend Questions," he announced, gathering up his notes.

"But, sir ..." Aden said, looking at the body slumped on the floor.

"The show must go on – the show must go on," the Prime Minister smiled, patting Aden on the shoulder. He opened the door and, with a spring in his step, left the room.

Chapter 73

Sweet Rewards

Pearl stood in front of the mirror in a hotel room in Hong Kong.

She raised her glass of Champagne and smiled. Droplets of bathwater dripped to the floor from beneath her bathrobe.

She couldn't believe this moment had come. After all these years, here she was with evidence that the French Navy had conducted illegal experiments which had destroyed the reef. They had sent in so-called experts who had said it was rogue bacteria, but now she knew the truth and soon the world would too.

She thought about her mother and father and how proud they would have been of her. She thought of Sinead. She fingered the lapel of her white robe and felt an empty sensation – the last time she had seen Sinead was beneath those blood-soaked sheets.

She snapped herself out of it. It was a time to celebrate. She toasted herself in the mirror and took another sip of Champagne.

She thought about Aden. He had lost someone too and she owed him a debt of gratitude she could never repay. If it hadn't been for him she'd be dead, and if it hadn't been for

Pat they would both be dead. And yet, here she was, drinking Champagne with a memory stick full of data.

"To you, Aden, thank you for your help." She toasted the mirror again. "I hope the information you found will be useful."

She walked over to a table in front of the window. She gazed at her mother's necklace, neatly coiled up in front of her. Thank heavens she had decided to put it on before leaving the island. It had seemed so symbolic to wear it as the data collection was nearing completion. Beside it was the memory stick loaded with crucial evidence. It was amazing that something so small could contain so much.

"Petit poisson deviendra grand," she said as she picked it up between her fingers.

She remembered her exchange with Aden on the island and how they had translated the French sayings. She imagined Aden translating it for her now: "The little fish will grow big."

She placed the memory stick back down and picked up the other one beside it.

She turned it between her fingers and saw the letter 'A' on the label. A for Algorithms. There was no way she could have let years of hard work be destroyed. On this memory stick were the all-important algorithms for the data capture and encryption routines.

Both keys were encrypted and only she knew the code. There was little chance of this information ever falling into the wrong hands now.

Pearl looked at the clock. She was due to meet her friend, Meriel at the newspaper offices in forty-five minutes.

Chapter 74

The Dirty Laundry

Aden pressed the mute button on the TV remote control and put it down beside him on Pat's sofa.

"Thanks," he said as Pat handed him a glass of beer. "That was one long day."

"You're telling me – and what was the highlight of your day, Aden?" Pat said in a cheeky tone. "Oh, yes," he continued, "when the Chief Inspector gets a phone call – from who? Only the Prime Minister no less, telling him what a brilliant officer Aden Fitch is and how he recommends Fitch gets a special commendation for his actions."

Aden beamed a smile.

"Well, I hope you get something too," Aden said. "You deserve it – you saved my life."

"Well, in fact, the Chief Inspector did say there might be something for both of us."

Aden nodded. "Good."

"Cheers, Spud." Pat raised his glass of Guinness.

"Cheers, Pat." Aden chinked his glass.

"He must have been shitting himself," Pat said.

"He was white as a sheet when it all started to kick off. Then he just brushes himself off and goes off to his Questions meeting. I was really impressed."

"Well, I suppose it takes a special kind of person to be the Prime Minister, so it does," Pat said.

They sat back on the sofa and sipped their drinks in silence. They watched the images on the TV. It was the tail end of a programme before the news.

"I wonder how Pearl is getting on?" Pat said.

"Yes, I hope she gets what she wanted," Aden replied.

"Truth?" Pat asked.

"Peace," Aden answered.

"Aye, I 'spose you're right," Pat said. "But what about you?"

"What do you mean?" Aden replied.

"Will you find peace?"

Aden bit his lip and pondered the question. "I miss her so much. I can't sleep. I hear her voice in my head all the time and there are little reminders everywhere. I went to phone you earlier and there was her name in my recent calls list – she's gone ... It's left a big hole in my life."

"I bet – who's gonna boss you around now then?" Pat said.

"Yep, indeed," Aden said and lowered his head.

"You're gonna to stay though, right?" Pat asked.

"Stay?"

"You're going to stay in the job?"

"Yeah, of course," Aden said positively. "This is my life. I don't know anything else. Even without Caren, this is still me – it's what I do."

"Grand," Pat said, raising his glass for another swig of Guinness. "Ooh – here we go. Put the sound on, put the sound on." Pat nudged Aden in the ribs.

Aden picked up the remote and pressed a button.

"In the news tonight ..." introduced the well-groomed female newsreader, "the Deputy Prime Minister, Greg Willis leaves office after it is discovered that a large sum of money has been paid into an off-shore account in his name, as payment in the form of a bribe to keep the UK in Europe."

Pat slapped Aden's leg. "Well done, me ole mucker!"

"Not quite the same thing as being involved in a plot to assassinate the PM, but I guess the public's not ready for that yet." Aden raised his glass.

"Also in the news – data supplied from an unrevealed source ..." Pat slapped Aden's leg again, "... is alleged to shine light on a Europe-wide criminal operation involving big business, banks and even, it is reported, possible government officials. This information has been handed to the authorities who will investigate further," the newsreader said. "A *Panorama* special looks at data leaks and whether they're a risk to the fabric of our society or, in fact, a benefit.

"And in France," the newsreader continued, "the Minister for the Economy has reportedly gone missing ..."

Aden stabbed the mute button and turned to his partner.

"It's a veritable shit-storm, so it is," Pat said.

"Aye – it is that," Aden said in his best Irish accent.

"That, my dear fellow, was an awful impression," Pat replied in his best English accent.

Aden smiled, sipped his beer and watched the images flash up on the silent TV.

"Innit amazing how the actions of one can affect the lives of others?" Pat said with a philosophical tone.

"How so?"

"Oh, I was just thinking about Pearl and her team, beavering away with her computer stuff, and then how that data ends up effectively saving the Prime Minister's life and uncovers your Raven fella's operation."

"Yeah," Aden nodded. "We were very lucky."

"How did you know she'd have stuff about the bodyguard and the Raven anyway?"

"It was when she told me she was collecting data from the world and not just France. With so much data from so many sources, I figured there must be something on there about what's been going on."

"Quick thinking that," Pat said.

"I'm just glad I had time to grab it."

"Yep – a moment longer and you'd have been toast. Just like the Raven's goons up there – toasted."

"Well, all of that information is now with the Chief Inspector, so hopefully it'll get through to the right people," Aden said.

"Yep, there could be another Anglo-French operation soon," Pat said.

Aden nodded. "Yes, I guess there will be."

"It would be funny if that was our next job."

"Yeah, wouldn't it?" Aden said. He stopped short realising what Pat had said. "What?"

"What, what?" Pat replied.

"You just said *our* next job."

"Yeah, I did, yeah," Pat nodded.

"What do you mean, *our* next job?" Aden was confused.

"Oh, of course, you don't know, do you?" Pat said. "Probably something to do with you missing one of the meetings earlier."

"I don't know – what?"

"I, me ole mucker ..." Pat leant across. "I'm your new full-time partner!"

Aden rolled his eyes. "Oh, great – I've got a forgetful Irish clown as a full-time partner!"

"Well, póg mo thóin," Pat replied.

Aden looked quizzical. "What the hell does that mean?"

"I'll tell you later," Pat winked.

Chapter 75

The Truth

Pearl walked out of the hotel and into the busy street. She skipped along the pavement like a young girl and imagined her parents by her side.

She was last in Hong Kong six months ago, to see her friend, Meriel and to give her an update on how it was all going. They had planned for this very moment and now it had arrived. It was Meriel's newspaper's chance for a world-wide exclusive. They were going to reveal the cover-up about the reef and what had happened to Pearl's parents.

Pearl touched her pocket to make sure the memory sticks were safe.

A crowd spilled out onto the pavement. Revellers queued to get into clubs. Neon cast a rainbow of light across the street.

"Sorry. Sorry," a young girl said, full of the party mood as she fell back against Pearl.

Pearl instinctively caught her and helped her upright.

"Thank you. Thank you," the girl said, embarrassed.

Pearl smiled and slowly weaved her way through the crowd.

She was pushed and shoved and, at one point nearly fell over herself, but she smiled and took it all in her stride. She felt a hand rub up against her and then grab her arm. She felt a jolt of panic. Her stomach turned over and her mouth went instantly dry. She turned to face a man staring directly at her.

"Sorry. I thought you were someone else," the man said and let her go.

Pearl, startled, snatched her arm back and turned. She fought her way through and breathed a sigh of relief to be on the other side of the crowd.

Then she realised where the hand had touched her – on her side, near her pocket. Her stomach turned over. *Oh my God*, she thought. All of this work, all of this time, all of this effort, all the people who had given their lives to help her search for the truth. Thoughts whipped through her mind at the speed of light – then despair.

She lowered her hand. Her fingers paused at the edge of her pocket – the desperation – the hope … She placed her fingers inside. Nothing. She probed. Her fingers made contact with something, something smooth to the touch. She continued to reach around inside her pocket – something else. She pulled the shapes out – *thank God*. Both memory sticks – she still had both memory sticks.

As she clutched her beating chest with one hand, she kept a firm hold on the memory sticks in the other.

She walked along the pavement until she was finally looking up at a large building in front of her. She knew Meriel was inside, waiting.

She strode up the steps in front of the main entrance.

She reached underneath her jacket and caressed her mother's necklace.

"Mummy – Daddy – this is for you," she said as she pushed her way through the revolving door.

Acknowledgements

Thank you to my friend, Pearl for her initial inspiration.

Thank you to my friend, Tina for her friendship, advice, support, proofreading, and especially the gift of the genuine Tahitian pearl that graces the front cover of this book.

And last, but by no means least, thank you to Heather for supporting me with encouragement and love throughout this whole process.

Rob Wassell

Rob Wassell is the writer of the best-selling *The Story of the Belle Tout Lighthouse*, which is now in its second edition and holds the claim of being the first book ever written specifically about the old lighthouse at Beachy Head. He followed this with *The Story of the Beachy Head Lighthouse*, which helped raise money for the re-painting of the stripes.

Writing is Rob's first love and, despite a busy career in business, he still finds the time to write.

Rob published his first novel in 1997.

Rob lives near Worthing in West Sussex with his partner Heather and their Jack Russell, Dottie.